Reverence

Raena Rood

One Foundation Publishing

ISBN: 978-1-952431-14-2 (paperback)

ISBN: 978-1-952431-13-5 (e-book)

ISBN: 978-1-952431-21-0 (hardback)

Cover Design by Ampersand Book Cover Designs

Map Design by Ben Rood

Edited by Kimberly Murphree

http://raenajrood.com

REVERENCE

Raena Rood

"I (Darius, King of Persia) issue a decree that in every part of my kingdom people must fear and reverence the God of Daniel. For he is the living God and he endures forever; his kingdom will not be destroyed, his dominion will never end. He rescues and he saves; he performs signs and wonders in the heavens and on the earth. He has rescued Daniel from the power of the lions."

— Daniel 6: 26-27 (NIV)

For my husband and best friend.
I finally dedicated a book to you.
You're welcome.

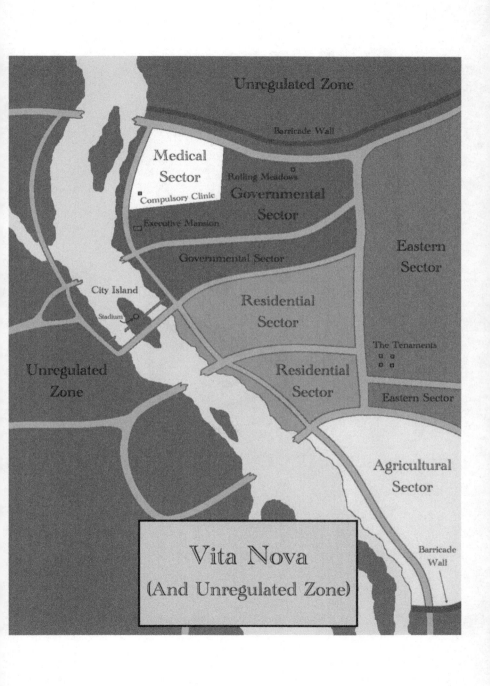

Chapter One

My mother will be dead within the hour.

The words played like a song in Kira Liebert's mind, drowning out every groan, every cough, and every muffled sob of the Compulsory Clinic's waiting room. Looking from one face to another, she observed the silent multitude of thinning hair, sunken cheekbones, and hollow eyes with a passive sorrow, unable to generate a single tear for anyone other than her mother. In another part of the room, a baby wailed—an unnatural, strangled sound—but she refused to look.

She would not consider, even for a moment, why an infant would be in this awful place.

Two months earlier, a city physician had discovered a golf ball-sized mass in an x-ray of her mother's right lung during her mandatory semiannual health screening. Inoperable cancer, he'd explained. Too large to remove. The notification had arrived on their doorstep within the week like a cruel joke.

Nothing moved quickly in Vita Nova—except for Compulsory Notifications.

Madison Liebert had accepted the manila envelope from the courier, and after reading the letter, she'd gone to the Governmental Sector to apply for a sole parental exemption. Exemptions had become rare in recent years, especially when the children living in the household were nearly adults themselves, as was Kira, but she'd held onto hope. What else could she do?

Another letter had arrived a week later, hand-delivered by the same grim-faced man who'd dropped off the Compulsory Notification.

Exemption Request Denied.

They had only one other option, but Kira's mother couldn't bring herself to do what needed to be done, so Kira had done it for her.

She'd called her father's office and left messages. Dozens of messages.

He returned none of her calls.

"MADISON LIEBERT?"

A tiny whimper escaped Kira's throat.

Her mother glanced at her, eyes narrowed in warning, and Kira swallowed back her emotions. This wasn't the time or the place. She kept her head down as she followed her mother across the waiting room.

They arrived at a tiny cubicle and lowered themselves into two cushioned chairs opposite a thin brunette with freckled skin and a pixie-cut. The woman pecked at the buttons on her keyboard, refusing to acknowledge their presence for a full minute.

"Paperwork," she mumbled, without raising her eyes from her computer screen.

Maybe that's how she copes with the horrible things she sees, Kira thought. *By not looking.*

Her mother slid a stack of forms across the desk. As she retracted her hand, Kira placed her palm on top of her mother's, feeling delicate bones beneath tissue-paper skin. Offering comfort in any way she could.

"Age?" Brown Pixie-Cut asked.

"Forty-seven."

"Marital status?"

Madison Liebert cleared her throat. "Never married."

An older gentleman sat in a neighboring cubicle, answering similar questions. There weren't many old people left in Vita Nova. You could go months seeing no one over the age of fifty. Those individuals fortunate enough to celebrate their sixtieth birthdays were automatically selected as Compulsories—as were those with chronic medical conditions—since the city government considered them a strain on the city's limited resources. Only those people deemed *essential* to the city's survival were allowed to live past the age of sixty.

The leadership of Vita Nova considered the Compulsory Program to be a humane alternative to simply tossing all the old and sick people over the wall.

Kira craned her neck around the barrier to steal a glimpse of the man. He looked to be in his late fifties, with bone-white hair and a kind face. He wore a wrinkled navy-blue suit and a red tie, and although it was way too big for him, it was probably the nicest outfit he owned.

The chair beside him was empty.

Unlike the older gentleman, Madison Liebert would have someone by her side during her last moments. That was something, at least.

The day before, Kira and her mother had spent the entire day outside, kneeling in their tiny backyard garden, tearing weeds from the dirt so they wouldn't choke out the flowers. Afterward, they'd ridden the bus to the market and splurged on two T-Bone steaks, fresh zucchini, a pound of strawberries, and a small basket of potatoes.

They'd pulled two kitchen chairs outside and eaten dinner on the front porch, watching the sunset together for the last time. Kira had made her mother's favorite dessert—homemade strawberry shortcake. The strawberries sold at the market were bulbous and watery and more sour than sweet, but she'd sliced them extra thin, drizzled them with a little honey, and let them sit in the fridge all afternoon.

Her mother had spooned the strawberries over her slice of cake and then poured a little milk on top. "This looks wonderful, Kira," she'd said, bringing a spoonful to her lips. "You outdid yourself."

Although she hadn't been hungry, Kira had cut herself a generous slice and forced herself to eat, taking small bites and chewing slowly, trying to focus on the flavors. Such a decadent dessert was a rare treat in their household. But then her eyes had landed on the cake pan. Only two slices were missing, and the thought had hit her: *My mother will never eat another piece of strawberry shortcake.*

She hadn't been able to swallow another bite.

"Is anyone here with you, Ms. Liebert?" Brown Pixie-Cut asked, as if she couldn't see Kira sitting in front of her.

"Yes. My daughter."

"Her name and age?"

"Kira Liebert. She's seventeen."

The intake officer refused to meet Kira's eyes. Instead, her eyes flitted between her computer screen and the paperwork. The lack of eye contact felt deliberate, and Kira leaned forward and stared at the woman, silently daring her to make eye contact.

Look at me, she thought. *Look at me, you coward.*

The woman didn't look.

After the intake officer finished entering her mother's information into the database, a heavy-set female nurse in black scrubs materialized behind their chairs and escorted them to an elevator. After a bumpy ascent, the doors opened, and the nurse led them into the eerie quiet of the third floor. Only the high-pitched squeaking of the woman's purple clogs against the polished floor broke the silence of the hallway. Other officials in black scrubs hurried past them, their eyes fixed on their clipboards.

Most of the doors in the hallway were closed. All except for one. When Kira peered inside the room, she saw a young woman huddled over the bed, her tears falling onto the body of the motionless young man who lay buried beneath the clinic's linens.

Kira's mother grabbed her hand and squeezed. "Come on, honey. Don't look at them."

The nurse veered off to the right, leading them into a private room with a window overlooking the clinic's crowded rear parking lot.

A small sign hung over the door: *Room 317.*

The tiny room had no television, no dresser, and no medical equipment. Just a single bed and an uncomfortable plastic chair. A clock—the closest thing the room had to a decoration—hung above the door. A hospital gown, a plastic bag, and a pair of gray socks with treads on the bottom lay on the neatly made bed.

Kira's stomach twisted at the sight. "Mom..."

Her mother silenced her with one word. "Quiet."

Lingering in the doorway, the nurse regarded Kira with wary eyes, as if trying to decide if she was going to be a problem. Then the woman tipped her head toward the hallway.

"None of these rooms have private bathrooms. If you need to use the restroom, it's down the hall on the right."

Madison Liebert nodded. "Thank you."

Kira struggled to hold herself together after the nurse left. Collapsing onto the plastic chair, she dropped her head into her hands while her mother dragged the privacy curtain around the bed.

Her mother emerged a few minutes later wearing her hospital gown and socks. She'd folded her clothing and placed it inside the plastic bag. She had left what little jewelry she owned on the kitchen counter at home.

"I'm going to use the restroom," Madison Liebert said. "I'll be back."

"Okay," Kira choked the word out.

After her mother slipped out of the room, Kira released the emotions she'd kept bottled inside since the Compulsory Notification had arrived on their doorstep. She wept until her eyes hurt, her chest heaving with great, body-wracking sobs. Anguish poured from her body, hot tears stealing through the gaps in her fingers and falling onto the thin fabric of her t-shirt.

She gave herself two minutes. Two minutes to lose control. Two minutes to be angry. Two minutes to grieve a loss that hadn't happened yet. The clock was nothing but a blur of black and white on the wall, so she counted the seconds off in her head. When her time was up, she pulled a handkerchief from her mother's purse and wiped the remaining tears from her cheeks, forcing the powerful emotions deep inside her chest where they would remain until this was over.

Until her mother was gone.

The door to the hospital room swung open. Madison Liebert scuffed across the room on her anti-skid socks and crawled into the bed, pulling the blanket over herself. When she spoke, her voice was distant and dreamy. "Well, the bed feels good. And the rooms are nicer than I expected."

Kira swallowed a few angry responses before the bitter words slipped past her lips. "We shouldn't be here. We should've run when we had the chance."

Her mother gave her a look sharp enough to cut glass. "Run where? Outside the barricade?" She shook her head. "Don't be ridiculous."

Kira said nothing. Her mother was right.

They had nowhere to go.

"Refusing the Compulsory Order would've only made things worse, Kira. They would've thrown me in the Confines and killed me anyway. This way, you get to be by my side until the end. We had a beautiful day yesterday, didn't we?"

"Oh, Mom..." Kira remembered their dinner on the porch and began to cry again. So much for being strong for her mother. "What am I going to do without you?"

Her mother flapped a hand at her, shooing the idea away. "You're going to be fine. You've got the townhouse and there's enough money to carry you through until you start working in a few months," she said, referring to Kira's upcoming job as a volunteer advocate for the city. "I'm glad you got that job. There's lots of room for advancement in the Governmental Sector. Plus, the pay is decent."

"That's not what I meant, Mom," Kira cried, swiping the handkerchief along her leaking nose. "How will I go on without you?"

Raising herself up on her elbows, Madison Liebert gave her daughter a penetrating look. "You will go on because you don't have a choice. Life doesn't always give us options, but the strongest ones among us keep moving forward, no matter how difficult things get." Her mouth hung open, as if she had more to say, but she closed her lips and swallowed hard. "There's a lot you don't understand about the world you're living in. So much you don't remember. You were too young. What I wouldn't give to spend a few more days with you."

A few more days? Kira glanced at the room's only window. There were no bars. No alarms that she could see. They weren't *that* high off the ground. Only three floors. What if they climbed out the window? Could they make it to the ground without breaking their legs? And then what? "Mom? What if we—"

"It's not going to happen," her mother cut her off. "I know what you're thinking, and I'm not jumping out any windows. Running isn't an option. We have to face this together." The anger on her mother's face dissolved into compassion. "Sweetheart, I never wanted to leave you—not if I could help it—but now that it's happening, you need to know that I'm not afraid to die."

The fantasy of breaking her mother out of the clinic fizzled like a fire doused with water, leaving only steam that burned Kira's eyes. "You're not afraid to die? You expect me to believe you?"

As the faint ticking of the wall clock counted off the last minutes of her life, Madison Liebert raised her gaze to the window. "I know you won't believe me, and that's my fault. I should've explained everything a long time ago, but I couldn't do it. I was a coward. One day, hopefully, you'll realize I did what I thought was best. Not for me, but for you."

"Explained what?" Kira demanded. "What did you do?"

A soft knock on the door interrupted their conversation.

"Come in," her mother called out. "We're ready."

No, we're not! Kira wanted to scream. *Go away! We're not ready!*

The door swung open, and a doctor entered the room, identifiable by his white lab coat. Middle-aged and handsome, with chestnut hair and tanned skin, he offered Kira a bright smile that reminded her of the toothy hosts on the old game shows the city ran on Saturdays after the morning broadcast. Two junior nurses followed him, both wearing black scrubs. One nurse carried a tray with a single syringe and a small silver vial.

"Good morning, Ms. Liebert. I'm Dr. Stern."

Kira shot out of her chair, imploring the doctor with her eyes. Hoping to appeal to whatever shred of humanity existed within the man. "Please. I'm begging you. Don't do this."

"Sit," her mother ordered. "Right now."

Rebellion didn't come easily to Kira. She never disregarded her mother's commands, but this was different. She couldn't allow this to continue, no matter what her mother wanted. "No! I will not let them kill you."

"That's enough." The doctor's megawatt smile disappeared, and he narrowed his dark eyes at Kira. "Young lady, if you can't control yourself, I'll have clinic security escort you from this room and your mother will die alone."

Your mother will die alone.

Closing her eyes, Kira saw the doctor's words scrawled in crimson on the backs of her eyelids, and she realized there would be no last-minute escape attempt for Madison Liebert. No hero swooping in to save the day. The only way her mother would leave this building was in a disposal van, and Kira could do nothing about it.

It wasn't fair.

But she couldn't let her mother die alone.

When Kira opened her eyes, the doctor had a hand on her mother's shoulder, that brilliant movie-star smile affixed to his lips once again. "How are you feeling today, Ms. Liebert? Any concerns or questions about the process?"

"None. Thank you, Dr. Stern."

"Good. I've reviewed your paperwork, and everything is in order for your procedure."

A powerful wave of nausea swept over Kira, and she collapsed into the plastic chair, tiny droplets of sweat forming on her forehead. Her peripheral vision diminished until nothing remained but a small circle of light with her mother and the doctor in its center. Leaning forward, Kira dropped her head into her hands and willed the feeling to pass. She wanted to find a bathroom to be sick in, but leaving her mother wasn't a possibility.

Not even for a second.

A female voice. One of the nurses. "Miss? Are you alright?"

Kira lifted her head from her hands and leaned back in her chair. With her eyes closed, she concentrated on taking slow, deliberate breaths—in through her nose and out through her mouth. She visualized the oxygen flowing through her body, reviving her cells.

"Kira?" Her mother sounded concerned. "What's wrong?"

The dizziness and nausea abated. She opened her eyes, and the world swam back into focus.

"I'm fine," she said, wiping the sheen of sweat from her forehead.

"Are you sure? You're white as a sheet."

"I'm okay."

The doctor stared at her, his lips a slim white line against tan skin. He wanted to kick Kira out of the room—she could see it in his eyes—but she hadn't given him enough of a reason. Instead, he nodded at the nurse holding the tray. "The medication, please."

The woman carried the tray to the doctor, and he picked up the syringe and inserted it into the vial, which was filled with an innocuous-looking clear liquid. After he extracted the liquid, he placed the vial back on the tray and flicked his finger against the syringe to clear out the air bubbles.

Pulling her gaze from the needle, Kira focused on her mother, expecting to see fear or hesitation. Tears forming in her eyes. A slight trembling of her lips. But Madison Liebert watched the doctor preparing her method of execution with an expression that could only be described as peaceful.

"Nurse, please note...I'm delivering a lethal dose of Somnumbutal via syringe at seven-thirteen a.m., in accordance with the Compulsory Order."

Madison Liebert closed her eyes as the doctor plunged the syringe into her arm. In less than five seconds, it was over. The doctor pulled the needle out and placed it on the tray. Then he stepped aside as one nurse placed a small plastic bandage over the tiny pinprick of blood.

The drug was no longer inside the vial. Now, it was inside Kira's mother's body, traveling along an elaborate network of veins on the way to their ultimate destination. The Somnumbutal would first render her mother unconscious, and then it would drift from organ to organ, meticulously shutting everything down. Kira imagined her mother's body as a well-lit house, and one-by-one, a little old man was going from room to room and switching off the lights.

The doctor placed his hand on her mother's shoulder. "You did wonderful, Ms. Liebert. We'll leave you two alone now."

"Thank you, Dr. Stern," her mother replied in a soft voice, her eyes already glazing over. "Thank you for being kind."

As the doctor and nurses exited the room, Kira perched on the edge of the bed and took her mother's hand. "Mom? Are you okay?"

It was a foolish question. Her mother wasn't okay. She was dying.

"I'm sorry," Madison Liebert whispered, her eyes drifting shut.

Pressing a hand against her mother's forehead, Kira said, "You don't have to be sorry, Mom."

"They made him leave, Kira."

Kira stared at her mother's chest, watching it rise and fall. Dreading when it wouldn't rise again. "I don't understand. Who made who leave?"

"He wasn't sick..."

Her mother wasn't making any sense. Probably a side effect of the drugs.

This wasn't right. Her mother didn't have to die like this.

"Mom, listen to me. Try to keep your eyes open, okay?" Kira begged. "I'm going to find the doctor and I'm going to tell him I want to volunteer in your place. They might let me do that. Then, I'll have the doctor bring you back. I'm sure they have an antidote, but you have to keep your eyes open a little longer. Okay? Please open your eyes."

"Can't... Going to sleep now..."

Kira grabbed her mother's shoulders and tried to meet her gaze. "Mom?"

But there was nothing. No spark of recognition. No awareness.

Nothing.

Then Madison Liebert's eyes rolled backward and her head flopped onto the pillow.

"Mom?"

Lowering her ear to her mother's chest, Kira listened as her heartbeat slowed. One missed beat. Then another. Finally, her mother's chest rose and fell for the last time.

Death was a horrible thing.

"Mom?"

Kira waited for a response, for one more word.

Nothing.

She held onto her mother's hand for as long as she could, not letting go until a grim-faced sanitation engineer entered the room and transferred her mother into a body bag, and then slid her onto a stretcher.

Unlike the Volunteers, whose bodies were cremated and their remains launched into the sky during the fireworks display at the weekly Reverence Ceremony, the Compulsories were given no such honors. There would be no casket for her mother. No funeral procession. Just a trip into the Unregulated Zone in a black disposal van filled with other dead Compulsories to be disposed of like trash in a landfill.

Kira didn't move until the man rolled her mother's body out of the room. When the door clicked shut behind him, she collapsed onto the bed and sobbed into the sheets.

"I'm so sorry, Mom."

The bed still carried the faint floral scent of the handmade soap her mother always bought at market.

Soap that smelled like roses.

Chapter 2

Two Years Later

They made him leave, Kira. He wasn't sick.

At the sound of her mother's whispered voice, Kira's eyes snapped open.

Bolting upright on the couch, where she'd been dozing, her heart hammered against the inside of her ribcage as she searched the living room for her dead mother.

"Mom?" She placed a hand over her heart, as if pressing on her chest would prevent her from having a heart attack if her mother responded.

Of course, no one answered.

Madison Liebert had been dead for two years.

Kira lowered her face into her hands and massaged her temples. She'd been plagued by headaches for the last few weeks, but that wasn't anything new. Her allergies were always bad in the early fall months. At nineteen, however, she was old enough to be selected as a Compulsory, so she had no desire to register her headaches with one of the local pharmacies just to get a bottle of aspirin.

Too many headaches might lead to a Compulsory Order with her name on it.

With aspirin off the table, Kira had stretched out on the couch after dinner and closed her eyes, hoping a brief rest would lessen her headache. But she must've dozed off, and now she had no idea what time it was.

Or what day.

A familiar sound pierced the fog in her head, bringing Kira back to reality, and she lifted her face from her hands.

The sound of people in the street outside her townhouse.

Lots of people.

Of course! It was Sunday. How could she have forgotten?

How long had she slept?

She pressed the button on the side of her watch, cringing as the screen lit up with the time.

Six-forty-two.

Oh, no.

She was late.

Very late, but she could make it if she hurried.

Rushing to her bedroom, she kicked off her sweatpants and pulled on a pair of jeans—the same wrinkled pair she'd worn the day before and hadn't gotten around to washing. She tore off her t-shirt and pulled on her navy polo with the tiny blue rose sewn over the heart, which identified her as a volunteer advocate. Without bothering to glance in a mirror, she grabbed an elastic from her nightstand and jogged downstairs, pulling her hair into a ponytail. She tied a cardigan around her waist—it would be dark and chilly before she returned home—and slipped on her sneakers.

She was going to need them.

In the street, a few people rode bicycles, but most hurried toward the river on foot. Because of the limited resources— which included fuel—only people with high-level city jobs owned personal vehicles. Everyone else used the city bus system. Since the buses didn't operate on Sundays to conserve fuel, most of Vita Nova had to walk—or run—to the island.

After locking the front door, Kira dashed down the steps and into the street. She fell in with the crowd, catching a quick glimpse of the barricade wall between two neighboring town-houses. A concrete monster twenty feet high and ten feet thick, the wall formed a protective barrier around the entire city, leaving only a small section of the land that bordered the river unfortified.

THE BARRICADE EXISTED BECAUSE OF THE JOB VIRUS.

That was what the media had called it, after the Biblical character of the same name. The first cases had emerged twelve years earlier, first in Europe and then in the United States. A devastatingly lethal virus that killed its victims within three days of infection, their bodies breaking out in weeping, pus-filled sores that caused sepsis and eventually death. The federal government couldn't get a handle on it. Most of them were dying themselves. Vita Nova—then known as Harrisburg, Pennsylvania—went into lockdown, on the orders of the city's mayor. No one came into the city, sick or not. Anyone showing symptoms of the virus was exiled outside the city, in what the government now referred to as the Unregulated Zone. They blocked off all roads leading into the city. Engineers from a local Army unit conducted a massive demolition campaign to destroy all but one of the city's eight major highway and rail-road bridges. Only the Market Street Bridge survived the campaign and now stood as the city's sole link to the Unregu-lated Zone. Those same engineers had flooded the area near Three Mile Island to create a natural southern barrier against the disease and then erected an electrified fence around the perimeter of the city. Guards patrolled the fence twenty-four hours a day to keep anyone from sneaking in.

Not that anyone could sneak in.

The fence operated at thirty-thousand volts.

Eventually, a concrete barricade with concertina wire curled along its top had replaced the electrified fence. Because of those protective measures, Vita Nova had seen no cases of the virus inside the city limits for more than a decade.

A year after the last reported case of the virus, the city voted to rename itself Vita Nova—meaning "new life."

KIRA JOGGED TO THE STADIUM, PASSING SEVERAL struggling families along the way. Parents carried their young children on their shoulders or dragged them along, forcing them to walk faster than their little legs could carry them.

Everyone was rushing for good reason. On Sunday evenings, the entire population of the city migrated to City Island for the weekly Reverence Ceremony. The *mandatory* Reverence Ceremony, where the newest batch of Volunteers began their Final Week by receiving their blue roses in front of the entire city. Afterward, the city honored the Volunteers who'd given their lives the previous week with a memorial ceremony and fireworks display. The Guards locked the gates to the Stadium at seven p.m., no exceptions, and anyone who wasn't inside got a warning from the city. Too many warnings and you became a Compulsory.

She passed a mother carrying twin toddler boys, one in each arm. Both boys were crying and sweating in the early September heat, as was their mother. Kira ignored her instinct to stop. Most parents were on their own, with no help. Few children in Vita Nova grew up in two-parent households, and even fewer grew up with grandparents.

The walkway came into sight just ahead and, beyond that, the cerulean surface of the river shimmered as if coated with diamonds.

Almost there.

The crowds grew thicker when she reached Front Street, one of the city's primary arteries, which ran parallel to the Susquehanna River. People poured into the street from every direction, all converging on the Volunteer Memorial Walkway, which would take them halfway across the river to the Stadium on City Island. Pale blue lights outlined the old iron truss bridge, guiding everyone to the Stadium like landing lights on a runway.

Prior to the virus, the walkway was known as the Walnut Street Bridge, and it had once spanned the entire river, linking the city's eastern and western shores to the small island in the center of the river. The eastern span of the pedestrian walkway still connected the city to the island, but on the opposite side of the island, the western span dropped off with the unnaturalness of an amputated limb. A short section of the old bridge remained standing on the river's opposite shore, extending out from the Unregulated Zone like an arm beckoning the city for salvation.

Unlike the other city bridges, the Volunteer Memorial Walkway hadn't been destroyed by an explosive charge during the height of the virus. Instead, the western span had been destroyed by ice floes decades earlier. City leadership had erected a chain-link fence to prevent people from exploring the western span, but the teenagers of Vita Nova frequently scaled the fence at night and made their way to the end of the bridge, where they sat with their legs dangling over the rushing water and got their closest glimpse of the Unregulated Zone.

Several of her friends had done it, but not Kira. In nineteen years, she'd never climbed that fence, and she never intended to.

The island was as close to the Unregulated Zone as she liked to get. During the first few years of the pandemic, the city had remained on lockdown. No one went in or out. For months, the diseased tried to breach the barricade to get to the hospitals inside the city. Eventually, they had died off, and the virus had presumably died off with them. After a few years had passed, the city leadership established the Patrols—the city's version of military soldiers—with the mission of going beyond the barricade to look for supplies.

It was the Patrols who had first discovered them. The Lawless. People who had survived the virus by abandoning their humanity. Brutal bands of marauders and killers living in the Unregulated Zone, among the ruins of society. They prowled the empty streets of the forgotten towns, taking what they wanted and killing anyone who got in their way. The Lawless had murdered dozens of Patrol soldiers over the years, but they'd never breached the barricade. Although it was a dangerous job, the heavily armed presence of the Patrols in the Unregulated Zone prevented the Lawless from getting close enough to Vita Nova to attack.

As she entered the walkway, Kira veered to the right, bypassing the crowded concrete section to her left for the interlocking iron girders that comprised the right side of the walkway. The rough metal cut into the bottoms of her sneakers and made her feet ache, but there weren't as many people in her way, so she could move faster. Through the iron girders, she could see the river sweeping by fifty feet below. The sight made her dizzy, and she returned her gaze to the distant lights of the Stadium.

A horn blared—two long blasts.

The five-minute warning.

Everyone on the walkway increased their pace, and the entire structure trembled, as if it had enough sense to be afraid.

Less than a minute later, Kira stepped off the walkway and approached the gate to the Stadium, where a dozen Guards stood spaced at equal intervals, scanning the laminated identification cards that the citizens of Vita Nova—men, women, and children—were required to carry with them at all times.

Only after the Guard scanned her ID did Kira relax a little. She'd made it inside the Stadium with a few minutes to spare. The final horn blared, signaling the closing of the gates. Anyone who hadn't made it inside before that horn would be delinquent.

Following the crowd into the Stadium, Kira climbed high onto the bleachers and found a seat in the top row. Before the virus had ravaged the world, the Stadium had been a Minor League ballpark. Enormous crowds of people had once flooded onto the island to see a baseball game played in the middle of a river, with downtown Harrisburg as the backdrop.

But instead of baseball players, Guards filled the field. Vita Nova's version of police officers, the Guards defended the barricade wall and the checkpoint on the Market Street Bridge. During Reverence Ceremonies, Guards also provided security for the Volunteers and the deputy mayor.

Tonight, twelve Volunteers stood in the center of the field. The number of Volunteers varied per week, with the average number being between five and twelve. Kira had seen as many as nineteen Volunteers in one week, and as few as two.

Once on the field, they were lined up by age, oldest to youngest, with the most respect being given to the youngest among them. The younger the Volunteer, the greater the sacrifice.

The evening's oldest Volunteer was Elizabeth Currant, age fifty-seven. She was also Kira's client.

The gray-haired woman stood at the head of the line, wringing her hands. Kira had met Lizzy two weeks earlier when the woman had walked into her office and explained her reasoning for becoming a Volunteer. During a self-exam, she'd discovered a lump in one of her breasts. Despite her husband's pleadings, she'd been too frightened to go to the Medical Sector to see a doctor. The possibility existed that the tumor was benign, but since a cancer diagnosis would've led to her immediate selection as a Compulsory, Lizzy hadn't been willing to take that risk.

"If I'm going to die, I want to die as a Volunteer," she'd told Kira during their initial meeting, clutching her handbag against her chest. "I feel terrible leaving my grandchildren, but what choice do I have?"

Unlike most Volunteers, Lizzy had asked for little during her Final Week. Just a fancy dinner with her husband at the city's nicest restaurant—The Riverfront—and an overnight visit with her three grandchildren at Rolling Meadows, the beautiful estate where Volunteers spent their Final Week. On the night before her death, she would be invited to the Volunteer Ball at the Executive Mansion, but Lizzy had informed Kira that she had no intention of attending the ball.

She wanted to spend her last night on earth alone with her husband.

A breeze whipped through Kira's hair, raising goosebumps on her exposed arms, and the rich and earthy scent of the river filled her nostrils.

A deep voice came over the loudspeaker. "Ladies and gentlemen, please welcome the deputy mayor of Vita Nova!"

Deputy Mayor Sienna Graves walked into view, her high heels sinking in the grass as she strolled to the center of the field. Although she was in her late forties, Graves looked a decade younger. Tonight, she wore a gray pantsuit that flattered her slender frame, her curly red hair swept into a high chignon that exaggerated her sharp cheekbones. Tall and elegant, with a perfect body and piercing green eyes, Graves was the envy of the women in Vita Nova...and an object of desire for the men. Kira's male clients often admitted to becoming Volunteers just so they could meet her.

The woman stopped in the middle of the field and raised a microphone to her lips. "Good evening, citizens of Vita Nova!" She gave a little bow, a smile finding its way to her lips. "Thank you for attending tonight's Reverence Ceremony!"

The crowd launched into boisterous applause.

When the applause died down, Graves continued, "As always, we will open tonight's ceremony with the Distribution of the Roses. This will signal the commencement of Final Week for the Volunteers. If you see these individuals around the city in the coming days, please remember to thank them for their service. If you have any goods or services to offer them, please do. Treat them with the utmost honor and respect. Volunteers are the reason our city continues to thrive. We are blessed to live within the safety of the barricade, but our space and resources are limited. Without the Volunteers, more Compulsories would have to be chosen." She turned toward the line of Volunteers. "Ladies and gentlemen, the citizens of Vita Nova owe you a debt of gratitude. We shall revere our brave Volunteers for offering their lives for the good of all."

"For the good of all!" the crowd echoed.

Kira's eyes dropped to the blue rose embroidered on her polo shirt. A tiny piece of thread stuck up from the edge of one petal. Pinching the thread between her thumb and forefinger, she gave it a hard yank. Instead of breaking, the thread unraveled, ruining one of the outer petals.

"Oh, shoot!"

A man seated nearby shot her a disapproving look.

"Sorry," she mouthed, using her thumb to smooth the string into place. As if doing so would fix her ruined shirt.

"After I finish distributing the roses," Sienna Graves continued, "we will honor the Volunteers who sacrificed themselves for the good of Vita Nova this past week."

Two brawny male aides in black suits flanked the deputy mayor. One held a tray of boutonnieres, while the other held a tray of corsages. One of Graves's duties as deputy mayor was to distribute the Sacrifice Roses during the Reverence Ceremony. The Volunteers would wear the roses for the entire week, whenever they went out in public, to ensure that everyone they encountered would recognize them as Volunteers.

"Without further ado, let's begin with the Distribution of the Roses. Elizabeth Currant. Please step forward to receive your rose."

Lizzy ambled toward the deputy mayor on unsteady legs, and Kira wondered if the older woman was having second thoughts. Was she regretting not going to the doctor to have the suspicious lump in her breast checked? Not that it mattered anymore. It was too late to turn back. Volunteers who changed their minds after the Reverence Ceremony were arrested and held in the Confines until the city put them to death as Compulsories.

Graves gave Lizzy a sweet-as-apple-pie smile and shook her hand. "Elizabeth Currant, is it your wish to end your life as a Volunteer?"

Lizzy nodded. "Yes, ma'am."

"And have you arrived at this decision of your own free will?"

"Yes, I have."

"Very well. Elizabeth Currant, the city of Vita Nova

extends you its sincere appreciation for your bravery and sacrifice. Tonight and in the days to follow, this city will honor you. After you have made your Sacrifice, we shall revere you. Your name will always be remembered. We will never forget you."

The deputy mayor held the microphone to Lizzy's mouth.

The woman stared at the microphone as if she didn't know what it was for, and then she leaned forward and whispered, "Thank you."

Passing off the microphone to one of her aides, Graves retrieved a corsage from one tray and slipped it around Lizzy's wrist.

Even on the Jumbotron, Kira could see Lizzy's hand shaking.

Once the corsage was secure, Graves stepped back, grabbed the microphone, and shouted, "Revere the Volunteer!"

More than seven-thousand people—the entire population of Vita Nova—leapt to their feet. *"Revere the Volunteer!"*

Lizzy faced the people seated in the bleachers, her desperate expression displayed on the Jumbotron for everyone to see.

The crowd ignored Lizzy's obvious distress and cheered for her anyway, the sound loud enough to carry across the water and echo through the crumbling relics inside the Unregulated Zone.

Kira stood with them—applauding and cheering—but she felt like crying.

The countdown to Lizzy's death had begun.

One by one, the Volunteers stepped forward to receive their roses. The youngest was only twenty-six. With each successive Volunteer, Kira found it more difficult to stand. More difficult to cheer. More difficult even to breathe.

After Graves distributed all the roses, the crowd stood for the Memoriam. Kira formed a v-shape with the index and middle fingers of her right hand and placed it over her heart. She watched the faces of the previous week's Volunteers appear on the Jumbotron, one after another, along with their birth and death dates. Six brave souls who'd given their lives for the good of all.

After the Memoriam, fireworks exploded in the sky over the river, the flaming rockets carrying a combination of explosives and the cremated remains of the previous week's Volunteers into the heavens. Each subsequent detonation sent more ashes into the atmosphere. The breeze whisked some of the remains away from Vita Nova, into the Unregulated Zone, while the river carried others to their final resting place in the Atlantic.

Lives offered for the good of all—their bodies burned until nothing remained but ashes—followed by a formal ceremony where the population tilted their faces toward the heavens.

Sometimes, the Reverence Ceremony felt less like a celebration of bravery and more like a sacrificial ritual.

After the fireworks ended, the stadium erupted in one last cry of, "Revere the Volunteer!"

Kira could barely force the words from her mouth.

Chapter Three

The city bus rolled up to the curb near Kira's townhouse forty minutes late, its air brakes unleashing an angry *whoosh* as the door swung open. She rushed up the steps and craned her neck over the divider, searching for an empty seat on the overcrowded bus.

Every seat was full.

The crowd behind Kira surged forward, driving her down the narrow aisle and up two short stairs to an elevated platform, where a group of leather-skinned construction workers filled every seat. She felt their eyes roaming over her as she climbed the stairs in her pencil skirt and high heels, but when she glanced at them, they averted their eyes. She grabbed one of the yellow hanging straps and faced away from them, already wishing the day was over.

It hadn't even begun yet.

After everyone had boarded, the bus rolled onward, plowing through the city streets. Kira planted her feet to keep from falling into the lap of one of the construction workers. She glanced at her watch, hoping the rotating hands might've slowed to give her additional time, but they hadn't.

Seven-fifty.

She had ten minutes to get to work.

Unfortunately, it took twenty minutes to get to the Governmental Sector.

Because the city expected everyone to use the public transportation system, the city buses were always overcrowded and running late. Kira accounted for the frequent delays by taking one of the earliest buses, which arrived at her stop at ten minutes after seven in the morning. Even when the bus ran late, she still made it to work on time.

The bus had *never* been forty minutes late before.

The driver pulled up to the next stop and a young man climbed aboard and came to an abrupt halt beside the driver. His eyes widened as he studied the overcrowded bus, and then he smacked his lips together and removed his jacket, revealing the blue rose pinned to the front of his t-shirt.

A Volunteer.

"Revere the Volunteer!" echoed through the bus.

Those passengers who weren't already standing rose to show their respect. Everyone formed their fingers into v-shapes and placed them over their hearts. Even the driver lumbered out of his seat and took off his baseball cap, unleashing a mop of greasy hair onto his shoulders.

Kira watched as the people in the first few rows battled for the right to give the man their seats.

"Please, sir. Sit here."

"No. Take my seat. It's closer to the front."

"Sir, it would be an honor."

After taking a few moments to consider his options—and making the bus and its occupants even later—the Volunteer slid into the seat behind the driver, not even bothering to offer a thank you to the woman who'd vacated it. There were two seats in each row, but the Volunteer sat sideways and took up both of them.

Such blatant displays of self-importance weren't unusual when it came to Volunteers. Most found the public veneration aspect of volunteering uncomfortable. Those people usually spent their Final Week holed up inside Rolling Meadows with their families. But some Volunteers came to expect or even demand adoration from everyone they encountered. By the end of the week, their insatiable appetites for worship led them to spend most of their time prowling the streets, demanding to possess anything—or anyone—that caught their eye.

At ten minutes past eight, the bus came to a stop in the Governmental Sector.

Kira squeezed down the stairs and into the main aisle. "Excuse me," she muttered, pushing her way past the people huddled in front of the rear exit. She stepped off the bus and into the street. The morning air smelled sweeter than usual because she'd spent the past twenty minutes inhaling the various body odors of a dozen beefy construction workers.

Only four blocks separated her from the Volunteer Support Center, but she was already ten minutes late for her eight o'clock appointment. Once she reached the front entrance of the building, she would still have to wait in line at the security checkpoint.

Her supervisor of eighteen months, Carl, would not be happy, but would he be mad enough to fire her?

She kicked off her heels, picked them up, and broke into a sprint.

A few cars buzzed past her, their drivers ignoring the young woman jogging barefoot down the street. Kira's first instinct was to be angry with the drivers—any of them could've pulled over and offered her a ride—but she quickly tamped down her anger. The people behind the wheels of those cars were likely high-ranking city officials or medical professionals. They didn't have time to stop for some random girl.

At eight-fifteen, Kira came to a stop underneath the red awning of her office building. As she bent over to slip her heels on her feet, her hair fell over her face. Damp blonde strands adhered themselves to her cheeks like paper mache. She hadn't realized how sweaty she was until she stopped running. The silky material of her blouse clung to her body, and her skirt felt even tighter than usual.

At least the blouse was black. The sweat stains shouldn't be *too* obvious.

There was no line at security, thank goodness. Kira placed her purse on the conveyer belt and watched as it disappeared inside the x-ray machine. Kevin, the building's heavily tattooed security guard, peered at his computer screen as the contents of Kira's purse floated by.

Despite his intimidating persona, Kevin was one of the nicest people in the building.

Taking in Kira's sweaty and disheveled appearance, the security guard gave her a look that was pure pity and waved her through the metal detector. "Good morning, Miss Liebert. Don't you usually beat me to the building?"

"Yes, I do," she replied, brushing sweaty hair off her forehead. "But my bus was running forty minutes late today. *Forty minutes*, Kevin. If Carl fires me today, you'll have to escort me from the building. I promise to only kick and scream a little."

Kevin chuckled without making a sound, his signature laugh. "I'd appreciate that very much, Miss Liebert." He rose from his seat, retrieved her purse from the end of the conveyer belt, and handed it to her. "But you don't have to worry about Carl."

"Why not?"

"It's Thursday. All the department supervisors are at a mandatory management training today and tomorrow. Most of them were grumbling about it as they left the office yesterday." He gave Kira a conspiratorial wink. "Have a wonderful day, Miss Liebert."

Relief flooded Kira's body. She was still late for her client, but at least she would not be in trouble. "You're the best, Kevin."

"I know. Don't tell anybody."

Kira headed for the stairs, passing by the building's only elevator. A handwritten sign hanging on the wall declared it out-of-order. The elevator had been out-of-order for as long as Kira had worked in the building. Most of the elevators in the city didn't work anymore because they were too difficult to maintain. Kira's mother had told her that, in the days before the barricade, an out-of-service elevator in a public building would've been grounds for a lawsuit, due to people with physical disabilities and limitations.

But not anymore.

There were no disabled people in Vita Nova.

KIRA JOGGED UP THE STAIRS, A NEWFOUND SPRING IN HER step. When she reached the fourth-floor landing, she peered into the waiting room through the rectangle of glass in the door. From the plush gray carpeting, to the enormous picture window that allowed in an abundance of natural light, to the framed photographs of blue roses that adorned the canary-yellow walls, the room more closely resembled a nursery than a place where people began the process of killing themselves.

Kira had always assumed the atmosphere was intentionally

cheerful to deter the Volunteers from changing their minds at the last minute.

In the middle of the manufactured cheer, a young man sat in front of the picture window, his left leg bobbing in a nervous rhythm. As Kira watched, he reached for one of the Volunteer pamphlets on the table next to him. The pamphlet featured a group of Volunteers—each with a Volunteer rose or corsage— staring proudly into the camera, the words *For the good of all* imprinted on the cloudless blue sky behind them. The young man peered at the image on the pamphlet, absently running his free hand through his unruly golden-brown hair.

Kira's heart sank at the sight of the pamphlet in his hands.

He's really young.

And really cute.

From his clothing alone—a black t-shirt, olive-drab work pants, and steel-toed boots—Kira deduced that the young man held a low-level job within the city. Construction, maintenance, or janitorial services. But his face was clean-shaven, not scruffy like most of the city's blue-collar workers, and although he wasn't overly muscular, he didn't appear weak, either. Nothing about the young man's physical appearance gave Kira any indication that he wasn't in good physical health.

So, why did he want to become a Volunteer?

As she reached for the door, Kira glimpsed herself in the glass and recoiled in horror. She looked—and no doubt smelled —as if she'd just finished a marathon. Quickly, she set to work, combing her fingers through her damp hair, taming it as best she could, and tucking the most errant strands behind her ears. Then, she pulled one of her mother's old handkerchiefs from her purse and used it to remove as much of the shine from her face as possible.

There. Good enough.

She took a deep breath, put a hand on the bar of the door, and pushed it open.

The young man looked up as Kira entered the room, and if her disheveled appearance disgusted him, he didn't let on. He tossed the pamphlet onto the table and rose from his seat. "Are you Miss Liebert?"

Not only cute, but *tall*. At least six feet.

"Yes, I am." Kira lifted her chin, trying to look professional despite being late and a total mess. "I'm sorry. I feel terrible for keeping you waiting. My bus arrived forty minutes behind schedule today, however, that's no excuse for my being late for our appointment. I sincerely apologize and if there's anything I can do to make it up to you, please let me know."

The young man smiled, revealing a set of lopsided dimples —an imperfection that made him even more attractive. The smile lit up his eyes, which were the most beautiful color she'd ever seen. An impossible, vibrant blue. The same color as the Volunteer roses. "Don't worry about being late. I took the whole day off work to come here, so I don't have anywhere else to be." He extended his right hand. "I'm Will Foster, and I believe you're going to be my advocate?"

Kira's eyes traveled the length of Will's outstretched arm to his hand, and she watched as it closed around her own much-smaller one. His hand felt both rough and soft at the same time.

And he smelled amazing.

Like trees and dandelions and everything outdoors.

"Nice to meet you, Will. My name is Kira Liebert, and I'm going to help you through this process," she replied, slipping effortlessly into the practiced speech that she used to open her appointments. "My job is to answer any questions you may have and make your Final Week as rewarding and fulfilling as possible. From here on, if you need anything, just let me know."

He raised both eyebrows, the corner of his lips turning up in a grin. "Really? Anything?"

Kira felt the blood rush to her face at his vaguely suggestive tone, and she silently cursed her fair complexion for turning her into an overripe tomato at the most inopportune times. Since her face was already red from running the last four blocks to her office building, hopefully Will wouldn't realize how much his little innuendo—if that was what he'd intended it to be—had made her blush.

Glancing down, she realized that she hadn't let go of his hand. She released it and narrowed her eyes. "Anything *within reason,* Mr. Foster."

"Ah." He snapped his fingers. "Got it. Thanks for clarifying. That should save us both a lot of embarrassment."

Kira couldn't stop a tiny laugh from bursting through her lips. "You're not going to cause me any trouble, are you, Mr. Foster?"

Will held both hands up in surrender, a mischievous glint in his eyes. "You'll have no trouble with me. I promise."

"Okay. Good."

Why didn't she believe him?

Chapter Four

Kira unlocked the door to her office and flipped on the overhead lights, bathing the barebones room in a harsh, fluorescent glow she knew would magnify her sweaty hair and face. She hung her purse from a hook on the wall and motioned to the chair opposite her desk.

"Please. Have a seat," she said. "We better get started, since I kept you waiting."

Lowering himself into the chair, Will's eyes passed over the empty walls. "Did you just start working here?"

Kira used her hands to smooth the back of her skirt before settling into her chair. "Actually, I've worked here for eighteen months, but our office policy prohibits us from decorating or displaying any personal effects."

"Seriously? Why?"

"Because this process isn't about me, or the things I enjoy, or the people I love." She repeated the words verbatim from her employee handbook. "It's about the Volunteer."

Will rolled his eyes. "That's a stupid policy."

Kira fought to contain her smile. It *was* a stupid policy.

"Why don't we get started?"

She searched for Will's intake file on her computer, clicking on the rose-shaped Volunteer Registration Program icon and typing his name into the search bar. When an individual decided to become a Volunteer, they called the office to schedule an intake appointment. During that initial appointment, the intake officer collected the client's personal information, entered it into the system, and assigned each client a volunteer advocate who would book the client's reservation at Rolling Meadows and fulfill their Final Week requests.

But when Kira tried to find Will's intake file, the search yielded no results.

"Huh."

Will leaned forward and clasped his hands in his lap. "Something wrong?"

"I'm not sure." Kira typed his name again, in case she'd spelled it wrong. Still nothing. "I can't find your name here. When was your intake appointment?"

"Uh, I met with a lady on Monday and I filled out a ton of paperwork. Was that it?"

Kira nodded. "It's strange that I can't find your file, but maybe the intake officer forgot to save the information after your appointment." Nothing like that had ever happened before, but she supposed it was possible. She clicked through the program and opened a new file for Will. "Let's fill out everything we can, and the intake officer can finish the rest later."

"Sounds good." Will leaned back in the chair, his long legs splayed, and crossed his arms over his chest. "Fire away."

Will wasn't the first Volunteer to show no fear of dying, but Kira had never worked with anyone so *blasé* about the process. Perhaps he didn't have any doubts about his decision to Volunteer, or maybe he was looking forward to the perks of his Final Week and reality had yet to set in.

But it would set in, eventually. It always did.

"As I mentioned earlier," Kira began, "my job is to walk you through this process and advocate for you along the way. Before you leave today, I'll book your reservation at Rolling Meadows and schedule the time of your Sacrifice."

She glanced at him, hoping to see a reaction at the mention of Rolling Meadows, but Will only nodded.

"Sounds great."

She refocused her attention on her computer. And then—without knowing why she was doing it—she lowered her voice and asked the one question her supervisors had specifically trained her *not* to ask. "I usually begin my appointments by asking my clients why they've chosen to become Volunteers."

Never. I've never asked a client about that before. That question could get me fired.

Will raised his eyebrows, as if he could hear her inner thoughts. "Does the city really care about my reasons for wanting to die?" he asked, a hint of defiance in his voice.

Of course they don't. What had she been thinking, asking a question like that? Volunteer Advocates weren't supposed to interrogate potential Volunteers. The city *wanted* people to volunteer. They encouraged it. The broadcasts were constantly running segments about the strain of overpopulation on Vita Nova's dwindling resources. They claimed that if the population continued to grow at its current rate, within five years, there wouldn't be enough food for everyone. Citizens would starve to death and disease would take hold. A weakened city could not defend itself from whatever terrors existed beyond the barricade—and Vita Nova would fall.

But Kira had already asked the question, and now it hung in the air between them like a foul odor. It was too late to take it back. "I'm curious about your reason for volunteering because I care about my Volunteers. You're making a huge decision today, and I want to make sure you've considered every option."

Fire blazed in Will's eyes—an obscenity in an ocean of blue. "I appreciate your concern, Miss Liebert, but my reasons for volunteering are my own. Let's just say I want a nice clean death instead of a messy one and leave it at that."

Messy. That word conjured grotesque images in Kira's mind. Carved wrists. Bullet-shattered skulls. Rope-burned necks. Terrible things from the time before the barricade. Things she'd only read about in books. She shuddered at the methods people had employed to end their lives before the Volunteer and Compulsory Programs had eliminated such barbaric practices. No one—not the sick, the elderly, or the despairing—needed to suffer any longer.

Death had no power over them.

Since Will would not reveal his reasons for volunteering, she shifted gears to a different subject. "What about your family?" She posed the question flippantly, although she was genuinely curious about him. "Your parents? Your siblings? How do they feel about you becoming a Volunteer?"

Will lowered his gaze to her desk. "My parents died when I was very young, and I never had any siblings."

Kira didn't know what to say. She'd only just met Will, but she felt a strange sort of kinship with him. They were both orphans. The worst kind of orphans. Orphans with no siblings. "I'm sorry to hear that." She wanted to press him about his parents, but since Will seemed reluctant to share any personal details about himself, she decided not to push. "Let's try to get your basic information down, okay?"

"Okay."

"How old are you?"

"Twenty-two."

"What about a job? Are you employed?"

"For the past six years, I've worked as a sanitation engineer for the city." Will stuck his boot out and nudged the small trashcan next to her desk. "I take out the garbage."

Bodies. He disposes of the bodies.

Kira's mind flashed back to the room at the Compulsory Clinic, to the sanitation engineer who'd silently transferred her mother's body onto a stretcher and carried her away from Kira. Thrown her into a hole in the ground. Shoveled dirt on top of her. Left her in the dark forever.

"Miss Liebert?" Will shifted in his chair, a concerned expression on his face. "Are you alright?"

She bit her lip, forcing the emotions deep inside her chest where they belonged. She couldn't blame Will for his job. Like her, he performed his role for the good of the city. "Yes, I'm fine. It's just...my mother died as a Compulsory two years ago."

He looked stricken, his cheeks flushing red. "I'm sorry, Miss Liebert. That was a stupid thing to say. I wasn't thinking."

"Don't worry about it. You couldn't have known."

"Was your mom sick?" he asked.

Kira examined her fingernails. She'd painted them a deep mauve color the previous evening, but they were already chipping. This appointment wasn't supposed to be about her, but yet here she was, about to discuss her mother's death with a total stranger. "The doctors found a large mass in her lung during her semiannual health exam. It turned out to be a cancerous tumor. Inoperable. She got the Compulsory Notification soon afterward."

Will stared at her. "Did you believe them?"

"Who?"

"The doctors."

It was a strange question to ask. "Of course. Why would they lie?"

The intensity in his eyes was at odds with his indecisive shrug. "I'm not saying they did. I'm just wondering if you saw the x-rays. Or the CT scan, since I'm assuming they ran additional tests after finding a mass on the x-ray. They also should've done a biopsy of the mass."

"You mean like a surgery?"

"Exactly. It's not really possible to know if a mass is cancerous without a biopsy. That's why I was wondering if the doctors performed any kind of surgical procedure on your mother's lung before they sent her a Compulsory Notification."

"Well...no." Will's questions had thrown Kira off-balance. She felt dizzy, as if she'd just stepped off a moving carousel. She met Will's eyes, suddenly angry at him for the doubts swirling around in her mind. "Why are you asking these personal questions about my mother? What business is it of yours?"

His expression softened, the intensity fleeing from his eyes. "I apologize for pushing the issue, Miss Liebert. You're absolutely right. It's none of my business."

"It's fine." Kira forced a smile. "Let's just move on."

She continued with the appointment, moving swiftly through the rest of Will's information. He lived in a cramped apartment in a four-building complex known as the Tenements, in the city's infamous Eastern Sector. Will had no known medical conditions and appeared to be in good health. He had no immediate family, he wasn't married, and he had no next of kin, but the program wouldn't allow her to continue to the scheduling page until she entered an emergency contact.

"Is there a significant other in your life?" Kira asked casually, her eyes flicking back to her computer screen. "A wife or a girlfriend, perhaps?"

Will gave her a pained look, so brief she wondered if she'd imagined it. Then his eyebrows shot up, and he recoiled in his seat. "Who's asking the personal questions now? I'm sorry, Miss

Liebert, but that question is extremely inappropriate and unprofessional."

The heat in Kira's cheeks rivaled the sun. "I wasn't being unprofessional," she blurted out. "I'm only asking because I have to enter someone as your emergency contact."

Will's face relaxed into an amused smile. "Relax. I didn't think you were asking me out, although—for the record—I wouldn't say no if you did."

"Oh, good. That's...uh..." she stammered like a fool, uncertain how to respond. "Well, yeah."

Thankfully, Will saved her by continuing to talk. "To answer your question, I don't have a wife or a girlfriend. If you need an emergency contact, just put my boss at the sanitation lot. His name is Hank Jones, but he goes by Jonesy. However, he's a grumpy old man, and he doesn't like me very much, so I wouldn't recommend contacting him unless things get bad." He winked at her. "Like...life or death bad."

"Very funny." Her face still burning, Kira entered Jonesy's name and the number for the sanitation lot. "For the record, I don't care if you have a girlfriend."

"Duly noted."

Kira's eyes locked with Will's, and she saw mischief in his gaze. He was teasing her again. Maybe even flirting with her. A faint fluttering, like the wings of a tiny bird, flapped against the inside of her ribcage. Of course, her first thought was to wonder if something was wrong with her heart. A genetic anomaly that the doctors would uncover at her next semiannual screening. She'd never felt anything like it before, and as unsettling as the sensation was, it also made her feel alive.

Will made her feel alive.

But that wasn't good. In fact, it was downright terrible.

Because Will would be dead in eight days.

Chapter Five

After Kira finished entering Will's information into the system, the next step was to book his stay at Rolling Meadows, the lavish estate where he would spend his Final Week. "Do you have any requests regarding the timing of your Sacrifice?"

Will's expression grew serious. "As soon as possible."

For such a young man, Will seemed awfully eager to die. Kira double-clicked on the Rolling Meadows icon to login to the website and search for an available date. As the website loaded, she skimmed the promotional image at the top of the page. A long driveway wound through the woods before emerging into an impeccably landscaped front yard. After a few seconds, the image morphed into various images of Volunteers enjoying the estate's nine-hole golf course, indoor swimming pool, horse stables, and fishing pond. The slideshow concluded with several interior shots of the Volunteer suites, with their Egyptian cotton bedding, balconies, and floor-to-ceiling windows.

Rolling Meadows, she thought. *The most beautiful place to die.*

The place functioned more like a luxury hotel than a medical facility. There was a formal dining room on the first floor, but the staff at Rolling Meadows also provided twenty-four-hour room service for the guests. According to Kira's past clients, the food was superb and featured rare delicacies that only Volunteers got to experience. Most spent their entire Final Week living in luxury in one of the elaborate Volunteer suites, which were large enough to accommodate whole families.

Kira opened the scheduler and spotted a green slot in a sea of red. "Good news," she said, although that little slash of green didn't feel like good news to her. "There's an opening at Rolling Meadows for next Friday afternoon at three o'clock."

"Three o'clock is perfect. Schedule it."

Her fingers hovered over the keys. "You do understand that, once your Final Week begins, you cannot change your mind?"

What she didn't add—but which most people knew—was that if a Volunteer changed their mind after the Reverence Ceremony, they would be arrested and held in the Confines until their transfer to the Compulsory Clinic, where they would be put to death involuntarily.

"I know that rule," Will said. "But you don't have to worry about me. I won't change my mind."

Kira nodded and typed his name into the open slot, which then turned red.

There. It was done.

She exited out of the program. "Okay. You're scheduled for next Friday. A bus will take you and the other Volunteers to Rolling Meadows on Sunday evening following the conclusion of the Reverence Ceremony."

"Great." Will's left leg was bobbing again, as it had been doing in the waiting room. "I'm ready for this."

Kira wanted to ask him what he meant, but the familiar, queasy feeling she got every time she scheduled a Volunteer for their Sacrifice distracted her. The first few times she'd scheduled someone to die, she'd run to the bathroom immediately afterward and thrown up. Now, she just felt sick for the rest of the day.

Scheduling people to die was getting easier, and Kira wasn't sure how to feel about that.

"The ceremony begins at seven," she continued, "but all Volunteers should arrive by six-thirty. If you need transportation to the Stadium, let me know and I'll arrange it."

"Okay."

Kira interlaced her fingers on the desk. The next step in the appointment process was to get a list of the client's Final Week requests. "As you know, Mr. Foster, we do everything we can to keep our Volunteers happy during their Final Week. You're welcome to update me as the week goes on, but can you think of any specific requests right now?"

Will's leg stopped shaking, and he sat up straighter in his chair. "What if I make it really easy on you? What if I only want one thing?"

"Easy works for me. What do you want?"

Will held her gaze, the muscles in his jaw tightening. "I want to spend my Final Week with you, Kira. The whole week. That's what I want. That's the *only* thing I want. Do you think you can make that happen?"

At the sound of Will speaking her name, the faint fluttering in Kira's chest transformed into eagle's wings. The blood rushed to her cheeks again, a solar flare of embarrassment. "I'm sorry, Mr. Foster," she replied, hoping her voice sounded firmer to Will than it did to her ears. "But I'm certain that's not allowed."

"How do you know?" He smiled, his eyes crinkling at the

corners. "Have any of your other clients asked to spend the week with you?"

"Of course not. But I'm sure it's against the rules."

Actually, she wasn't sure. During her training period, her supervisors had drilled it into her head to never get too close to any of her clients, for obvious reasons. But they had also instructed her to always fulfill the client's demands, if possible. Those Final Week requests were the lifeblood of the Volunteer program. Without them, the program would flounder. However, none of her other clients had ever made Kira a part of their requests.

What did Will want from her?

She wasn't sure, but she had a pretty good idea.

He must've read her expression, because he rushed to say, "It's not like that. I'm not expecting anything...*physical*. That's not the type of person I am. As we've already established, I don't have any family to spend the week with, and I don't want to be alone."

Every part of her wanted to say yes. Not just because Will was an attractive guy who'd spent the last half-hour flirting with her, although that was part of it. But something intrigued her about him. She wanted to know him better.

But she couldn't do it. For precisely those reasons.

Reaching into her desk, Kira grabbed an appointment card with her name and work number on it. "I'm very sorry, Mr. Foster, but the answer is no. However, if you think of anything else you'd like for your Final Week, please call me as soon as possible and I'll arrange it."

Will lowered his head, his disappointment clear, but he accepted the card and rose to leave. "Thanks for your help, Miss Liebert," he said, hesitating in the doorway. "I appreciate it. And I apologize if my request made you uncomfortable. That wasn't my intention."

"Don't worry about it. Have a good day."

"You too."

He gave her a final nod before disappearing into the hallway.

After he left, Kira remained anchored to her chair, both hands gripping the edge of her desk for support. Her legs felt shaky and weak, incapable of supporting her weight, and the terrible nausea she'd experienced during her first few Volunteer appointments returned with a vengeance.

She dropped her head into her hands and breathed in through her nose and out through her mouth until the nausea subsided.

Will had eight days to live. Nothing was going to change that fact. He had no right to ask her to spend the week with him. Even if doing so wouldn't cost Kira her job, she still wouldn't want to do it. It was important for her to remain disconnected from her clients. That wasn't some arbitrary rule. She knew what it was like to watch someone die, and she never wanted to experience that again.

So why did she feel as if she'd made a mistake by refusing Will's only request?

And why did she want to run after him?

Chapter Six

"Wait. This guy wants to spend his Final Week... *with you?*"

In a corner booth of the South Street Cafe, Kira picked up her spoon and stirred her ice water, creating a swirling vortex that mirrored the uncertainty in her own mind. "Why is that surprising? I'm lots of fun."

On the other side of the table, Emma Castile grabbed her butter knife and wagged it in the air. "Let me get this straight. This client is the cutest guy you've ever laid eyes on—those are your words—and the only thing he wants for the last week of his life is to spend every waking moment with you. And you told him no? Is that really what you did?"

Kira stopped stirring her water and frowned. "If I say yes, are you going to stab me with that butter knife?"

"I'm considering it." Emma tipped her head forward, dark curls framing her face. "This poor guy is about to kill himself *for the good of all.* He should get anything he wants. And that includes you, my friend. Would you like to know what I would've done in your situation?"

"Not really."

"I would've jumped into his arms and let him carry me off into the sunset. "

Kira rolled her eyes. "Em, I'd known the guy for twenty minutes. He's not carrying me anywhere. Besides, why would this total stranger want to spend his Final Week with me? That makes no sense. He doesn't know me."

Emma shrugged. "Who cares? Maybe he thought you were pretty. Or maybe he saw something wonderful in your personality that the rest of us have missed."

"Very funny."

"Or maybe it's what he said. Maybe he doesn't have anyone in his life. Whatever the reason, I think it's romantic that this Volunteer wants to spend his last few days with you, and I think you're crazy for saying no. I would've said yes in a heartbeat."

"Yeah, well...you're not me," Kira shot back, dropping her spoon onto the table for emphasis. The loud clang of metal against metal drew the attention of several diners seated nearby.

This lunch wasn't going the way Kira had planned. She'd called Emma after Will left her office and asked to meet up, hoping lunch with her best friend would make her feel better. She'd expected Emma to assure her she'd made the right decision, but that wasn't happening.

Emma was making her feel worse.

"I'm not trying to upset you." Emma reached across the table and squeezed Kira's hand. "Besides, I'm only being half-serious. I don't expect you to drop everything in your life to spend a week with a total stranger. There's got to be a reason this attractive guy doesn't have anyone in his life. There must be something wrong with him. He's probably a serial killer. Or he eats onion sandwiches on the city buses.

Either way, he's a disgusting monster, and you made the right decision."

"Your sarcasm is not appreciated."

Smirking, Emma released Kira's hand. "I'm surprised no one has ever propositioned you before. I've always assumed that Volunteers request really crazy things for their Final Week."

"Most of them don't want much," Kira replied with a shrug. "I've had a few who've asked for weird things. This one guy's dream was for the city library to carry a book he'd written. That wasn't a problem. I arranged for it to be printed and bound, like an actual book, but when he brought me the manuscript, there was only one word on each page. And it was three-hundred pages long."

"Three-hundred?"

"Yes. Every word was upside-down and backward. It was a recipe for chicken cordon bleu. When I questioned him about it, he claimed the book was esoteric. It's in the city library if you want to read it."

"That's hilarious!" Emma raised her glass in the air. "To the Bill Shakespeare of Volunteers! I'm going to check the book out of the library tonight in memory of him."

Kira covered her mouth to stifle a laugh. This was why she'd invited Emma to lunch. "Most Volunteers aren't crazy, you know? They want sensible things. Things that will help their families. Survivor benefits for their spouse. Better jobs within the city for their kids. Stuff like that. But the crazy ones sure make the job more interesting."

"Do you always give them what they want?"

"If I can, yes," Kira replied, a hint of pride finding its way into her voice. She didn't love her job—it required more of her emotionally than she'd expected—but she was good at it. She did everything possible to fulfill her client's requests.

Except for today.

"Well, if I ever become a Volunteer—which I won't; I'm not that selfless—but if I do, I'm going to request to drive for my Final Week."

Kira took a sip of her water. "To drive? You already have a car."

Not just any car, but a Porsche. The car had been a gift from her father, who held an important position in the city. After he oversaw the building of the barricade, Emma's father was placed in charge of all construction operations for the city. The Castile family had a lot of money and lived in a beautiful house close to the Executive Mansion. Emma only worked because her father insisted she hold down a regular job so no one could say he was coddling his only child. However, for her seventeenth birthday, Stefan Castile had given Emma a salvaged Porsche. Despite being more than a decade old, the little white car ran like a dream. Overnight, Emma had joined the ranks of the city's elite—those rare few who didn't have to rely on bikes or buses to take them everywhere.

The first time Emma had allowed Kira to drive the car was after Kira's mother died. Emma had been trying to cheer her up —and it *had* worked—but it had also led to Kira asking to drive whenever they went somewhere. Emma usually insisted on driving, since Kira didn't own a vehicle and wasn't technically allowed to drive. But sometimes—usually late at night—Emma would relent and allow Kira behind the wheel of her Porsche. Then she would cling, white-knuckled, to the passenger door as Kira tore through the city streets, whipping around lumbering buses and flooring it for yellow lights, ravenous for the kind of freedom you could only get from driving a car.

Across the table, Emma grinned at Kira, her eyes twinkling mischievously. "I don't want to drive a car. I want to drive a bus."

Kira choked on her water. "A *city* bus?" she sputtered. "Em, you could drive a bus right now if you wanted. Go apply to be a driver."

"Oh, I don't want to drive *every day*," Emma replied. "I want to get behind the wheel of a bus just one time, and I want it to be loaded with passengers, and I want to give them the ride of their lives."

Kira cupped her cheeks with her hands. "If you become a Volunteer, please don't request to be assigned to me."

"Oh, I'm *definitely* requesting you, my friend, because you're the best." Emma slipped her arms out of her sweater to reveal a sleeveless blouse that highlighted her toned arms. She placed the sweater beside her in the booth and gave Kira an imploring look. "You know, I see why that client hit on you. You look cute today. Have you done something different with your hair?"

Kira narrowed her eyes. "Why did I just feel a shiver go down my spine?"

"Sheesh. Can't a girl compliment her best friend?"

"You want something, Em. I see it in your eyes. What is it?"

Emma lifted her glass and batted her eyelashes. "I was simply wondering," she said, keeping the glass close to her lips, as if trying to hide behind it, "if you would like to accompany me on a double date next Wednesday evening?"

Kira shook her head before Emma finished speaking. "Nope. No way. Absolutely not. Remember the last time?"

"Of course I do. We had a wonderful evening."

"The guy you brought along for me drank the leftover butter out of his empty dish of broccoli." Kira grimaced at the memory of her date dabbing melted butter off his chin with a napkin. The butter had left a gloss-like shine on his lips for the rest of the night. Thankfully, he hadn't tried to kiss her. "He drank it, Em. The broccoli was gone. I've never seen anyone drink melted butter in my life."

"Oh, don't be so judgmental. At least he wasn't wasteful. The next guy is going to be better, I promise. Much better."

"How do you know? Have you met him?"

"Well...no, but his friend is incredible, so I'm sure he's incredible." She rubbed her bare arms and winked at Kira. "Just like us. Incredible people have incredible friends."

"Stop trying to butter me up."

Emma snorted. "You said butter."

Kira rolled her eyes. "So gross. Anyway, tell me about this new guy of yours. How'd you two meet?"

Emma sat up straighter in the booth, excitement lighting up her face. Nothing excited her more than talking about guys. Especially guys who were interested in her. "His name is Alaric Render. Isn't that a noble name? Like something out of a Victorian romance novel. Anyway, he came into the hospital last week with this nasty cut on his arm. The cut needed stitches, but the emergency ward was full, so I got a bandage and wrapped it up for him. We chatted for an hour while he waited for a doctor."

"How did he hurt his arm?"

"He's on the Patrols," Emma explained, referring to the armed soldiers who patrolled the Unregulated Zone. "He was searching an old warehouse, and he cut his arm on a metal pipe."

Kira glanced out the window. Beyond the river, the decaying buildings of the Unregulated Zone appeared crooked and ominous, the gloomy skyline resembling the nightmarish imaginings of a mad person. She couldn't imagine setting foot inside those abandoned structures. How many still held the corpses of those who'd perished from the Job virus? How many were hideouts for the Lawless?

Kira pushed the thought from her mind. "Well, if this guy is brave enough to go into the Unregulated Zone every day, then I'm sure he can handle you."

Emma gave her a wolfish grin, revealing two pointy incisors —quirky vampire teeth that somehow made her more adorable. "I hope so, for his sake. Anyway, he's so handsome. You won't even believe it. Dark hair. Dark eyes. Mysterious. A little dangerous. My perfect guy."

"And what about his friend? I suppose he's my perfect guy?"

"Your perfect guy doesn't exist." Emma pressed her lips into a slight frown. "Not in this city, at least. You're too picky. I can't believe you're nineteen and you've never kissed a guy. I've kissed dozens."

"Did you want me to kiss butter lips?"

"Not him, obviously. But I've set you up with seven guys in the last two years, and none of them were good enough for you. However, this time it's going to be different. Your fella, Dayton Cowell, is also on the Patrols. And after Alaric left the clinic, I *might* have looked up Dayton's medical records—"

"Emma!" Kira gasped. "You can't do that. You could get into trouble."

She waved a hand at Kira. "Only if someone finds out. Besides, what's the point of working in the Medical Sector if you can't peek into people's medical files? Anyway, you'll be happy to know that Dayton is in excellent physical health. His cholesterol and blood pressure are both normal. His alanine transaminase levels were a little high, but we won't hold that against him. Oh, and he's very attractive. Not as attractive as Alaric, but close."

Dating was the last thing on Kira's mind, but she didn't like the idea of Emma going out with a mysterious and slightly dangerous guy on her own. "What would the four of us be doing? Just dinner?" Dinner shouldn't take long. An hour or two at most. As long as Dayton didn't drink his leftover butter, he'd be an improvement over her last date.

Emma's face brightened. "They want to take us to The Riverfront for dinner." She paused for a moment, eyebrows raised, as if expecting a big reaction that two Patrol soldiers wanted to take them on a date to the most expensive restaurant in the city. But when Kira only stared at her, Emma continued, "If we're having a good time, maybe we'll go dancing at The Grotto afterward?"

Situated at the north end of City Island, The Grotto used to be a city bathhouse in the early twentieth century. The place sat abandoned for decades before being converted into a dance club a few years after the barricade went up. Kira had been to The Grotto a handful of times with Emma and she hated it. The music was too loud. No air circulated inside the ancient building, which made it perpetually hot and stuffy, and it was always so crowded that you couldn't move without bumping into someone.

"No way. I told you last time that I'm never going back—"

"Oh, look!" Emma interrupted. "Our food's here!"

A harried-looking server appeared next to their table, carrying a plate in each hand. "Sorry that took so long, ladies. Here you go," she said, sliding the plates onto the table. A turkey on wheat with carrot sticks for Kira, and a grilled cheese and applesauce for Emma, who ate like a six-year-old. A huge pickle teetered on the edge of each plate, leaking green juice onto their food. "Can I get you ladies anything else?"

"We're good." Emma's nose wrinkled as she took in the bowl of chunky applesauce in front of her. "Everything looks wonderful."

After the server returned to the kitchen, Emma grabbed her fork and mashed the chunky apples into bits. "Ugh. I always forget that this place makes their applesauce extra chunky. They want us to think it's gourmet, but it's not gourmet. It's laziness."

Kira rescued one of her carrots from a river of pickle juice and popped it into her mouth. "Thanks for grabbing lunch with me today. It was a weird morning, and I needed to get out of the office for a bit. Although I got roped into another double date, I'm still glad I came."

Emma took a tentative bite of her applesauce. "Believe me, I know what it's like to need an escape from issues at work. I thought I was being smart by applying for an administrative job in the Medical Sector. I wanted something easy that wouldn't require me to do any manual labor. You know how I feel about manual labor. Plus, I figured I could spend all day flirting with cute doctors. Maybe I should've chosen a job in Agriculture instead?"

"Agriculture?" Kira tried to imagine her posh best friend— who practically lived in dresses and high heels—working on a farm and taking care of the livestock, and a laugh burst through her lips. She'd never seen Emma in a pair of sneakers, much less a pair of overalls. "Why Agriculture?"

"Um...lots of reasons." Emma counted them off on her fingers. "One, I wouldn't have a boss telling me what to do. Two, all the free food I can sneak. And three, have you seen the guys who work in agriculture? Two words, my friend: rippling muscles."

"Em, as hard as I try, I cannot picture you toiling all day in the scorching sun, collecting chicken eggs and bottle-feeding goats. Besides, you don't like animals. I once saw you throw a rock at a pigeon."

"Um, first of all, the rock missed the pigeon. And you're forgetting that the winged beast was *screeching* at me. It had the most evil red eyes I've ever seen."

"It had *pigeon* eyes, Em. That's how their eyes look. The poor bird couldn't help it."

"Whatever." Emma tucked a stray curl behind her ear, her face turning serious. "Forget the stupid pigeon. I'm not kidding when I say that I hate my job. Especially since they're always scheduling me to work at the front desk of the Compulsory Clinic. That place literally drains the life out of everyone who walks through the door, including the staff."

As if responding to Emma's sudden mood shift, a cloud drifted in front of the midday sun, casting the interior of the cafe in shadows. For the past two years, Kira's best friend had spent at least three days a week as a receptionist at the Compulsory Clinic, where her job was to check people in at the front desk and direct them to the waiting room.

For most Compulsories, Emma's was one of the last faces they ever saw.

An awkward silence fell over the table. Kira tore off a small piece of her sandwich, but she couldn't bring herself to eat it. Her appetite had disappeared. She hated not being able to help Emma. Her job was to give the Volunteers anything they wanted—to ensure their every happiness during their Final Week—but she couldn't even help her own best friend. "I'm so sorry, Em. My job has its own issues, but I can't imagine working in that awful place."

Emma pushed her applesauce around with her spoon. "Yeah. People who've never been inside that building don't understand how awful it is."

Kira knew what Emma meant. She hadn't returned to the Compulsory Clinic since her mother's death, and she never intended to go back...unless the city forced her. She even avoided walking past the building.

She only ever visited the place in her nightmares.

Kira gave up trying to eat and placed her sandwich on her plate. "You could always quit."

Frowning, Emma pushed her bowl of applesauce away. "My father won't hear of it. You know that." She sighed and shook her head. "I'm not one of your clients, Kira. I don't expect you to fix all of my problems."

Kira leaned back in her seat and crossed her arms. "What's that supposed to mean?"

Emma tore off a piece of her grilled cheese and stuffed it into her mouth. "Exactly what I said. You're great at what you do. You want everybody to be happy. Making people happy is a nice trait to have if you're a volunteer advocate, but in the end, all of your clients end up dead. It's like they're on this train that's heading for a thousand-foot drop-off into a ravine, and you're the steward or the conductor or whatever they're called on trains, and you're running around, trying to keep everybody happy, but the train is still heading for the ravine."

Kira opened her mouth to argue, but the broadcast screen built into the wall above the diner's front counter flickered and came to life. Most of the cafe's patrons left their seats and crowded into the tight space in front of the counter to see what was going on. Mid-day broadcasts were rare, and they usually meant something bad.

When Victor Devlin's face popped up on the screen, Kira averted her gaze and began absently picking crumbs from her sandwich.

She couldn't bring herself to look at him.

"Citizens of Vita Nova, I'm coming to you today with an urgent broadcast," Mayor Devlin began. *"As of this morning, six of our fellow citizens are missing. These individuals worked in the Agricultural Sector, and none of them reported for work this morning. Although we cannot be certain, every indication is that these six citizens are defectors. A thorough search of their apart-*

ments revealed the absence of clothing and nonperishable food items. According to interviews conducted this morning, several of their coworkers in the Agricultural Sector have overheard these individuals speaking against the leadership of this city for weeks. A few of them had even mentioned defecting to the Unregulated Zone."

"Yikes, look at them." Emma muttered, drawing Kira's attention to the screen. "They're all so young."

A lineup of photographs taken from the Vita Nova identification cards had replaced Devlin's face on the broadcast screen. Four males and two females, none older than thirty. Kira didn't recognize any of them, thank goodness.

"I don't understand." She looked at Emma. "How did they get out of the city?"

"I have no idea."

On the screen, the mayor intertwined his fingers and leaned closer to the camera. *"My fellow citizens of Vita Nova, I understand how difficult things can be inside the barricade. I share your frustration. None of us asked for this life, but we must not forget that the world outside of the barricade does not belong to us yet. It still belongs to the Lawless. They're our real enemy, not each other. If we remain united in our resolve for just a little while longer, we will be victorious. One day, we will reclaim the land beyond the barricade. On that day, our Compulsory and Volunteer programs will cease, and our lives will return to normal. On that day, we will be free. This is Mayor Devlin from the Executive Mansion. For the good of all."*

"For the good of all," the patrons of the cafe echoed.

After the screen went dark and the customers returned to their seats, Kira could still see the faces of the young men and women in her mind. She glanced at Emma, who looked uncharacteristically rattled. "Defectors sneaking out of the city at night? Does that make any sense to you?"

"It's possible, I suppose." Emma drew in a long breath. "Especially if they're from Agriculture. Those people have access to the river. All they would need is a boat."

Kira's hands felt like twin blocks of ice, so she rubbed them together underneath the table. "Something isn't right. Devlin isn't telling us everything."

One corner of Emma's mouth nudged into a half-smile.

"You're just saying that because he's your father."

Chapter Seven

Before leaving work that afternoon, Kira called Rolling Meadows to check on Lizzy Currant. She always phoned her Volunteers on Thursdays, the day before their Sacrifice, to see if they had any last-minute requests or needed anything from her.

This late in their Final Week, the excitement had usually worn off and the reality of their situation had set in. Even the most boisterous and outgoing of her Volunteers were subdued by Thursday afternoon, almost as if they could feel death slithering up behind them like a black serpent, fangs bared and ready to strike.

Lizzy was no exception.

"Hello, Kira." The woman's voice sounded gravelly, as if she'd been crying. "Thanks for calling. This suite is incredible, by the way. I've been spending most of my time out here on the balcony."

Kira heard birds chirping in the background, and she imagined Lizzy reclining in one of the lounge chairs, her eyes closed, the late afternoon sun warming her face. "It's a beautiful place, isn't it? So quiet. You forget you're still in the city."

"That's the best part," Lizzy agreed. "By the way, my three granddaughters stayed with us last evening, and we had a wonderful time. Thank you for arranging that. You don't know how much it meant to us. We took them swimming in the indoor pool. We didn't get back to the suite until almost midnight. I wanted to make the day last as long as I could." Lizzy's voice cracked a little. "They're wonderful little girls."

Kira's eyes burned. She closed them until the feeling went away. "Do they understand what's happening?"

"Oh, they're too young. The oldest is nine and the youngest is five. I don't think they understand anything. Maybe that's for the best. They loved the pool. And the room service." She laughed a little, the sound at odds with the sadness in her voice. "They've never experienced room service. When they left this morning, they kept asking if they could come back to spend another night this weekend. We tried explaining that I won't be here after tomorrow, but they kept asking."

Lowering her gaze to her chipped nails, Kira picked at the remaining polish. The worst part of being an advocate was figuring out what to say in those final hours, when nothing she said made any difference. "They'll understand with time, Lizzy. I know it doesn't feel that way right now, but they will. One day, they'll appreciate your Sacrifice."

Lizzy continued as if Kira hadn't spoken, her voice dense with grief. "The hardest part was saying goodbye. My daughter and my husband both said it's better that way. That if I see them tomorrow—before—it will be too difficult. For them *and* for me. I suppose they're right, but it guts me, Kira. The finality of it. I hugged those precious babies goodbye, and now I'm never going to see them again."

Flecks of nail polish littered the surface of Kira's desk, and she stared at them, overcome by the sudden urge to hang up the phone. "So, Lizzy," she said, clearing her throat, "the reason for my call is to let you know that I've confirmed your dinner reservation for this evening. I booked you and your husband a table at The Riverfront. You'll be right by the window with a beautiful view of the water, as you requested. Your reservation is at six-thirty, so I've arranged for a car to swing by and pick you up at six."

"That's sweet of you. Thank you, Kira. You've made this so much easier."

"Good. I'm glad to hear that."

But that statement—*You've made this so much easier*—rang in Kira's ears.

Maybe dying shouldn't be easy. Maybe she wasn't doing the right thing by making it easier.

No. Kira pushed the idea away, shoved it inside a closet, and snapped a padlock on the door. Keeping the Volunteers happy during their Final Week was an important job. It wasn't an easy job, but it was honorable.

"Are you certain you don't want to go to the Volunteer Ball tonight?" Kira asked. "I could easily move your dinner at The Riverfront up a little earlier so you could do both. You might not feel like going right now, but it really is a lovely event. I'd hate for you to miss it."

The woman sighed into the phone. "I don't think I could handle being around all those strangers tonight. I've felt nauseated all week, and I haven't been able to keep much food down. To be honest, I considered asking you to cancel our dinner reservation for tonight, but I decided against it. I know it's just my anxiety kicking in. Besides, I don't want to ruin tonight for my husband. This is our last night together. Did you know we've been together for forty years? We started dating when we were seventeen."

Kira brought a finger to her parted lips. To a nineteen-year-old, forty years sounded like an eternity. "I had no idea. That's amazing."

"It wasn't enough time. I keep telling Ron to finish out his last three years with another woman." Lizzy uttered a soft laugh. "Maybe I should've requested your help with finding a woman for him. Is matchmaking among your many talents?"

As Kira brushed the flecks of nail polish into her trash can, Will's face appeared in her mind. After lunch, she had tried to forget about Will by burying herself in work. She'd been successful for a little while, but he was still there, lurking in the back of her mind, waiting for an opportunity to step into the light. No matter how hard she tried, she couldn't forget the look in his ice-blue eyes or the hope in his voice when he'd made his only request.

"I want to spend my Final Week with you, Kira. The whole week. That's what I want. That's the only thing I want."

"Honey?" a male voice spoke up on the other end of the phone. "Are you alright?"

"I'm fine, Ron," Lizzy replied. "I'm on the phone with Kira."

"Who's Kira?"

"My advocate. Could you give us a few minutes? We were just about to say goodbye."

"Okay." Lizzy's husband sounded unsure, and Kira didn't blame him. Right now, every minute was precious. "I love you."

"I love you too, honey."

On the other end of the line, Kira heard the balcony door slide shut.

"Kira? Are you there?"

"I'm here."

A choked cry echoed in her ear. "I'm scared."

"Oh, Lizzy..."

Lizzy Currant wasn't the first Volunteer to struggle the night before her Sacrifice. That was why the city held the Volunteer Ball on Thursday, the night before the Sacrifices. The alcohol flowed freely at the ball, and the party went late into the night. By the time the Volunteers retired to their suites at Rolling Meadows in the early hours of Friday morning, most of them went right to sleep, too drunk to realize that midnight had passed and it was now the last day of their lives.

But Lizzy wasn't going to the ball. There would be no alcohol-induced distraction for her. Thankfully, Kira was well-trained on how to deal with clients who struggled near the end of their Final Week. "There's no reason to be scared, okay? Aside from the initial needle-stick, it's totally painless. As the Somnumbutal enters your system, you'll become tired, but you'll still have a few minutes of lucidity. Your husband will be by your side the entire time, holding your hand. You'll be able to say your goodbyes. Then, you'll drift off to sleep. It's the most peaceful way to—"

"Am I doing the right thing?" Lizzy interrupted, a hint of panic in her voice. "Because this doesn't feel right, Kira. When I look at my husband and those grandbabies of mine, it feels like I'm making a huge mistake. I don't know what I was thinking. When I found that lump in my breast, I was so scared. My first instinct was that I had to become a Volunteer before they made me a Compulsory..."

"I know, Lizzy. And I can't imagine how hard this must be for you, but you're doing the right thing. Everything will be fine, I promise. Your family will be okay. They have each other. They're going to get through this, and so are you."

Kira had given a version of this speech to dozens of clients over the last eighteen months, and each time, it got a little harder to force the words past her lips.

"I guess you're right," Lizzy sniffed. "Thank you, Kira.

You've been lovely to work with. I feel blessed that you were my advocate."

"It's been an honor to work with you, Lizzy."

A muffled sound, followed by a delicate honk as the woman blew her nose. "Sorry about that," she said. "I should get ready for dinner. My appointment is at eight-thirty tomorrow morning. I suppose this is the last time we're going to talk?"

"It doesn't have to be," Kira said, combing her fingers through her hair. "I could call you tomorrow, if you'd like. Before I go to work."

"Please don't. I want to spend every minute with Ron."

"Okay. I understand."

When Lizzy spoke again, she sounded far-away and dreamy. "I should've taken the risk."

Kira picked at a tiny knot in her hair, frowning. "What risk?"

"Scheduling a checkup after I found that lump. I should've taken the risk. The outcome might've been the same, but now I'll never know." Lizzy breathed a heavy sigh into the phone. "Stay awake, Kira. Don't let this city put you to sleep. Stay awake...and take risks. If you never take risks, you're as good as dead anyway."

"I want to spend my Final Week with you, Kira. The whole week. That's what I want. That's the only thing I want."

Kira banished Will's voice from her mind and tried to think of something to say to Lizzy. Something profound and meaningful that would carry the woman through the final few hours of her life. But the only thing she could think to say was: "Thank you for your Sacrifice."

The words sounded pathetic and empty, even to her own ears. After a long moment of silence, Lizzy whispered into the phone, "Stay awake, Kira."

And then the line went dead.

Chapter Eight

One of the longest and most confusing days of Kira's life concluded with a black Lincoln Continental parked outside her office building.

At four-thirty, she waved goodbye to Kevin at the security line and emerged into the late-afternoon sunshine, prepared for a long bus ride home. As she stepped out of her building, she saw a man in a neatly pressed suit and sunglasses leaning against the rear quarter-panel of the idling Lincoln, an open Vita Nova newspaper in his hands. Both the car and the man looked out-of-place in the city, as if someone had airdropped them in from another part of the planet where the Job virus and the barricade did not exist.

Kira was so mentally drained, so out-of-sorts, that she didn't recognize the man until he glanced up from his newspaper.

Victor Devlin, the Mayor of Vita Nova.

And Kira's father.

Devlin closed his newspaper and tucked it under his arm. "Hello, Kira."

The words broke out of her mouth before she could contain them. "What are you doing here, Victor?"

"You aren't happy to see me?"

"Why would I be? Shouldn't you be in the Executive Mansion with your wife and children?" Kira demanded, referring to Vance and Violet, the ten-year-old twins Devlin had fathered with his wife, Naomi.

Kira's father didn't seem disturbed by her attitude, but very little disturbed that man. He took off his sunglasses and dropped them into his breast pocket, revealing gunmetal-gray eyes that perfectly matched Kira's. His thin lips stretched into an amused smile that highlighted the deep pockmarks in his cheeks. "I can't believe how grown-up you are. You look so different from the last time I saw you."

"That's because I was twelve the last time you saw me," Kira shot back, recalling the brief period when Devlin had reappeared in her life, asking to spend quality time with the daughter he'd never claimed as his own. Although he hadn't come right out and said it, Kira had gotten the impression that raising his new children had made him feel guilty about having an illegitimate child running around the city.

At the time, Kira had wanted a relationship with her father, so her mother had reluctantly obliged, allowing Devlin to take Kira on a few day excursions. On one occasion, they'd gone to City Island to feed the ducks. On another, they had a fancy lunch in the Executive Mansion, where Kira had eaten a dandelion salad with roasted beets and goat cheese and felt sick for the rest of the day.

Despite her constant pleadings, Devlin had refused to introduce Kira to her brother and sister, insisting that it would be too confusing for them at such a young age. "In time," he would say. "Be patient, my dear." And she'd tried to be patient

—she really had—clinging to the promise that she would one day have a relationship with her siblings.

But one day had never come.

Devlin had put on a good show for a few weeks, but his enthusiasm for reestablishing a relationship with his oldest daughter had wilted like a flower left in the sun too long, and in the end, he'd faded out of her life as quickly as he'd reappeared.

Removing a handkerchief from his pocket, Devlin dabbed the beads of sweat from his brow. "Can you believe this heat? In September?"

"Did you drive all the way over here to chat about the weather, Victor?"

"Kira, would it kill you to call me Dad?"

"Actually, it might," she muttered. "I'll leave that honor for your real children."

His smile faltered a little, and he gestured to his car. "I thought I'd offer you a ride home."

"I'm fine. I enjoy the bus."

"The bus?" Devlin's face contorted in disgust, as if she'd just admitted to crawling home through the city's sewer system. "You can't possibly enjoy the bus. The public transit system is a horror show, as I'm sure you're aware. I could get you home in ten minutes."

Kira glanced in the direction of the bus stop, weighing her options. Out of loyalty to her dead mother, she wanted nothing to do with her father. Although she wondered why he'd picked today to stop by her office, she wasn't curious enough to accept a ride from him.

But the idea of spending thirty or forty minutes on a sweltering and overcrowded bus wasn't appealing.

"Kira, I know you're upset with me—you have every reason to be—but please let me drive you home." Devlin opened the front passenger door and motioned for her to climb inside. "We need to talk."

Getting inside the car felt like the worst betrayal of her mother, but after an extremely long and confusing day, she just wanted to get home as quickly as possible. Plus, she'd forgotten to pack her sneakers, and her feet were throbbing after walking across town in her high heels to meet Emma for lunch.

Without looking at Devlin, Kira slid into the passenger seat.

The car appeared brand-new, although like all other cars in Vita Nova, it was over twelve years old. However, the leather upholstery looked and smelled as if it had come straight off the assembly line. Like her father, the vehicle was smooth and unmarred by personal effects. There were no half-empty mugs of coffee in the center console, no children's toys or books lying on the backseat, and no crumbs scattered across the floor mats.

Devlin climbed behind the wheel and stuck the key into the ignition. The engine purred to life, a distinct sound and vastly different from the guttural grumblings of the city buses. He shifted the vehicle into drive and pulled into the street.

As they abandoned the crowds and bustle of the Governmental Sector for the Residential Sector, Devlin said, "Weren't you supposed to be done at four? I've been waiting outside your building for thirty minutes."

Kira crossed her arms and slouched in her seat, aware she must look like a sulking teenager and not caring. "I had to work late today." She didn't add that she'd stayed an extra half-hour to make up for being late to work this morning. "Plus, I didn't know you were coming to my office, so I don't see how your having to wait is my fault."

"It's not." Devlin shook his head. "You're right. I apologize."

"What do you want, Victor?" she demanded. "I'm sure you didn't come here today just to offer me a ride."

Devin's right hand dropped from the steering wheel to his

leg. "I've been thinking about you a lot lately," he explained, scratching his thigh through the delicate material of his suit. "I suppose I wanted to check up on you. See how you're doing, you know? Find out if you need anything from me."

Kira's eyes flitted from Devlin's slender fingers to her own, which were short and a little stubby, like her mother's. "Out of curiosity, did you ever consider checking up on me a few years ago? Like say...right after Mom died? That would've been helpful since I'd essentially become an orphan overnight."

"Now, don't say that." Her father actually had the gall to sound offended. "You're not an orphan, Kira. I've always been here if you needed me."

The nerve of this man, to suggest that he'd ever been anything but absent from her life. A lifetime of anger bubbled up inside Kira's chest, a volcano of rage threatening to spew out of her. "You've always been here? Victor, you dated my mother for six months and got her pregnant. When you found out about the pregnancy, you left her, because having a child out-of-wedlock wasn't convenient for your political aspirations. You wanted nothing to do with me until you started having kids with your wife, and even then, you abandoned me after a few weeks. Do you know how difficult it was for my mom to allow you back into my life, knowing what kind of man you are? And you repaid her kindness by abandoning me just like you abandoned her."

"Kira, that's not what—."

"Tell me something," she cut him off. Outside her passenger window, the Residential District flew by, a blur of indistinct colors with the solid mass of the barricade wall rising up in the background. "Did you ever consider wielding that political power of yours to save my mother's life? Don't you think that's the least you could've done for me?"

"By the time I heard about your mother's Compulsory Notification, it was too late for me to intervene—"

"That's a lie!" Kira shouted. "I called your office and left dozens of messages. Don't deny it. You know how stupid we were? We honestly believed that you would intervene and save her life, but you never even called me back. Why? Why didn't you call me back?"

They were only a few blocks from her townhouse now, so Kira grabbed the door handle, preparing to launch herself out the door the moment Devlin brought the car to a stop. Accepting a ride from her father hadn't been a good idea. She might've avoided the hassle of the bus, but this was so much worse. She couldn't stomach being in such close proximity with a man who had abandoned her mother—twice—when she'd needed him the most.

As he turned onto Kira's street, Devlin cleared his throat. "I'm not proud of my behavior, Kira. You have every right to be angry with me for ending my relationship with your mother when she got pregnant. I couldn't accept responsibility for a child at that point in my life, so I left her to raise you alone. After I met my wife and we had our children, I realized what a mistake I'd made. That's why I tried to get to know you when you were a child, but I could never figure out how to incorporate you into my life. I was selfish, and because of that selfishness, I missed a lot of time with my daughter that I'll never get back."

Kira's townhouse came into view ahead, on the left side of the road.

Thank goodness this terrible ride is almost over.

Thank goodness this day is almost over.

"And I know you don't believe me about the messages you left after your mother received her Compulsory Notification, but I'm a busy man and my office receives dozens of calls every day. It takes time for my secretary to sift through them all. I swear on my children's lives, I did not find out about your mother until it was too late. If I had known, I would've done everything in my power to save her, Kira. You have to know that."

She opened her mouth to argue and then closed it again. What if Devlin was telling the truth? What if the voice messages really hadn't reached her father in time to save her mother? Could she still hold him responsible? Was that fair?

Devlin angled the Lincoln into a parking space across the street from Kira's townhouse. He shut off the engine and folded his hands in his lap. "Say something. Please."

Kira hesitated, one hand gripping the door handle. She couldn't go until she asked her father one more question. "Why did you come to my office today? I want the *real* reason."

He twisted sideways in his seat. "I'd like to invite you to stay with my family in the Executive Mansion. Starting today."

"To...what? Stay?" His words made no sense, not after all this time. "You want me to stay with you?"

"Your mother is gone, Kira, but you're not alone in this city. You're not an orphan. It kills me to hear you say that." Devlin reached across the center console and grasped her hand. "I'm still here, and you've got two half-siblings that you've never met. My wife is eager to meet you. We both want you to live with us. To be a part of our family."

Devlin's hand felt unnaturally cold, and the way his long fingers curled around her small hand made her think of a mouse trapped in a nest of vipers. It was all she could do not to rip her hand away from his. "Victor, I needed you when I was a child, but things are different now. I'm an adult. I don't need you anymore."

Devlin's shoulders sagged, his body deflating like a popped balloon. "Kira, I understand your feelings, and I wasn't going to mention this because I didn't want to worry you, but there's another reason for my visit today. I'm sure you've heard that six workers in the Agricultural Sector defected to the Unregulated Zone last night."

"Of course. I saw the broadcast."

He nodded. "Please don't share this information with anyone, but we believe the defectors intend to provide the Lawless with critical information about our city. Specifically, the locations of our Guard checkpoints and potential weaknesses in the barricade. We're concerned the defectors may even try to sneak the Lawless into the city. We believe they used the river to leave, so the Guards have increased their boat patrols, but there's a chance they escaped somehow."

Escaped.

It struck Kira as a strange word to use when describing people leaving the protection of Vita Nova.

"Why are you telling me this?"

Devlin blew out a breath. "When the Guards searched one of the defector's apartments, they found your name and address written on a piece of paper. Underneath your name, they'd written: *Mayor's secret daughter. Can we use her?*"

Devlin might as well have thrown a glass of cold water in Kira's face. "You think I'm in danger?"

He shook his head. "We don't know anything for certain. It's possible they decided against targeting you, but we must take every precaution to ensure your safety. That's why I'd like for you to stay with me for the next few weeks. Longer, if you wish. I've already spoken to your supervisor and arranged for a two week leave of absence from your job."

"You what?"

"We have twenty-four-hour security at our house," he continued. "It will be safer for you there."

Lockdown.

Devlin wanted to put her on lockdown at his house.

But none of this made any sense. Why would the defectors want her? What could she possibly do for them? She wasn't close to her father. She barely knew him.

And that wasn't even her biggest question.

She snatched her hand away from Devlin, unable to stand the feeling of his icy fingers wrapped around hers for another second. "How?" she asked. "How could anyone know I'm your daughter? You've never acknowledged me publicly. My mother never told anyone. I only told my best friend, and I know she wouldn't tell anyone."

White-hot anger ignited in Devlin's eyes, his patience with her wearing thin. It wasn't the first time Kira had seen that expression on her father's face. She remembered this side of him from when she was twelve. He'd always tried to be nice during their little excursions, taking her out to fun places and buying her anything she wanted. But if she pushed back at all, or if she gave him the slightest amount of grief, his candy-coated exterior would melt away, revealing the darkness underneath.

Devlin tugged at the gray necktie that matched his eyes. "I don't have all the answers, Kira. I wish I did. What's important is your safety. Why don't you run inside and pack what you need to get you through the next few days? First thing in the morning, I'll send my people over to collect the rest of your belongings."

She didn't even hesitate. "No."

Before her father could protest, she opened the car door and stepped onto the sidewalk. "I'm sorry, Victor, but you've never helped me before, and I'm not interested in your help now."

Devlin stared at her, his upper and lower jaws sliding over each other like tectonic plates. Grinding his teeth in anger was one of Victor Devlin's signature moves. After a moment, he dug into his breast pocket, pulled out a business card, and handed it to her. Written underneath his name was a nine-digit number. "Take this."

Kira ran her fingers over the white letters and numbers ingrained in the black cardstock. "What's this for?"

"That's my personal phone number," Devlin explained. "Call that number and you'll be connected to my office in the Executive Mansion. You'll be able to reach me anytime, day or night."

She stared at him, slack-jawed.

"If you change your mind—"

Kira slammed the door, cutting her father off mid-sentence.

As she crossed the street, Devlin started the engine and pulled away from the curb. She paused on her front steps and watched it go, the taillights growing dimmer until the car disappeared from view.

Lowering her eyes to the card in her hand, she glared at the phone number that could've saved her mother's life.

Then she tore the card into dozens of tiny pieces and let the breeze carry them away.

Chapter 9

Sunday

"**W**hat am I doing? Seriously. I can't believe I'm doing this."

Kira mumbled to herself as she made her way across the Volunteer Memorial Walkway, limping along in a pair of wedge sandals she'd liberated from her mother's closet. The sandals looked cute, but they were too tight for her feet, and she had a feeling she'd be sporting some impressive blisters in the morning.

She'd left her townhouse ninety minutes before the start of the evening's Reverence Ceremony. Unlike the previous Sunday, when Kira had battled the crowd to get into the Stadium on time, only a few other people were on the walkway this early, and thankfully none of them were close enough to hear her mumbling to herself.

"This is crazy, Kira. You've officially *gone* crazy."

She tugged at the hem of her skirt—which barely touched the middle of her thighs—in a vain attempt to add inches to the dress. As if the sandals weren't making her uncomfortable enough, she'd chosen to wear a yellow sundress to the cere-

mony instead of her usual polo shirt, jeans, and sneakers. She'd
brought a lightweight cardigan along to slip over her shoulders
after the sun finished its descent. Or sooner, depending on how
uncomfortable she felt. Like the sandals, the sundress had
belonged to her mother. Besides having smaller feet, Madison
Liebert had also been two inches shorter than her daughter.
The length of the skirt hadn't seemed like an issue back at
home, when Kira had spent an hour studying herself from
every angle in her bedroom mirror. But now that she was out in
public, she felt as if she was walking around half-naked.

What had she been thinking, dressing like this for a Reverence Ceremony?

Simple.

She'd been thinking about Will.

Glancing to her left, Kira saw the stone arch expanse of the
Market Street Bridge, which ran parallel to the Volunteer
Memorial Walkway and cut across the southern tip of City
Island before continuing into the Unregulated Zone. Armed
Guards manned a checkpoint at the middle of the bridge
twenty-four-hours a day. Only the Patrols—and sanitation engi-
neers like Will—could use the bridge to access the Unregulated
Zone.

At the checkpoint, a Guard leaned against the barrier rail,
clutching a rifle in his hands. He appeared to be watching Kira,
his head turning to follow her progress.

You're being paranoid, she assured herself. *He isn't looking
at you.*

Turning away from the Guard, Kira continued forward, her
wedge sandals clomping against the concrete walkway. She'd
spent the past three days in her townhouse with the doors
locked and the curtains drawn. An unofficial lockdown, of sorts,
inspired by her father. The thought of her name written on a
piece of paper inside a defector's apartment gave her chills, but

fear and paranoia hadn't been the only thing holding her prisoner in her home.

The other thing had been Will.

Ever since the moment Will Foster stepped into her office, with his beautiful eyes and heartbreaking smile, Kira hadn't been able to get him out of her mind. It broke her heart that he didn't have any family—she knew what that felt like—and she'd spent all weekend weighing her options and trying to figure out the right thing to do. In the end, her decision had come down to her father and the two-week leave of absence he'd already arranged for her. She couldn't really call her supervisor and tell him she didn't want the leave because he would not defy an order from the mayor. And she wasn't about to spend the next two weeks alone in her townhouse with nothing but her thoughts to keep her company.

Finally, she'd made a decision.

She would spend the week with Will.

As she neared the end of the walkway, Kira saw a dozen guards milling around the Stadium's entrance, scanners in hand, waiting for the citizens of Vita Nova to descend upon them like a plague of locusts. A horn sounded—a single blast—signaling the opening of the Stadium gates. The Guards moved into position, holding up their scanners and waving the early arrivals into the Stadium. Kira hung back a little, searching for Will in the small crowd of early arrivals. But she couldn't find him.

"Miss?" One of the Guards gestured for her to enter the gate. "Come on through."

She considered telling the Guard that she was waiting for someone, then decided against it. More people were pouring onto the island, and as the crowd swelled around her, she realized how easy it would be to miss Will if she waited for him outside the gate. Once inside the Stadium, she could break off from the crowd and wait near the Volunteer entrance. If any Guards questioned why she was waiting outside the special entrance, she would explain that she was an advocate who needed to meet with her client prior to the ceremony.

She held out her ID for the Guard. He stared at it, his eyes darting from the card to her face. Satisfied, he scanned the unique barcode, checking her in for the ceremony. "For the good of all," he said.

"For the good of all."

After passing through the gate, Volunteers entered the Stadium through a side door, where staff members waited to greet them and line them up by age. Kira slipped away from the crowd and planted herself near the door to wait for Will. Leaning against the building, she twisted her cardigan in her hands, her nervousness building with each passing minute.

Just after six-thirty, the first Volunteer trudged up to the entrance. He was a man in his forties or fifties, wearing a suit and tie, with a military-style buzz cut and a neatly trimmed goatee. She'd seen the man in the waiting room of her office a few weeks earlier. He'd been there with a woman and a teenage girl, all three of them crying.

"Revere the Volunteer," Kira said, raising her fingers to her heart as the man passed by.

He gave her a curt nod and stepped through the door.

Other Volunteers followed. An older woman in a lovely gold dress who offered Kira a sincere smile, followed by a skinny young man who avoided Kira's gaze. Three middle-aged women came next. Friends, perhaps? They traveled in a pack, arms joined in an unbreakable chain. Soon after, a young woman with pink hair appeared, holding the hand of an adorable boy with blond hair and freckles. The boy wore a pair of black pants, a red plaid shirt, and a pair of shiny dress shoes.

Kira's heart sank at the sight of the boy. Did he have a father? Someone to look after him when his mother was gone?

"Revere the Volunteer," Kira said.

The young woman glared at her. "You got that right." Then she and the boy disappeared inside the Stadium.

When only ten minutes remained before the start of the Reverence Ceremony, Kira finally spotted Will in the crowd gathered outside the gate. Unlike the other Volunteers, he hadn't bothered to dress up for the evening's ceremony, but he still looked incredibly handsome in a gray button-down shirt, dark jeans, and work boots. After the guard scanned his ID card, Will passed through the gate and began walking in Kira's direction, his hands jammed deep into the pockets of his jeans. He was so focused on his destination that he didn't seem to notice Kira, passing close enough that she caught a brief whiff of the same dandelion-woodsy scent that had accompanied him into her office on Thursday morning.

"Will?"

He did a quick double-take, the purposeful expression on his face giving way to confusion. His gaze dropped to her sundress before returning to her face. "Miss Liebert? What are you doing here?"

"I was hoping to talk to you before the ceremony," she said. "If you have a moment."

He glanced at the Volunteer entrance and shrugged. "Sure. They'll have to wait for me."

As Kira led him away from the entrance, she wished she hadn't worn the sundress. Back at home, the dress had made her feel confident. Self-assured. Maybe even pretty. Now she felt ridiculous. The dress was too short, and it highlighted her bare arms and shoulders, putting every mole and imperfection on display for the world to see.

Taking a deep breath, Kira launched into her prepared

speech. "Here's the thing. I couldn't stop thinking about what you said you wanted for your Final Week. Obviously, I've never had a client request to spend time with me, so that caught me off-guard, and that's the reason I said no. But the more I thought about it, I realized I didn't want you going through this week alone." The words poured out of her, filling the space between them. "No one should have to face this week without a friend by their side, and if you still don't have anyone, I'd like to be that friend for you."

When she finished speaking, Will only stared at her, saying nothing.

She contemplated throwing her sweater over her head and running away. "So, uh...what do you think?"

Finally, Will's lips stretched into a warm smile, and those lopsided dimples melted her heart. "Sorry. I just wanted to make sure you were finished before I said anything. That was a brilliant speech. A little wordy in the middle, but the ending was great."

She tried to glare at him, but it was a struggle not to laugh. "It's not too late for me to change my mind, you know."

"All kidding aside, I'm glad you reconsidered my request, Miss Liebert."

"Do you mind calling me Kira? If we're going to be spending the entire week together, we should be on a first-name basis."

"No problem. But in the interest of propriety, I must insist that you refer to me as Brave and Benevolent Volunteer. And don't forget to curtsey whenever I enter a room."

She rolled her eyes. "Or I could just throw something at you. How does that sound?"

"That works, too." At the sound of the five-minute warning horn, Will's smile faded. "I better go inside. Wouldn't want to be late to my own funeral."

"I've only got one rule for this week," she said. "No funeral or death jokes."

Will gave her a thumbs-up. "Kira doesn't like death jokes. Got it. Before I go, how do you feel about spending a little time together tomorrow? The market will be open. Do you want to get lunch?"

Before coming out this evening, Kira had vowed to do whatever Will asked of her this week. Within reason, of course. Lunch was within reason. "That sounds great. I'll meet you outside the market at eleven."

"Okay. See you then."

But instead of going inside, Will hesitated, his eyes locked on hers. "Before I go, I really need to tell you something."

"What's that?"

He smiled. "You look amazing in that dress."

Chapter Ten

"William Foster, please step forward to receive your rose."

From her spot in the bleachers, Kira watched as Will strolled across the field and came to a halt only a few inches away from Sienna Graves.

The deputy mayor took a step back, casually increasing the distance between herself and Will, before plastering a saccharine smile on her face and extending her hand. "Good evening, Mr. Foster."

Will shook the deputy mayor's hand, but he did not return her smile.

Graves smoothed out the front of her suit jacket, as if the heat from Will's gaze had caused wrinkles to appear in the fabric. "William Foster," she began. "Is it your wish to end your life as a Volunteer?"

"Yes, it is."

"And have you arrived at this decision of your own free will?"

"Yes, I have."

The woman's grin broadened while her eyes remained dark, an expression that reminded Kira of a cartoon villain. "The city of Vita Nova extends you its sincere appreciation for your bravery and sacrifice. Tonight and in the days to follow, this city will honor you. After you have made your Sacrifice, we shall revere you. Your name will always be remembered. We will never forget you."

She held the microphone out to Will, the smile frozen on her lips.

Will's eyes darted to the crowd before returning to the deputy mayor. He leaned forward and spoke into the microphone: "I'm counting on that."

Sienna Graves cocked her head to the side and squinted at Will, clearly trying to figure out what he meant. Then—with a shrug—she grabbed a blue rose boutonniere from the tray and pinned it on his gray shirt, directly over his heart. "Revere the Volunteer!"

"Revere the Volunteer!"

Kira rose, applauding Will's Sacrifice with the rest of the crowd. But unlike those around her, she felt no happiness. For Will, the time to change his mind had passed. The rose was on his chest. The countdown had begun.

When the cheering died down, Kira returned to her seat. On the western side of the river, the sun had descended behind the neglected buildings of the Unregulated Zone, painting the decaying landscape in a reddish-hue that made the area appear to be on fire. The spire of an old church jutted out from among the buildings, stretching skyward, as if imploring the heavens for rescue from the flames.

With the sun nearly gone, the temperature fell several degrees, and Kira slipped her sweater over her shoulders. She only had to get through the Memoriam and then she could go home.

Her eyes fell on the tray of boutonnieres.

Still one left.

As if on cue, Sienna Graves said, "It's time to meet tonight's last Volunteer. This young man isn't comfortable with the bright lights and the crowd, so we wanted to give him a few minutes to prepare before bringing him onto the field."

A murmur swept through the Stadium. Whoever this young man was, why wouldn't he be required to join the other Volunteers on the field?

With the microphone still in her grip, the deputy mayor silenced the crowd with a loud clap of her hands that reverberated through the Stadium's speakers. "Theodore Easton, please step forward to receive your rose."

The young woman with choppy pink hair stepped onto the field, still holding the hand of the little boy Kira had seen earlier. As the woman tugged the boy along, he gazed up at the crowd, his eyes growing wide.

He clutched a red lollipop in his free hand.

A single word slipped from Kira's lips. "No."

A hush fell over the Stadium, the abnormal absence of sound mirroring the eternal silence of the Unregulated Zone. Except for her own heartbeat in her ears, the only noise Kira could hear was water rushing over rocks and downed tree limbs as the river continued its never-ending journey to the ocean. Unless she was imagining it, the river sounded as if it was speeding up, eager to leave this dark patch of earth behind.

Nothing like this had ever happened before.

Kira surveyed the faces of the people seated nearby. A few looked surprised, but none reflected the horror she felt inside. The vast majority were *smiling*, tears glistening in their eyes, as if a little boy volunteering to be murdered by his own city was the most magnificent thing they'd ever seen.

And then the crowd applauded.

On the field, the boy raised the lollipop and jammed it into his mouth.

When the little boy and the pink-haired woman reached the center of the field, the camera zoomed in on the child, giving the entire city a close-up view of his sticky face and red-stained lips. He continued to suck away at the lollipop as if his young life depended on it, and judging by the frightened look in his eyes, the lollipop was the only thing keeping him from crying.

Deputy Mayor Graves rested her hands on either side of the boy's neck, her long nails curling over his shoulders like bloody talons. "It is my honor to introduce Theodore Easton and his mother, Trinity. At age six, Theodore is about to become the youngest Volunteer in our city's history."

The applause started up again, louder this time, but Kira refused to join in. She had done many questionable things for Vita Nova, but she would not applaud the death of a child. Any citizen, regardless of age, could become a Volunteer, but no children had ever volunteered before. The youngest Volunteer that Kira was aware of had been a fourteen-year-old girl. Still a child, yes, but she wasn't *six*.

Six was a baby.

"Theodore Easton, is it your wish to end your life as a Volunteer?"

The little boy blinked at the deputy mayor. Then he pulled the lollipop from his mouth and looked at his mother. "Is it, Momma?"

"Yes, baby." The pink-haired young woman uttered a nervous laugh and crouched in front of her son. "Remember? You've been asking to become a superhero for the city for months. Ever since you turned six."

The crowd responded with a collective *aww* that soured Kira's stomach.

"Yes, Momma," he said. "I'll be a superhero who saves everybody."

"That's a good boy," his mother responded. "So, baby, if this is what you want to do, then you just have to tell Deputy Mayor Graves that this is your wish."

The boy looked at the deputy mayor and nodded. "I wish to be a superhero."

Sienna Graves's delighted gasp was echoed by the crowd. "Aren't you just adorable? Theodore, have you arrived at this decision of your own free will?"

Again, the little boy looked at his mother for guidance. "Momma?"

The young woman nodded. "Yes, baby. Just keep saying yes when she asks you questions."

"Okay. Yes."

Trinity Easton rose, a satisfied smile on her lips.

Kneeling as best as she could in her pantsuit and stiletto heels, the deputy mayor pinned the blue boutonniere to the little boy's shirt.

Kira didn't hear the deputy mayor's rehearsed speech or the shouts of *Revere the Volunteer!* that followed. Her mind couldn't comprehend what was happening, so her body took over, going through the motions, bringing her to her feet with the rest of the crowd when it was time to applaud.

But she did not applaud.

Her hands hung at her sides like anchors, too heavy to lift.

Only when the Memoriam began and the faces of the previous week's Volunteers appeared on the Jumbotron did Kira come back into herself. Along with the rest of the Stadium, she rose and placed the fingers of her right hand into a v-shape over her heart. She watched as images from Lizzy Currant's life played out on the screen, set to music. From childhood through adulthood, the entire population of Harrisburg watched as Lizzy grew from a curly-haired toddler to a dignified woman. A few pictures from her luxurious final days at Rolling Meadows showed her relaxing poolside with her three granddaughters. The adorable trio of a frizzy-haired blonde girls were pint-sized versions of their grandmother.

Lizzy's slideshow concluded with a photograph of her and her husband dining at The Riverfront, the shimmering indigo surface of the Susquehanna visible in the background. They held hands across the table and stared into each other's eyes; the picture taken from far enough away that the couple probably didn't realize they were being photographed. The image was breathtakingly beautiful, like something from one of the glossy pages of the old magazines Kira sometimes paged through at the library.

I booked that table for them, she thought to herself, her pride swelling for a moment before being replaced by sadness. Sadness for a love lost.

As the image faded to black, Lizzy's name materialized on the screen in bold letters, alongside the dates of her birth and death.

The screen flickered, and the music shut off.

Deputy Mayor Graves glanced off-field and frowned. She raised the microphone to her lips. "I apologize, ladies and gentlemen. We seem to be experiencing...uh...technical difficulties. Please be patient. I'm sure everything will be back to normal very—."

At the far end of the field, the Jumbotron came to life with an emergency broadcast from the Executive Mansion. Victor Devlin's face filled the screen. *"Citizens of Vita Nova, please accept my sincerest apologies for interrupting the Memoriam, but this message is of the highest importance. A few minutes ago, I received word that one of our Patrol units located six bodies in the Unregulated Zone. They delivered the bodies to the Medical*

Sector for examination, and although they haven't been formally identified yet, we believe that these six individuals are the same individuals who defected to the Unregulated Zone four days ago."

Kira's fingers fell away from her heart.

"The person—or persons—responsible strategically placed the bodies across the entrance to the western span of the Market Street Bridge, so that one of our Patrol vehicles nearly ran them over as they returned to the city for the night. Preliminary evidence suggests that all six individuals endured various forms of torture immediately prior to their deaths."

The Stadium echoed with gasps and whispers.

Torture?

Devlin squinted into the camera. And for reasons she couldn't explain, Kira felt as if he was watching her.

"These defectors chose the Lawless over their own city, and they paid the ultimate price for that act of treason. However, no citizen of Vita Nova deserves such a cruel fate. Effective immediately, I am increasing the number of daily Patrols into the Unregulated Zone. The Patrols will screen any Lawless they capture for the Job virus. Those who test positive will be euthanized. Those who test negative will be brought to the Confines for interrogation. If we apprehend the individuals responsible for these murders, we will execute them."

Tearing her eyes from the screen, Kira searched the field for Will and found him standing near the little boy. Even from a distance, she could see the hostility on his face. The young man who'd told her less than an hour earlier that she looked amazing in her dress was gone. This Will was different. Colder and harder, somehow.

A rock with sharp edges.

"We cannot know what information the enemy elicited through their methods of torture," Devlin continued. *"We also*

cannot know if there are more potential defectors among us. But the Patrols and Guards will do everything within their power to keep our city safe from sabotage. I'm asking that every citizen remain vigilant. If you see or hear anything suspicious, report it. If you hear your neighbor speaking ill of our city, report it. All treasonous activities must be thwarted. If we work together, as we always have, Vita Nova will endure. We will survive. For the good of all."

"For the good of all."

Victor Devlin's face vanished, replaced by a baby photo of one of last week's dead Volunteers. Bald-headed and rosy-cheeked, the little boy extended his chubby arms toward the camera, his bright-blue eyes possessing no hint of the knowledge that his premature death would one day make him a hero.

Moving of their own volition, Kira's fingers found their way to her heart, but her eyes drifted beyond the Jumbotron, to the Unregulated Zone. It hypnotized her—all of that unrestrained darkness—so that she couldn't tear her eyes away from it, not even when the fireworks lit up the night sky and the remains of Lizzy and the other Volunteers rained down on the river.

What had the defectors gone into the Unregulated Zone looking for?

And why had the Lawless repaid them with slaughter?

Chapter 11

Monday

Kira left her townhouse early, giving herself plenty of time to make the long trek across town to the Broad Street Market. She didn't want to be late for Will on their first day together.

She also didn't want to spend another minute alone.

Nightmares had plagued her sleep. In the worst one, she'd stood on a residential street in the Unregulated Zone, gazing up at one of the abandoned houses. Black mold crawled up the damaged siding, creeping higher as Kira watched, an insatiable monster intent on devouring the house and its contents. Rotting boards swung from rusty nails, having long ago given up the pretense of protecting the shattered windows. Kira glimpsed her reflection in a shard of broken glass—she looked terrified— and then movement drew her attention to a different first-floor window.

Something drifted past the broken glass. A subtle shifting of fabric, moss-covered and stiff with age. The funeral garments of a spirit that paced the empty house, unable to rest.

Not a spirit, she assured herself. *Just curtains moving in the breeze.*

Someone had sprayed a series of red slashes on the front door. Kira had seen enough broadcasts about the Unregulated Zone to know the slashes meant the Patrols had searched this home for supplies. The number on the door indicated how many bodies they had found within.

12.

With dawning horror, Kira watched the door creak open.

Skeletal fingers curled around the doorframe, revealing nails mottled with dirt and grime. Pale fingers clutched a wilted blue rose. A face emerged from the darkness. Burnt white skin sloughed away from white bone. A toothless mouth hung open in a silent scream.

It was Lizzy Currant.

Kira tried to scream, but no sound emerged.

Join us, Kira, Lizzy's corpse beckoned. *It's dark and terrible and wonderful in here.*

Kira had awoken gasping for air and thrashing at her sweat-soaked sheets. According to her watch, it was three-twenty in the morning.

She hadn't slept the rest of the night.

As the Broad Street Market came into view, Kira resolved to push the nightmare from her mind so she could focus on Will's Final Week. The nightmare had meant nothing. Lizzy Currant's spirit wasn't haunting a house in the Unregulated Zone. She'd been cremated, her ashes shot into the heavens with the other Volunteers. Naturally, Kira had been upset after learning of the defectors and their tragic deaths, and finding out from her father that one of them had written her name on a piece of paper before dying hadn't helped matters. That news—coupled with the sadness of seeing Lizzy's face in the Memoriam—had inspired a terrible dream.

But she didn't need to be afraid.

Whatever the defectors's reasons had been for sneaking out of the city, they were no longer a threat to Kira or anyone else. If they had intended to use her for a nefarious purpose, that would not happen now.

They were gone, consumed by the Unregulated Zone.

Kira spotted Will leaning against the brick building, his hands stuffed inside the pockets of a moss-colored military jacket. He hadn't noticed her yet. He was too busy studying the ground beneath his boots, clearly trying to avoid eye contact with everyone walking into the market.

He wasn't wearing his rose.

"Good morning, Will."

He lifted his head, his eyes finding hers in the crowd of people approaching the market. The left corner of his mouth ticked into a half-grin, and he pushed away from the wall and walked up to Kira. "Good morning, Miss Liebert."

"Why aren't you wearing your rose?"

"What?" Feigning surprise, he patted the front of his jacket as if realizing he'd misplaced the flower. "Oh, it's under here somewhere. It was cold when I left my apartment."

Kira raised one eyebrow. "It's sixty-five degrees."

"Really? Must be colder in the Eastern Sector."

Kira folded her arms over her chest, hoping she'd heard him wrong. "Please tell me you stayed at Rolling Meadows last night and not in the Tenements."

"I'm more comfortable in my apartment."

"Will!"

"It's *my* Final Week. And if I'm happy in my bed. I don't see why it should matter to you where I spend my nights." A suggestive smile dangled on the edge of his lips. "But I'm open to other suggestions if you have them."

She rolled her eyes. "You're going to be a problem for me, aren't you?"

"More than you realize."

Will was flirting with her. The realization made her bold, and as people moved around them, heading into the market, Kira grabbed the zipper to his jacket and yanked it down to reveal the blue rose pinned to his black t-shirt.

"Hey!" he protested. "Undressing me in public is inappropriate, even for you, Miss Liebert."

Pressing her lips together to keep from laughing, Kira drew her hands away from his jacket—and the solid curves of his chest. "First, I've asked you to call me Kira. Second, you're supposed to make sure everyone can see the rose when you're outside."

"What if I don't want them to see it?"

She narrowed her eyes. "Why wouldn't you want people to see it? One of the biggest benefits of volunteering is having the entire city honor you. Now, stop being a stick in the mud and take that stupid jacket off."

With an irritated groan, Will removed the jacket and draped it over his arm. "There. Happy? Now, people are going to yell at me all—"

"Revere the Volunteer!"

A man jogged past them, placing his fingers in a v-shape over his heart.

"Thanks, man." Will gave him an embarrassed wave and leaned toward Kira. "Can we go inside now? Please?"

"Absolutely."

They fell in with the crowd heading into the market. Even before they reached the doors, Kira could smell the food. The myriad of delicious aromas, all competing for dominance, made her stomach growl.

"You know, I still can't believe I agreed to this," she said.

Will ran a hand through his hair. "Honestly? I can't believe you agreed to it, either."

"Most Volunteers want free stuff for themselves and their families. No one has ever requested the pleasure of my company before."

"Well, that's their loss, isn't it?"

As they reached the entrance, a man exited the building clutching a reusable grocery bag. He turned to say something to the woman behind him, and his left shoulder slammed into Will's chest. "Whoa. Sorry, buddy."

"No problem."

When the man spotted Will's rose, his eyes widened, and he almost dropped his groceries in his rush to put his fingers over his heart. Then, digging into his grocery bag, he pulled out a paper-wrapped loaf of bread and presented it to Will like a religious offering.

"Revere the Volunteer!"

Will stared at the loaf of bread in his hands. "Uh...thanks?"

After the man continued on his way, Will turned to Kira. "See? Revere the Volunteer means nothing to him. They're just words the city has taught him to repeat like a parrot." He shifted the bread to his other hand so he could open the door for Kira. "Giving up a loaf of bread isn't a big deal—he'll just buy another one—but what you're doing means something. You aren't obligated to spend a week with me. No one would expect you to do this, simply because I'm a Volunteer. That you're willing to sacrifice your time to be with me says a lot about you as a person."

Kira nodded, understanding what Will meant. The *Revere the Volunteer* salute often came across as disingenuous, but it truly meant something to her. The Volunteers gave up their lives so she could live, and she wanted to honor that Sacrifice.

"Come on," she said. "I'm starving. If we don't get lunch soon, I'm going to steal your bread."

They entered the immense building and were swallowed up by the crowds of people navigating the narrow aisles between the vendor's tables. Without saying a word, Will placed a hand on the small of Kira's back and guided her down the main aisle.

She told herself not to dwell on it—the unfamiliar but pleasant pressure of his hand—but she couldn't think of anything else.

Long before the Job virus and the barricade, the Broad Street Market had been a Harrisburg landmark. It prided itself on being the oldest continuously operating market house in the United States, having first opened its doors in 1860, when local farmers at the market had helped feed Union soldiers. Every Monday, Thursday, and Saturday, the old building on the corner of North Third and Verbeke Streets came to life as vendors of all kinds took up residence beneath its cavernous roof. Baked goods, soups, flower arrangements, homemade candles, even clothing and accessories could be purchased for a price. The market was one of the few places in Vita Nova that the city leadership allowed to operate as it had before the barricade.

When they broke free from the crowd, Will removed his hand from Kira's back.

She immediately missed it.

"What can I buy you for lunch?"

"*You* aren't buying *me* anything for lunch," Kira said. "I'm buying you lunch. You're the Volunteer, remember?"

"Oh, I remember. But Volunteer or not, my father would roll over in his grave if he knew I'd let a nice young woman buy my lunch. Sorry if that offends you, but I'm a little old-fashioned that way."

Stepping closer to Will to allow a group of people to pass by, Kira breathed in his earthy scent. "It doesn't offend me. My mother used to say that men should be more chivalrous and women should let them. Your father sounds like a good man."

Will's smile dimmed. "Yeah, he was. So, what sounds good to you?"

"I'm not sure. Do you mind if we walk around a little first?"

"Not at all."

When Kira met up with Emma at the market, they usually bought salads for lunch. A stand at the far end of the building allowed customers to build their own salads from a variety of toppings, and the woman who owned the stand made delicious homemade dressings. But Will didn't strike Kira as a guy who ate a lot of salads, and her own hunger was too great to be satisfied by a bowl of lettuce.

They moved deeper into the market, winding through the aisles and passing by a series of butcher stands operated by individuals from the Agricultural Sector. Vita Nova took most of their profits, since the animals were owned by the city, but the butchers earned a little money selling the meat to the citizens. Kira gazed longingly into the glass cases at the fresh chicken and turkey breasts, lean cuts of beef, and smoked jerky and sausage sticks. She tapped her chin with one finger, debating whether to purchase a chicken breast for dinner that evening, but the meat was so expensive she couldn't justify it.

Only the wealthiest of the city could afford to eat meat daily.

She spotted a flower stand on the left side of the aisle, her eyes drawn to the day's fresh bouquets, all featuring roses in uncommon pastel hues. Pink and yellow and lavender roses, blending together into a rainbow of colors. Above the display, a sign read: *Vita Nova Floral: Proud Purveyor of the Blue Roses for Volunteers.*

There were no blue roses for sale, of course. They only gave those to Volunteers.

When Kira's eyes settled on a lavender rose, the woman stationed behind the table stood, her lips peeling into a predatory grin. "Do you like them, dear?"

"I love the lavender ones."

The woman's eyes shifted from Kira to Will. She opened her mouth to speak—probably to guilt him into buying a rose for Kira—but then she noticed the blue rose pinned to his shirt and her fingers snapped to her heart. "Revere the Volunteer."

"Thanks," Will mumbled, taking Kira's hand and tugging her away from the flower stand.

"Excuse me?" the woman called after him. "Would you like a fresh bouquet of lavender roses for the young lady? Flowers are always free for our brave Volunteers."

"No, thanks. We're good."

When they were out of earshot of the woman, Will paused in front of a candle stand. "Sorry. We just finished talking about chivalry and then I refuse to get you a free bouquet. For the record, I'd love to buy you a dozen lavender flowers. Just not roses...and not from Vita Nova Floral." He pointed at the rose on his chest. "Do you know how they make these?"

"Don't they grow them that way?" Kira asked. "I always assumed it was some sort of rose interbreeding program."

Still holding Kira's hand, Will led her into the next aisle. "Actually, blue roses start out as white roses," he said. "To color them, they cut the stem and place the flower in a cup filled with blue dye. A day or two later, after the rose petals have absorbed the blue dye, they cut the stem and add more dye. It's a rough process for the rose. They end up dying much faster than normal roses. Fitting, right?"

"That's kind of depressing."

"That's Vita Nova."

They came to a stop in front of a vender. The sign taped to the counter read *Randolph's Soup Kitchen*. A rail-thin man with white hair sat behind the counter on a rusted lawn chair, a stained dish towel tossed over one shoulder, his legs splayed out in front of him. He was definitely the oldest person in the market. Possibly in the entire city. With his head canted awkwardly to one side, his eyes closed, and his mouth hanging open, he looked...

Kira drew in a breath. "Oh, goodness. Is he—"

"Dead? Nah. Randy always looks dead." Will turned to Kira, a mischievous twinkle in his eyes. "Okay, so I'm going to let you in on a little secret. What I'm going to tell you will affect everything you've been led to believe for your entire life, but you have to promise to keep an open mind. Will you do that for me?"

Studying the old man's chest for signs of movement, Kira nodded. "Sure. I'll do my best."

"Okay. So, the secret is...none of the food vendors in this market are any good, except for Randy. Don't feel bad if you didn't know. Most people don't. But fortunately for you, I know the truth, and I feel obligated to make sure you have a great lunch today. The best lunch of your entire life, in fact."

"And the best lunch of my life is going to be..." Kira squinted at the dry-erase board and read the Soup of the Day. "A five-dollar bowl of creamy vegetable soup?"

Will wagged a finger at her. "Not just any five-dollar bowl of creamy vegetable soup. Randy makes the *best* creamy vegetable soup in the city." He leaned over the counter and shouted, "Isn't that right, Randy?"

The old man jolted awake, kicking out with both legs. One skinny arm slammed into the counter, knocking a metal soup ladle to the floor. It landed with a heavy clang that was lost in the noise and bustle of the market.

Randy's eyelashes fluttered, his face a mixture of confusion and fear, until he noticed Will. Then his eyes narrowed, and he slumped into his chair. "Ack. Shoulda known it was you, kid. You're becoming a real a pain in my—"

"*Randy*," Will chided. "Is that a nice thing to say when one of your most loyal customers is out here trying to drum up new business for you?" He gestured to Kira, who offered Randy an embarrassed wave that was not returned. "I was just telling my friend here that you make the best soup in Vita Nova."

"Sure do." Randy rose from his chair, joints popping, and bent over to pluck the ladle from the floor with a shaking hand. "Everybody knows it."

As Kira watched, the old man pulled the hand towel from his shoulder and used it to half-heartedly wipe the dirty ladle, his eyes flicking between Kira and Will, as if daring them to say something about the cleanliness of his kitchen.

Which, of course, they didn't.

"Two bowls?" Randy asked.

Will nodded. "And fill them all the way up. I'm trying to impress this girl. Don't go cheap on me like you usually do."

With a loud grunt, Randy tossed the towel back over his shoulder and shuffled over to one of the metal soup kettles. Then he plunged the ladle inside and dished out two generous bowlfuls of soup.

As Kira observed Randy's slow and methodical movements, she couldn't help but wonder how a man in his physical condition had avoided becoming a Compulsory. And although she didn't know Randy's exact age, he had clearly waved goodbye to sixty many years ago.

The old man placed the bowls of soup on the counter. "That'll be ten even." He grabbed two spoons and dropped them into the thick soup. Then he tilted his head forward and squinted at Will. "You got something stuck to your shirt, kid."

Will smirked. "You noticed? I thought maybe you couldn't see the rose, what with those failing eyes of yours. You should make an appointment at the Medical Sector to get them checked out."

"Ack. My eyes ain't failing and neither are my fists. If you think I can't see good enough to knock that weaselly grin off your face, just give me a reason."

Kira bit her lip to keep from laughing.

She liked Randy.

Digging into his wallet, Will pulled out a twenty-dollar bill and laid it on the counter. The old man snatched it up and stuffed it inside the front pocket of his soup-stained apron with neither a thank you nor any effort to make change.

"Come on, Randy. I'm a Volunteer. Can't you at least salute me?"

The old man tutted and dropped into his lawn chair. "I ain't saluting you, kid. I'll let the Guards come in here and drag me to the Confines before I put my fingers over my heart for your snotty little—"

"Keep the change, Randy," Will called out as he and Kira picked up their bowls and walked away.

———

THEY HEADED FOR THE NEAREST EXIT, WHICH OPENED into a brick courtyard featuring a series of low stone benches. The sudden quiet of the outside world was a welcome change from the noise and commotion of the building. Will led her to a bench and placed his jacket down for her to sit on. They sat side-by-side with steaming bowls of soup in their laps.

"Be careful," Will warned. "Randy's tastebuds still work, but his nerve endings don't, so he doesn't realize how hot the soup is."

"Okay..." Kira stirred the soup to cool it off, hypnotized by the swirling greens, reds, and oranges of the diced vegetables. When she thought it was cool enough, she raised a spoonful to her mouth, blew on it, and took a bite.

Wow!

A multitude of flavors, many of which she'd never tasted before and couldn't identify, made up a creamy broth so delicious she could've easily drank it on its own. The vegetables were diced so small it was as if they weren't there, yet the abundance of vegetables added a heartiness to the soup that Kira would've normally only attributed to meat. She took another bite, and that's when she tasted something different. Something besides the vegetables. Something soft and chewy.

"Are there noodles in this?" she asked.

"Rivels." Will nodded. "Little pieces of dough. Randy drops them into the pot while the soup is still cooking. Good, right?"

Good didn't even describe it. Kira raised another spoonful to her mouth. The soup wasn't just good; it was incredible. The chewy bits of dough reminded her of the sticky buns her mother used to make from scratch every year for her birthday. Flour wasn't easy to come by in Vita Nova, and neither was sugar, so sticky buns had been a once-a-year treat in the Liebert household.

"How have I never heard of Randy?" Kira asked, stirring her still-steaming soup before taking another bite. "I must've walked past him hundreds of times and never noticed him."

"Randy's good at blending in. Always has been. He used to be an Army soldier, back in the days before the barricade. Doesn't hurt that he spends all of his time sleeping in that lawn chair. People pass him by without looking, but he's got enough loyal customers to keep him in business."

"But he's so old. No way he's under sixty."

"He claims to be fifty-five, but he's been claiming that for as long as I've known him." Will scratched his head. "All I can figure is that someone important is protecting him. Maybe they like his soup?"

Kira glanced at her bowl and realized it was already half-empty. "I don't suppose you'd be willing to buy me another bowl after I finish this one?"

She'd intended it as a joke, but Will picked up his own bowl, which he hadn't even touched, and placed it next to her on the wall. "Here. You can have mine."

"No!" Kira half-shouted, pushing the bowl back to him. "I let you buy me lunch, but I draw the line at eating yours. Don't you understand how this Volunteer thing works?"

Unwrapping the bread he'd gotten from the man exiting the market, Will broke off a sizable chunk. "I don't want the soup. I've been eating too many rivels lately." He patted his flat stomach for emphasis and held up the bread. "Besides, I might as well eat this before it gets stale."

She knew she should argue with him—Will was just being nice—but she *really* wanted more soup. "Okay," she said, picking up the bowl. "But for the record, I don't feel good about this."

"Your discomfort is noted. Now, eat."

Before he took a bite of his bread, Will bowed his head and closed his eyes for a few seconds. Kira was about to ask him if he was okay when his eyes opened.

"Do you mind?" he asked.

Kira's face caught on fire—Will had noticed her staring at him—but then she realized he was wagging the chunk of bread over her bowl of soup.

"Uh...sure," she muttered, not entirely sure what he intended to do. "Go ahead."

He dunked the bread into the soup, allowing it to soak up as much of the creamy broth as possible. Lifting the dripping bread to his mouth, he took a huge bite that was both uncivilized and endearing at the same time.

Kira stared at him, practically drooling, until Will noticed her watching and passed her the rest of the bread.

"Try it. It's even better this way."

He didn't have to tell her twice. Ripping off a small chunk of bread, she dipped it into her soup, popped it into her mouth, and closed her eyes. "Oh, wow. That's *so* good. Randy is a good, good man."

"He really is, isn't he?"

They ate in silence, pausing between bites to toss bread crumbs to the sparrows hopping along the ground at their feet. The birds snatched the crumbs from the pavement, gobbled them down, and looked up for more.

Will eventually broke the silence. "So, do you have anything else going on this week?" he asked. "Aside from hanging out with me, I mean."

"My week is pretty open," Kira replied, lifting a sopping piece of bread to her mouth. "Well, except for Wednesday night."

"What's on Wednesday night?"

"Nothing really. I agreed to this double date thing with my friend, Emma."

"A date?" Will stopped eating and looked at her. "Where are you going?"

"She wants to go to The Riverfront for dinner and then dancing at The Grotto."

"That old bathhouse?" He flung a piece of bread at the birds, a pinched expression on his face. "That place is a dump."

"I know. Between you and me, I'm not looking forward to

the date, but I'm doing it for Emma. However, I'm yours for the rest of the week."

As the words left her lips, she realized how they sounded. Leaning forward, she allowed her hair to fall in front of her face. A blonde shield so Will couldn't watch her as she died of embarrassment.

But Will continued talking, unfazed by her statement. "Well, I have a suggestion for what we should do tomorrow, but I don't think you're going to like it."

Kira tore off another piece of bread and used it to sop up the last of her soup. "If it's as good as this soup, I'm on board."

"I want to take you into the Unregulated Zone."

The bread slipped through Kira's fingers and landed in her empty bowl. She looked at Will. "The Unregulated Zone? Are you crazy? You mean the place where six defectors were just murdered by the Lawless? No way. Absolutely not."

"I drive out there all the time, Kira. It's not dangerous."

"It *is* dangerous! Besides, your job is driving *bodies* into the Unregulated Zone," she sputtered. "You want me to help you transport bodies?"

He waved the idea away. "Of course not. I'm not working this week, but I can still get us out there. The Guards won't give us any trouble. They all know me. I understand it's scary for you, Kira, but this is important to me. Please. As my dying wish."

"Dying wish?" She glared at him. "That's a little manipulative, don't you think?"

Will plucked the discarded chunk of bread from Kira's bowl and popped it into his mouth. "I have no shame," he said through a mouthful of bread.

Kira's stomach churned. She wished she wouldn't have eaten two enormous bowls of soup, plus half a loaf of bread. The idea of driving into the Unregulated Zone with Will terrified her. She hadn't been outside of the barricade since she was seven. Vita Nova was her whole life. It was all she knew. What if they encountered the Lawless? What if they came under attack, as the defectors had?

But another part of her—the same part that had agreed to violate every rule of Volunteer advocacy in order to spend the week with one of her clients—was curious about the Unregulated Zone. What would it be like to set foot on the soil beyond the barricade? A place she hadn't gone in over twelve years.

Will smiled at her. "You look a little sick."

"You don't know what you're asking me to do," she whispered. "Just last night, I had an awful nightmare about the Unregulated Zone. And now you expect me to go out there?"

"Kira, I wouldn't ask you to do this if I couldn't keep you safe. I know why you're afraid, but you'll just have to trust me."

I only just met you, she wanted to argue. *How can I trust you?*

But something in his eyes made her believe him.

He would keep her safe.

With a heavy sigh, Kira relented. "Okay, I'll go with you, but only if you promise that this is the worst thing you're going to ask me to do all week."

"I make no promises." He crumpled up the paper that had once held his loaf of bread. "So, now that you've agreed to come with me, there's one catch. But you're *really* not going to like it."

She groaned. "What's the catch?"

"If the Guards on the bridge see you in the passenger seat of the disposal van, that's going to be a problem. We aren't allowed to take civilians out there."

"Okay. So, how do we keep the Guards from seeing me?"

Will's eyes met hers. "Remember how I said you weren't going to like it?"

She stared at him, waiting, but he seemed hesitant to say

more. And that's when the realization hit her. "Wait. You're not suggesting that I...?" She let the question hang in the air because she couldn't bring herself to speak the words.

He nodded, his face grim.

"You'll have to ride in the back of the van."

Chapter 12

Tuesday

There won't be any dead bodies in the back of the van, Kira kept reminding herself as the bus deposited her in the city's Eastern Sector, a few blocks south of the sanitation lot. She kept her head on a swivel as she walked through one of the roughest neighborhoods in Vita Nova. Fourteen-story apartment buildings rose on either side of her, casting their shadows across the empty roadway.

The Tenements.

Will's home.

For nineteen years, Kira had existed in a twelve square-mile area, yet she'd never walked through this neighborhood. Never felt the cracked sidewalk beneath her boots. Never seen it up close.

Most of the Compulsories came from the Eastern Sector.

So did most of the Volunteers.

Now Kira could see why.

Each block contained two dumpsters, one on each side of the street, leaving barely enough room in the narrow roadway for the city buses to creep by. Every dumpster overflowed with refuse, and the building's residents had begun tossing their garbage into the street. Ripped bags cluttered the sidewalk, spilling spoiled food into the road, where it would be crushed beneath the bus's churning wheels.

Through filthy windows and tattered curtains, Kira caught brief glimpses into the lives of the people who lived in these overcrowded high-rises. On the second floor, a woman strutted past an open window, a shrieking baby balanced on one hip. A few seconds later, a man lunged into view, his face beet-red as he shouted, *"What am I supposed to do? She's sick! What do you want me to do?"*

On the next block, Kira glimpsed a face staring at her from a closed window on the third floor of the apartment building. A little girl with dark braids falling over her eyes, the breath from her nostrils fogging up the glass as she followed Kira's progress along the sidewalk.

Kira raised her hand in a silent wave, but the girl darted out of view.

Kira picked up her pace, eager to get away from the Tenements. How could anyone as sweet and funny as Will have grown up in such a depressing place? She understood now why he'd become a Volunteer. He had no family, an awful job, and he lived in one of the worst sections of the city. Besides—given the unsanitary conditions of the Eastern Sector—it would only be a matter of time before he became ill and the government forced him to become a Compulsory.

A few minutes later, the chain-link fence that surrounded the sanitation lot came into view, and Kira breathed a sigh of relief. She'd made it out of the Eastern Sector without getting robbed or attacked.

The day was starting out better than she'd imagined.

An unmarked black disposal van idled inside the fence, its

rear doors hanging open, and Kira froze in place as the realization of what she was about to do finally set in.

This is crazy, she thought. *I can't do this. I can't go into the Unregulated Zone.*

At that moment, she wanted to turn on her heels and run. She wanted to go back to her depressing office and her empty desk. She wanted to forget all about Will Foster and his insane plan of sneaking her into the Unregulated Zone.

Will stepped out of the van carrying a rag and a bottle filled with blue liquid. He didn't spot her right away. Humming to himself, he walked to the side of the van, opened the door, and tossed the rag and the bottle onto the front passenger seat. He wore the same battered work clothes he'd worn to her office that first day—black t-shirt, olive work pants, and boots—and his golden-brown hair appeared almost blond in the morning sunlight.

The fluttering sensation returned, like dozens of little hummingbirds had taken up residence in her stomach. Her feet moved on their own, drawing her closer to the sanitation lot.

After he closed the passenger door, Will spotted her walking through the entrance to the lot. His face lit up as his eyes swept over her. "I wasn't sure you'd actually show up today."

"I wouldn't miss it for the world. Besides, I'm your advocate and this is one of your requests."

"Yeah, but leaving the barricade for the first time in the back of a meat wagon is a lot to ask of someone."

The tiny hummingbirds in Kira's stomach transformed into bats. Bloodthirsty bats with tremendous, leathery wings. "Please don't call it a meat wagon, Will. I'm barely holding it together here."

He laughed. "Sorry. Gallows humor is a requirement for this job."

Kira's gaze dropped to the empty spot on his shirt. "Aren't you forgetting something? Again?"

Will wiped his hands on his work pants. "Before you yell at me, I'm not wearing the rose because I don't want the Guards on the bridge to know I'm a Volunteer. They won't believe I'm still working—especially in *this* job—and they won't let us through the roadblock. But I promise to put the rose on as soon as we get back to the city."

She nodded. "I suppose that's acceptable."

"You'll be happy to know that we thoroughly clean these vans at the end of every shift, but I just wiped the floor down to make you feel better."

"Ugh," Kira groaned. "The idea of you needing to *wipe the floor* down doesn't make me feel very good."

Will's expression wavered between amusement and pity. "The Compulsories aren't just laid out in the back. They're placed inside body bags before we load them into the van." He paused, studying her expression. "I'm not sure how much information you want."

"As little as possible."

"Okay. Want to look inside? Maybe that would help."

Not really. She hadn't allowed herself to think about her mother until this moment, but now everything was becoming too real. She wasn't sure she could handle seeing where her mother's body had ended up after the sanitation engineer had wheeled it out of the room at the Compulsory Clinic.

What if this was the same van?

"Kira? You okay?"

"I'm fine," she said, a little too harshly. She stepped around Will, grabbed the edge of the door, and peered inside.

"See? It's just a regular van."

Kira didn't know what she'd expected to see. Maybe blood spatters or mystery liquids on the floor, or discarded body parts jutting out of ripped garbage bags. What she saw instead was a windowless van with a metal floor. It didn't look comfortable, but it wasn't the blood-soaked nightmare she'd imagined.

Will spoke up from behind her. "We should really get moving if we're going to do this."

She spun around to face him. "I don't know about this, Will. Going outside the barricade is illegal. What if someone sees and reports us?"

"Who's going to see?" He held his arms out and rotated in a circle. "There's no one around. It's just the two of us here."

He was right. No other workers had arrived at the sanitation lot yet. The Tenements were a few blocks away, and the only building nearby was an abandoned warehouse on the other side of the street.

"But won't your boss realize that one of these vans burned gas on a day when it wasn't supposed to be used?"

"You'd think so, but no." He leaned against the side of the van and crossed his arms. "My boss, Jonesy, doesn't track the mileage of the vans. I've gone into the Unregulated Zone a bunch of times on my days off, and he's never said a word about it."

Kira stared at Will, waiting for him to elaborate. When he said nothing, she asked, "Uh, this is probably a dumb question, but why would you *ever* go into the Unregulated Zone on your day off?"

Will chewed on the inside of his lip as if considering how much to say. Finally, he pushed away from the van and stepped closer to her.

"If you're ready," he said, "I'd like to show you."

Chapter Thirteen

Kira rode into the Unregulated Zone with her back pressed against the side of the disposal van, clutching her knees against her chest. She couldn't talk to Will because there was no window between the front and back of the van. But two small windows built into the van's rear doors enabled her to see the buildings flashing by, and she could track their progress through the city.

She tried to keep her eyes on those windows.

But once—just once—she lost focus.

Her gaze fell to the floor of the van, and she imagined a pile of bodies lying beyond the tips of her boots. All of them zipped into body bags. All of them heading for the Unregulated Zone. And then she imagined her mother's beautiful body at the bottom of that pile, still wearing her hospital gown and socks, crushed beneath the weight of the city's Compulsory dead.

The van swerved to the right.

Kira tore her eyes away from the van's floor—which was, of course, empty—and returned her attention to the rear windows. Judging by the grouping of government buildings that poked like dirty fingers into the sky, and that the road had gotten noticeably smoother beneath the van's tires, Kira was pretty sure they'd just merged onto the Market Street Bridge.

The vehicle slowed.

This is it, she realized. *We're at the checkpoint.*

If the Guards on the bridge searched the rear of the van, they would discover Kira. She had nowhere to go. Nowhere to hide.

Over the idling engine, she recognized Will's muffled voice as he spoke with one of the Guards. There were two other voices: one female and one male. They spoke with Will for a long time, their discussion punctuated by the occasional burst of laughter. Although she still didn't understand *why* he did it, Kira no longer wondered how Will could travel back and forth freely into the Unregulated Zone without raising any eyebrows. From the sound of it, the Guards on the bridge found him every bit as charming as Kira had the day he'd entered her office.

A few minutes later, the van rolled forward again.

Kira expelled a breath and stretched out her legs, the anxiety leaving her body. But her relief was short-lived. Seconds later, the vehicle's tires abandoned the smooth bridge for a heavily rutted roadway, and the sunlight disappeared, blanketing the van's interior in shadows.

A wave of fear swept over Kira. She tried to tell herself that a cloud had moved in front of the sun, but what if that wasn't true?

What if the sun didn't exist on this side of the river?

She tried not to think about the six dead defectors, their tortured bodies strewn across the same roadway they'd just driven over. Their only sin had been sneaking out of the city— the same sin Kira was now committing—and they'd suffered immensely for it.

What was she doing? Why had she agreed to this?

For the first time in her life, she was no longer safe inside the protective bubble of Vita Nova.

She was in the Unregulated Zone.

WHEN THE VAN'S REAR DOORS SWUNG OPEN FIFTEEN minutes later, Kira scrambled out of the van and fell into Will's arms.

"Whoa! Are you okay?" Holding her at arm's length, Will brought a hand to her face and lifted her chin, forcing her to look at him. "What happened?"

She gripped his muscular forearms, her fingers digging trenches into his skin. "Why is it so dark over here?"

"It's just cloudy," he assured her. "There's a storm moving in. The city is dark, too."

Peering over Will's shoulder, Kira saw what had once been the business district of a modest town. A broken stoplight hung overhead, the colored glass destroyed in some long-forgotten conflict. Lush vines twisted around the pole that extended over the street, green tendrils dangling like the apocalypse's version of streamers at a child's birthday party.

She hated riding inside the disposal van, but standing outside of it was so much worse. She wanted to crawl back inside and slam the door.

"Will...?"

"Kira, it's safe here. I promise."

Will had parked the van at the junction of two main streets. Dozens of rust-covered vehicles blocked the narrow intersection, their front ends all pointed in the same direction. The drivers must've been trying to make their way out of town. Among the abandoned vehicles was an old school bus, the words *Evacuation Transport* spray-painted on its right side.

The bus's lower-half still retained patches of its original yellow coloring, but a dozen years spent baking in the unyielding sun had bleached the entire top-half of the bus white. Thick weeds punched through cracks in the road, obscuring the asphalt from view.

To Kira's right was an old grocery store. White paint on the front windows identified the store as Musser's Market. Through the dingy glass, Kira could see barren shelves, drooping ceiling tiles, and unidentifiable dark lumps on the floor that she hoped were dead animals and not dead people. According to the time-faded cardboard sign hanging in the window, Musser's had been running a special on ribeyes when the world ended.

Kira's breath caught in her chest. It was one thing to view the Unregulated Zone from a distance with the vast expanse of the Susquehanna River as a barrier, but it was another thing to stand in the middle of all that death and destruction.

Will reached for Kira's left hand, his warm fingers wrapping around her cold ones. "We have to walk from here. The Patrols moved most of the abandoned vehicles off the main highway so our disposal vans can reach the burial pits. As you can see, most of the roads in these small towns are completely impassable. The Patrols search them on foot, when they search them at all."

"Okay." Even though they were standing in what amounted to a graveyard, Kira couldn't help but be distracted by how perfectly her hand fit inside Will's. "So, where are we going?"

"A few blocks north. It's not far."

They meandered through the sea of vehicles, passing an old credit union, a diner, and a mom-and-pop pharmacy. Of the three businesses, the pharmacy had fared the worst. Looters had hurled garbage cans through the large front window and picked all the shelves clean. The glossy climbing vines that had overtaken the exteriors of most of the buildings in town had wormed their way into the pharmacy through the broken front window and were growing on the empty shelves.

Will spoke up beside her. "This town is called Emmitsburg. It used to be a beautiful place, filled with families. Most people who lived here commuted to jobs in the city, but Emmitsburg was their home. Their sanctuary. However, there weren't any hospitals in this town. No emergency rooms. When the virus hit, these people had nowhere to go. They couldn't get into the city, and they couldn't risk going too far because of the virus. Many of them tried quarantining inside their homes, but that only worked until they ran out of food and medicine. Every time a need forced them from their homes, they risked exposure to the virus. Many of them got sick during those supply runs. Or they carried the virus back to their families."

The businesses fell away, replaced by several blocks of single-family dwellings separated by narrow alleyways. Most of the houses had red numbers spray-painted on their front doors, indicating the number of bodies the Patrols had found inside. Most of the numbers were low—between one and five—but Kira noticed the number thirteen scrawled on one door.

"The media gave people hope about potential cures," Will continued. "There was a rumor that one hospital in the city had found a treatment for the virus, but that's all it was. Just a rumor. The reason the infection rates inside the city remained so low was because anyone who displayed any sores—or even a hint of a rash—were sent outside the fence to die. Those who didn't go willingly were shot."

Kira nodded grimly, her stomach winding itself into tight knots. She'd been young when the virus hit—only seven—and she remembered little about those early years. But she recalled seeing one live news report of Patrol soldiers firing on a group of sick people who had refused to go outside the electrified fence. As the sound of gunfire filled the living room, Kira's mother had rushed in from the kitchen and snapped off the broadcast screen.

Soon afterward, the news reports had ceased altogether.

Will stopped in front of a smallish, one-story house with yellow clapboard siding, its porch only wide enough to accommodate a single rocking chair. The house also had the distinction of being the only one on the block without a red number spray-painted on the front door.

"After being expelled from the city," Will said, releasing her hand, "the bad people—the *real* Lawless—ended up in towns like this one, breaking into houses to steal supplies. Hurting the people inside. Spreading the virus. Making things worse. Some folks had the means to defend their homes, but bullets don't last forever. And they won't stop a virus. Or starvation."

Kira could hear something strange in Will's tone. A sorrow she couldn't understand. "Will?" she ventured. "Why did you bring me here?"

Slowly, he turned to face her, and the sadness she saw in his eyes mirrored his sorrowful tone. "This was my home," he said, gesturing to the squat yellow house without a number on the door. "I lived here with my parents."

Chapter Fourteen

Kira blinked, certain she'd misheard him. "You what?"

How could Will—a man who lived and worked in Vita Nova—have lived with his family in the Unregulated Zone *after* the virus?

She shook her head, eager to deny his claim for reasons she couldn't explain. "No. That's not possible. What you're saying isn't possible."

Will stared at her, a piercing intensity in his gaze. "I was ten when the virus hit. We tried to get into the city—we'd heard the same cure rumors as everyone else—but they wouldn't let us past the blockade on the bridge. By that time, the outcasts from the city had flooded into our neighborhood, so we went into lockdown in our homes, boarding up the windows and doors and shutting off the lights. My father was the only one who ever left the house, and he only left to search for food and supplies. Otherwise, he slept during the day and stood watch every night with my grandfather's old hunting rifle. Nights were the worst. I couldn't sleep because of the horrible sounds coming from outside our front door. Gunshots. Screams. Crying. We wanted to help our neighbors, but we couldn't do anything. We couldn't even go outside."

Kira wanted to stop him—she had so many questions—but she stayed quiet, afraid that if she said anything, Will would shut down and stop talking.

She needed to know who he really was.

Will remained anchored to the sidewalk, as if unable to cross an invisible threshold only he could see. "We lasted two years here. I'm not sure why they didn't find us sooner, but by the time we tore the boards off the windows, the neighborhood was empty. All of our neighbors were dead or gone. The only good part was that we could finally move freely throughout the town. It became easier to search for supplies or anything else that might be useful to us. I was twelve by then, so my dad let me go with him as long as he was staying close to the house. Things were better for us. We had a few good months. And then the Patrols reached our town."

Kira raised her eyebrows. "The Patrols?"

Will nodded, his shoulders sagging beneath the weight of his memories. "My dad wasn't home when they showed up in our neighborhood. He'd gone out scavenging that day, searching for penicillin. The medicine was for me. I'd gotten an ear infection."

He sounded penitent, as if by getting sick he'd committed a grave sin.

"My mom and I heard the Humvees before we saw them. We watched from the window as they pulled onto our street. Three of them. At least fifteen Patrol soldiers got out, all wearing these full-face protective masks. They looked terrifying. They searched the neighborhood on foot, going from house to house and carting away anything that might be useful in Vita Nova. I kept thinking they might skip our home as the looters had, but I was wrong. When two Patrol soldiers came up the sidewalk, my dad revealed himself. He must've been hiding nearby. I don't know what he intended to do, but he wasn't aggressive toward them. He didn't even have his rifle—he must've stashed it somewhere. He just walked toward them with his hands in the air. I heard him saying something about his family. And then one Patrol soldier shot him in the head."

Tears blurred Kira's vision, but they didn't prevent her from imagining the scene playing out in the overgrown front yard—a man sprawled on the ground, blood pouring from a bullet hole in his forehead, and Will's devastated face peering out from a first-floor window.

Will's gaze went cloudy, his body rigid. "My mother told me to stay put, and then she ran outside. She only wanted to get to my father." Then he closed his eyes and pressed his lips together. "They executed her, too. I watched it happen, but I couldn't stop it. My father had our only gun. So, I ran and hid in the basement while the Patrols searched the house. They took everything. Our food stores. The rest of our ammunition. Our medicine. Everything that mattered. Even after I heard the Humvees pulling away, I didn't come out. I only came out after it was completely dark. I spent the rest of the night burying my parents."

Kira rubbed at goosebumps on her arms, but it was no use. They wouldn't go away. She didn't want to believe Will's story because it went against everything she believed. The people living in the Unregulated Zone were the brutal ones. The dangerous ones.

With one shaking hand, Will pushed the sweaty hair from his forehead. "I figured the Patrols would return, but I didn't care. I hated myself for not protecting my mother, and I wanted to die. But they never came back. They'd taken all the food, and I had no way of hunting, so it wasn't long before I was starving."

Every part of Kira wanted to hold Will—to wrap her arms around him and comfort him—but she wouldn't allow herself to do it. Partly because it wasn't appropriate and partly because he would be dead in three days. Instead, she plucked a piece of lint from the sleeve of her jacket and dropped it, watching as it vanished into the weeds. "I'm so sorry," she whispered. "I can't imagine how terrible that must've been for you. Can I ask how you ended up in Vita Nova?"

"It was Jonesy, my boss at the sanitation lot," Will explained. "He wasn't a supervisor back then. He was still driving bodies to the burial pits. About a month after the Patrols killed my parents, Jonesy found me wandering near the pits. I was so malnourished, I could hardly walk at that point. Jonesy was there, unloading bodies, and he spotted me. I don't think he gave a thought to what he was doing. He just helped me into the back of his van and drove me to his apartment building. I couldn't go to school or anything, but he did his best, trying to teach me stuff at home. He's been like a father to me. When I was old enough to drive, I became a sanitation engineer like him."

The back of Kira's neck itched, and she scratched it, her eyes darting from the empty house to Will. She couldn't think of how to ask her next question without sounding rude.

Will rubbed his forehead, studying her expression. "Are you wondering why I would pick a job that brought me back out here?"

She gave him a guilty nod. "Especially a job that required you to transport bodies."

He shrugged. "I appreciated everything Jonesy did for me, but Vita Nova isn't my home. I needed to come back here. To see for myself that this place really existed and wasn't just something I'd dreamed up. Only two jobs go into the Unregulated Zone: the Patrols and the sanitation engineers." His eyes darkened. "And I definitely wasn't joining the Patrols."

A chattering drew Kira's attention to a nearby lamppost, where a gray squirrel was furiously shaking its tail at them.

"Come on," Will said. "I need to show you something else."

Leaving Will's old house behind, they continued in silence. A few blocks up the street, a large stone church came into view, its bottom-half entirely obscured by green vines. The church took up most of the block, and a wrought-iron fence separated it from the sidewalk. Set atop the building's prominent bell tower, a metal cross extended into the sky.

"That's where we're going." Will pointed at the church. "There's something inside that I need you to see."

Kira followed him, driven by curiosity. She'd never been inside a real church before. The leadership of Vita Nova had repurposed all the old churches in the city into something else —either into additional housing units or offices for government officials. While she understood the basic tenants of Christianity, it had never been a part of her life, and she knew no one who adhered to it. Christianity had been on the decline in the decades prior to the pandemic, but after the Job virus wiped out most of the population, it had all but disappeared.

In Vita Nova, only the government—and the brave Volunteers—were deserving of worship and praise.

Information about the controversial religion wasn't easy to come by. None of the books in the city library mentioned it. However, after her mother's death, Kira had discovered a few devotionals buried at the bottom of a box of old clothes in her mother's closet. The little books paired brief excerpts from the Bible with inspirational stories about how to live as a Christian.

She had no idea why her mother had those books or why she'd kept them so well hidden.

As Kira followed Will up the concrete steps, the sun finally broke free of the clouds and shined on the front entrance, lighting their path.

Pushing the door open, Will stepped into the dim vestibule and Kira followed, eager to get off the street. The door closed behind her with a heavy thud. There were no windows in the vestibule, save for a narrow pane of glass built into the wall above the door. That window only allowed in enough light for Kira to see the wooden bench to her right and an old coat rack to her left. A coat hung from the rack, stiff with dust.

Will continued toward a set of double doors at the other end of the vestibule. "This way. It's right through here."

"What is?"

Instead of responding, Will grabbed both handles and pulled the door open.

Dazzling light flooded the hallway, impossibly bright after the darkness of the vestibule. Kira stumbled forward and grabbed Will's arm. Touching him made her feel safer, as if nothing could harm her as long as he was with her. She leaned around his body and peered into the next room.

For a moment, she couldn't understand what she was seeing.

And then she gasped.

Chapter Fifteen

K ira had never seen so many flowers.

Bright-yellow blossoms resembling a cheer-leader's pom-poms grew from planters scattered around the sanctuary. Dozens of them filled the center aisle and the space beneath each of the church's stained-glass windows. Most of the flowers were a cheerful canary-yellow, but several of the planters stationed at the front of the church featured gorgeous multicolored flowers: purple swirled with yellow and delicate specks of azure on the outer tips. Eight stained glass windows lined the sanctuary, each window segmented into three distinct sections, with the smallest windows set high near the ceiling. Someone had propped each of these top windows open to allow direct sunlight into the church, and then strategically placed flowers in locations that received the most sunlight.

When Will spoke, he kept his voice low, as if this building were still a church instead of a greenhouse. "I know you mostly see roses in Vita Nova," he said. "I thought you'd like to see different flowers."

"You were right." Kira lowered her voice to match his. She hadn't realized how much she'd grown to dislike roses until she'd stepped inside the sanctuary. "What are they?"

"Dahlias. They bloom during the summer months, but you can store the tubers over the winter to replant. You can also eat them. Not just the tubers, but the whole flower. They don't have much of a smell, which is good when you're trying to avoid being discovered, but from what I understand, dahlias are difficult to keep alive indoors. This place is a miracle."

"It looks like a miracle," Kira breathed, running her fingers over the tiny yellow petals. Unlike the rest of the buildings she'd seen today, the church felt alive. The flowers weren't the only thing that made it feel alive. The pews weren't covered in a thick layer of dust but were polished to a high shine. The stained glass windows were in perfect condition, not cracked or shattered. And the metal lectern stood at the head of the main aisle, as if someone had used it recently.

"I don't understand," Kira said. "What is this place? Who is growing these flowers?"

"Is that you, Will?"

With a gasp, Kira wheeled around, startled by the sound of an unfamiliar voice.

A petite woman with stringy white hair squinted at them from the rear of the sanctuary, her body positioned in front of the vestibule doors to block their exit. She wore a pair of faded bib overalls that drooped on her tiny frame, and a metal bucket dangled from her right hand, sloshing droplets of water onto the wood floor at her feet. Although Kira had no way of knowing the woman's age, judging by her white hair, leathery skin, and the way her upper back curved so that she stood hunched over, she was at least in her upper seventies.

It was shocking to see such an old person in real life—no

one inside the city lived past the age of sixty—but the elderly woman didn't appear to be much of a threat.

Then Kira's eyes dropped to the woman's narrow hips, and she sucked in a breath.

The black grip of a handgun jutted from the front pocket of the woman's overalls.

Will headed for the rear of the sanctuary. Either he hadn't noticed the gun yet or it did not bother him.

"Will?" Kira whispered. "What are you—?"

"It's me, Aunt Reeva," he said, negotiating the cramped space between two flower pots. "It's Tuesday, remember? I always come on Tuesdays."

Aunt Reeva?

Kira took a step back, her legs bumping into one of the wooden pews. How did Will know this woman? According to the story he'd just told her, he'd been alone when Jonesy found him wandering near the burial pits. She felt the sudden urge to run, to shove her way past Will and the elderly woman and sprint out of the church.

But even if she made it outside without the woman shooting her in the back, where would she go?

She was in the Unregulated Zone...

...and Will had the keys to the van in his pocket.

With great effort, the woman bent over and placed the bucket of water on the floor, wincing as she straightened back up. "I knew you'd be stopping by," she muttered, leveling her suspicious gaze at Kira. "But you didn't mention bringing a friend."

"I know, Aunt Reeva." Will pulled the woman into a quick hug, but she kept her arms at her sides, unwilling to embrace him. He released her and picked up the bucket, moving along the aisle and pouring a little water onto each plant. "But you know as well as I do that it's always better to ask for your forgiveness instead of your permission. Besides, your hospitality knows no bounds, even when it comes to the young women of Vita Nova."

"That's what you think."

As Will approached Kira with the bucket, their eyes met and she whispered, "What's going on?"

He waved his free hand toward the old woman. "Kira, that beautiful woman over there is Aunt Reeva. In case you're wondering, she's not my real aunt. Over here, everyone calls her Aunt Reeva. She tends the flowers...and the sick. In the days before the virus, she worked as a nurse. An excellent nurse."

The woman winced a little, either at the memory of her previous life or at some hidden pain. "Flattery will get you nowhere, Will Foster." She gave Kira a pointed look. "Your charms don't work on everyone."

"Aunt Reeva, this is Kira. She's my volunteer advocate."

The old woman gave Kira a brisk nod before returning her attention to Will. "Wonderful. Now that we've dispensed with the pleasantries, perhaps you could explain to me what your volunteer advocate is doing on the wrong side of the river?"

"I wanted to show her the church," he replied. "And I wanted her to meet you. She's never met anyone from the Unregulated Zone before. Well, except for me."

"Will? What is this?" Kira demanded, no longer frightened of the old woman. Now she was just angry. "Why did you bring me here?"

Before he could respond, the woman grabbed his arm. "You should've come alone, but at least you came. Pastor Alwyn doesn't have much time. A few hours at most. I was coming up here to cut him some flowers."

The smile vanished from Will's face. "I didn't realize he was that sick. Last week—"

"A lot can happen in a week, Will. Especially over here. You know that."

The old woman picked a pair of ancient-looking scissors off one pew. Leaning over the nearest plant, and cut off three of the yellow blooms. "Your name is Kira, right? My hearing isn't what it used to be."

"That's right."

"Okay, Kira. Call me Aunt Reeva. Everyone else does. Since Will has upset us both today, why don't we let him finish watering these flowers while you and I go downstairs to check on Pastor Alwyn? How does that sound?"

Kira glanced at the rear doors that led into the vestibule. Nothing blocked her escape anymore, and she had a feeling that neither Will nor the old woman would try to stop her if she made a break for it. She couldn't drive the van, but she could certainly find her way back to the bridge by following the river.

But she didn't want to run.

She wanted to go with Aunt Reeva. She wanted to see whatever it was the old woman had to show her.

"Okay."

"Good girl." The woman put a hand on Kira's shoulder and guided her toward the vestibule. "The way I figure it, if you're going to help my Will kill himself in a few days, we might as well get to know each other."

———

ONE DOOR IN THE VESTIBULE—A DOOR KIRA HADN'T noticed before—opened into a stairway.

She followed the old woman down the stairs and into a darkened hallway. There was enough light that she could make out the outline of a closed door a few feet in front of them.

Aunt Reeva passed the flowers to Kira, and a few seconds later, Kira heard a padlock pop open.

"The lock isn't for keeping things inside," Aunt Reeva explained, dropping the padlock—the key still inside of it—into her front pocket next to the pistol. "It's for protecting what's inside from what's outside."

Before Kira could ask what she meant, the older woman continued, "I know a padlock won't stand up to those guns the Patrols carry, but it makes me feel a little better. Besides, if they make it this far unaccosted, we've got bigger problems than some rinky-dink padlock."

"Unaccosted? What do you mean?"

Aunt Reeva ignored the question, pushing the door open and motioning for Kira to step inside.

The basement of the church had been converted into a hospital ward. Beds lined each side of the large room, the mattresses covered with linens that looked impossibly clean, given that they existed in the Unregulated Zone. Beside each bed was a metal rolling table with a battery-powered lantern. On the wall to Kira's left, a glass-front cabinet stood six-feet tall, filled with bottles of medications, both over-the-counter and prescription. Many of the labels had faded to nothing. On those bottles, someone had scrawled the name and dosage of the medication over the faded label with a black Sharpie.

There were plenty of battery-powered lanterns scattered around the basement, but only one of them was lit. It sat on a metal table on the right side of the room, illuminating the gaunt face of the makeshift hospital ward's only occupant.

"That's Pastor Alwyn." Aunt Reeva's voice was low and filled with reverence. "He's been with us since the beginning. This used to be his church, before the virus. He helped guide our group through this nightmare, and he's been the glue holding us together ever since."

Kira hovered in the doorway, the dahlias still clutched in her hands, nervous to go any further into the room. "He's a Christian minister?"

"A wonderful Christian minister. A true man of God." The woman glanced at Kira. "Are you a believer, honey?"

"Believer?" For a moment, Kira didn't understand what Aunt Reeva meant. "You mean do I believe in God?"

The woman nodded, her eyes burning into Kira's. "Do you?"

Shriveling under the intensity of the woman's stare, Kira didn't know how to answer that question. After finding the devotionals hidden in her mother's closet, curiosity had driven her to read the stories, and she had to admit that she'd found them intriguing. "I like the *idea* of God," she finally said. "But I have a hard time understanding why He would allow a virus to wipe out most of His creation."

Aunt Reeva's face softened, and she closed her eyes. "Those whom I love, I rebuke and discipline. So be earnest and repent." Her eyes fluttered open and settled on Kira. "That's from the Bible. Those are the Lord's words to the lukewarm church at Laodicea. Because they were neither hot nor cold, He warned the church that He would spit them from his mouth. Perhaps this virus wasn't intended to destroy us, but to inspire repentance in our hearts."

Repentance? Repentance for what?

Kira was about to ask when the man in the hospital bed gasped for air.

Aunt Reeva rushed over to the man, whose eyes were open and wild and searching the room. "Melanie?" he called out, his voice gritty from disuse. "Melanie? Where are the boys? You shouldn't let them play near the river."

The old woman placed a hand on the man's forehead and smoothed back his sweat-dampened hair. "It's okay, Pastor. It's

Reeva. Everything is okay." She glanced over her shoulder at Kira. "Come on, honey. Come closer. He won't bite."

Kira moved forward...and then stopped.

What was she doing? What if the man was sick? What if he had the virus? What if she got too close to the man and he sneezed or coughed on her? She imagined her skin covered in pus-filled sores and shuddered.

The white linens concealed most of the man's body, but Kira's eyes traveled from his face to his bone-thin arms, searching for any sign of the virus's telltale sores and finding none. Finally, her gaze landed on his hands, which were an unnatural purple color, but which also had no visible sores. "What's wrong with him?" she asked Aunt Reeva. "Does he have the virus?"

Aunt Reeva took the flowers from Kira and placed them in the small glass vase on the metal table next to the lantern. Then she picked up the man's delicate wrist and held it in her hand. She remained quiet for a few seconds before gently placing his hand beneath the sheet. "He's not sick, honey; he's dying. That happens over here. People grow old, their bodies give out, and they die. Sometimes, they don't get to grow old first. If it's the virus you're worried about, let me assure you, this man doesn't have it. We might not have any scary walls to protect us, but no one's died of the virus for a long time."

Kira inched closer to the bed, and as she moved into his field of vision, the old man turned his head and studied her with rheumy eyes.

"Melanie?"

"No, I'm not—"

"You can't let the boys play at the river, Melanie," he said, his voice cracking like twigs beneath a heavy boot. "I told you, it's not safe. The undercurrent is too strong."

Confused, Kira glanced at Aunt Reeva.

The older woman leaned closer to Kira and lowered her voice. "He's disoriented, honey. That happens near the end. He thinks you're his wife, Melanie. She died of cancer in her late-thirties. They had four sons, but the youngest drowned in the river when he was a little boy. The other three died of the virus."

Kira covered her mouth with her hand. "Oh, that's terrible."

The dying man's face mirrored Kira's own, his lip quivering, unshed tears sparkling like jewels in his emerald-green eyes. With great effort, he pulled a hand from beneath his blanket and reached for her. "Come closer, Melanie. I can't see you very well."

Kira couldn't imagine the gaunt shape in the hospital bed as a strong husband and father, but as she gazed deeper into his eyes, she could see flickers of the man he used to be, like the last embers of a dying fire.

And she knew what she had to do.

Casting aside her fears of the virus, Kira moved toward the bed and took the old man's hand. His fingers were ice cold, and she closed both of her hands around his to warm it. "It's Melanie. I'm here."

"His first name is Daniel," Aunt Reeva whispered in her ear. "But his wife called him Danny."

Kira nodded and gave the man what she hoped was a reassuring smile. "I'm here, Danny."

"Melanie, I'm worried about the boys. Are they alright?"

"Don't worry. They aren't at the river. I just checked, and they're all safe. They wanted me to tell you they love you. You're a good father, Danny."

Tears slid down the old man's cheeks. "Thank you," he whispered. "Thank God for you, Melanie. I've missed you so much."

He closed his eyes, his lips parting a little.

Gently, Kira returned the old man's hand to its spot beneath the blanket. She felt someone squeeze her shoulder, and she looked up to see Aunt Reeva.

"Thank you for doing that," the woman said, tears glistening in her own eyes. "That was kind of you. Don't take this the wrong way, honey, but I can't believe you're from that awful city."

Another voice spoke up: "Neither can I."

Kira turned to see Will in the doorway, the metal bucket in his hand, his expression unreadable. He placed the bucket on the floor and pulled the door shut behind him.

Will Foster remained a mystery to Kira. He'd kept so much hidden from her. His past, for one. And this church. She didn't know who he really was or what he wanted with her, and part of her was angry with him for being deceptive.

Yet there was something about Will that she trusted. An abnormal goodness about him that made her yearn to be close to him.

He walked across the room and stood over the bed. "How long?"

"Not long," Aunt Reeva replied. "A few hours, at most. Can you two stay a little while?"

Will looked at Kira and raised his eyebrows. "Can we?"

The decision was hers, apparently.

"Of course," she said. "We'll stay."

Chapter Sixteen

Pastor Alwyn died two hours later.

At the end, the old man's breaths came in frantic gasps, punctuated by a guttural rattling noise that emanated from deep within his throat. His legs writhed beneath the blankets; his hands clenched into fists. The veins in his neck protruded, as if he were fighting not against his own failing body, but death itself.

Kira remained by his side the entire time, in case he opened his eyes and searched the room for his dead wife. During the worst of his struggles, she put a hand on his arm and said, "Shhh. It's okay, Danny. It's okay." And although he didn't open his eyes and look at her again, she felt his muscles relax beneath her fingers.

On the other side of the bed, Will sat in a folding chair, his head buried in his hands, unable to watch.

Seeing the old man struggling for each breath, Kira wished for one of the drug-filled needles that had ended her mother's life. If she had one in that moment, she would've plunged it into his arm and put him out of his misery, whether or not Aunt

Reeva approved. Death was a horrible thing, but it didn't have to be like this. The leadership of Vita Nova wasn't perfect—Kira knew that better than anyone—but at least they'd made death into a process. A quick, clean, and painless process.

But this...

This wasn't natural. This was barbaric.

Before he breathed his last, Pastor Alwyn opened his eyes. Expecting him to look for her, Kira softened her expression, trying to affix some emotion to her face other than horror.

But the old man looked at the ceiling.

The terrible guttural sounds coming from his throat ceased, his chest relaxed, and his nearly translucent lips drew into a smile.

Kira peered at the ceiling, wondering what had caught his attention.

But there was nothing there.

At least, nothing that Kira could see.

The dying man lifted a hand toward the ceiling.

Kira leaned forward to take the minister's hand, but Aunt Reeva caught her arm.

"Let him reach, honey," the woman said, tears shimmering in her eyes. "He's worked so hard for this. Let him reach."

Kira had no idea what Aunt Reeva was talking about. *Let him reach? Reach for what?* But she obeyed, lowering her hand to her side and watching as the last seconds of Pastor Alwyn's life played like the end of a sad movie.

"Reach, honey," Aunt Reeva whispered. "Reach."

And right up to the end, he reached.

———

They left Aunt Reeva alone with the minister's body and climbed the stairs to the vestibule. Will headed for the church's front door, but Kira paused at the entrance to the sanctuary. After the dimness of the basement, the light streaming through the stained-glass windows was brighter, the yellow flowers more alive and more stunning than when Kira had first seen them. She wanted to go home, but she knew she would never see anything so beautiful again.

Not in Vita Nova.

"Shouldn't we help her bury him?" Kira's voice broke on the last word. Pastor Alwyn had already been gone for twenty minutes, but she was still crying. Although he'd been a stranger to her, watching the old man die had brought up a host of emotions that she'd worked hard to repress after her mother's death.

"Nah, she'll be fine." Will glanced at his watch. "We need to get back to the van. I never planned on staying this long."

"But I don't feel right leaving her. Are you sure—"

"Yes, I'm sure." He marched across the vestibule, grabbed her hand, and pulled her toward the door. "*Let's go.*"

Kira wrenched her hand from his. "What's wrong with you?"

The urgency disappeared from Will's face, and he looked at her as if seeing her for the first time. "Kira, what you did here today..." His voice trailed off. "That was incredible. I never imagined you would do something like that."

She tugged her sleeves over her hands and used them to wipe the tears from her cheeks. "I only wanted to help him."

"Well, you did. You gave him peace before he died. And I'm sorry for not telling you the truth about this place. Or about me. But I thought you needed to see it for yourself."

"What is the truth?" she asked. "Why did you bring me here?"

Will joined Kira in the sanctuary's entrance, and they stared at each other, their feet straddling the border between darkness and light. He moved closer to her—close enough that Kira could feel his breath against her cheek, drying the remaining tears from her face. His fingers trailed along her arms before finding her shoulders. "I'll tell you everything when we get back to the city, okay? I promise."

Standing this close to Will, with his hands on her shoulders, Kira felt vibrant and colorful, like the roomful of dahlias. Her sadness at the death of Pastor Alwyn drained away, replaced by the same longing she saw reflected in Will's eyes.

This isn't a good idea, she warned herself. *He's a Volunteer. He'll be gone in a few days.*

But then Will tucked a loose tendril of hair behind her ear, and Kira no longer cared if it was a good idea. As he lowered his fingers to her chin, she went up on her tiptoes, put her hand on the back of his neck, and guided his lips toward hers.

"Aww. How romantic."

Kira pulled out of Will's arms and whirled around.

A man—a *Lawless* man—stood inside the vestibule. Massive in build and stature, with a beard that reached almost to the center of his chest. A mane of reddish-brown hair topped his head, but he'd shaved the sides and back of his skull right down to the scalp. Although it was dim in the vestibule, the light from the sanctuary illuminated the dark red stains on his hands.

Blood.

The man had blood on his hands.

Will moved in front of Kira, blocking her body with his own.

Reaching for his hip, the Lawless man pulled a hunting knife from its sheath and ran his index finger along the blade. His cold, soulless eyes raked Kira with freezing contempt.

"Well, well, well... What do we have here?"

Chapter Seventeen

When she was ten, Kira had suffered the same recurring nightmare nearly every night for a year. In the dream, a Lawless man had climbed through her bedroom window in the middle of the night and crouched over her bed, exhaling rotten breath into her face. He'd explained that his own children had died of the virus, and he was taking Kira to the Unregulated Zone to be his new daughter. He warned her that if she screamed, he would kill her mother. Fearing that the man might follow through with his threat, Kira had remained silent as he threw her body over his shoulder and carried her out of the townhouse.

At that point, the dream always flashed forward to the river crossing. In the gloomy night, the water of the Susquehanna had looked as thick and dark as oil. After attaching Kira to his back with ropes, the Lawless man had waded into the freezing water.

Halfway across the river, the man began to struggle. As her captor sank lower into the rushing water, the river sloshed over Kira's head and into her mouth, choking her. In desperation, she searched the murky river for the lights of an approaching Patrol boat, but there was nothing.

No one was coming to save her.

Finally, the man's strength gave out, and he slipped beneath the water's surface with Kira strapped to his back. She flailed and fought against his sinking weight, trying to free herself from the ropes that secured her body to his, but he was like an anchor dragging her down. The pale lights of the city reflecting on the water's surface disappeared as Kira drifted to her watery grave at the bottom of the Susquehanna.

That's when she would awaken from the nightmare, gasping for air, her mouth filled with the earthy taste of the river. She would cry out and her mother would come running, pulling Kira into her arms and assuring her that everything was going to be okay.

But now her mother was dead...and the Lawless man standing in front of her bore a striking resemblance to the man from her nightmares.

Kira lowered her gaze to the dark red stains on his knuckles and wrists.

The man returned the knife to its sheath and dug a filthy-looking rag from his pocket. "Sorry about that," he said, wiping his hands. "Guess I missed a little."

With his body still positioned between Kira and the Lawless man, Will spoke over his shoulder. "Kira, this is Brack. You don't have to be afraid of him. He's not going to hurt you."

The Lawless man's smile broadened, revealing yellow teeth and a missing incisor. "I wouldn't be so sure about that, city boy," he said, his words punctuated by a slight whistling sound. "Whether or not I hurt her depends on what she does for us."

For us?

"Change of plans," Will said. "We're going back."

The yellow-tinged smile evaporated. "Going back? What do you mean, you're going back?"

"Exactly what I said. We're going back to the city."

The Lawless man charged at them.

Kira cried out and stumbled backward into the sanctuary, but Will didn't move.

Although Will wasn't short, the Lawless man towered over him, teeth bared in rage. "You're not going anywhere, and neither is your little girlfriend. Not until we decide what to do with her."

Will stood his ground, arms crossed over his chest. "You heard what I said, Brack. The decision is already made. I'm taking her back."

"That's not your decision to make," the Lawless man growled.

"Yes, it is. I'm the one making the sacrifice here. Not you. Which means I decide what happens this week."

Kira couldn't understand what was happening. How did Will know this man? And what had he meant when he said there'd been a *change of plans*? What plans?

"I'm done arguing with you, Foster."

Suddenly, the man lunged past Will and grabbed Kira's arm, his jagged fingernails digging into her skin. "Let's go, sweetheart."

"Let go of her!" Will shoved Kira's attacker with surprising force, hard enough to make the man stumble backward. "Don't touch her!"

The Lawless man regained his balance and went perfectly still. His mouth fell open, the anger on his face giving way to bewilderment. Then he let out a dejected sigh, jerked the hunting knife from its sheath, and advanced on Will. "Sorry about this, Foster, but you've left me no—"

"You've got mud all over your boots."

A husky voice broke through the madness.

Aunt Reeva.

The old woman stood at the top of the stairwell, her eyes red-rimmed and raw. The grip of the pistol still poked out of the pocket of her overalls, but she didn't reach for the gun. If she feared the Lawless man, she didn't show it. She just looked tired. "Brack, what have I told you about cleaning off your shoes before you come in here? Your wife might let you get away with that, but I certainly won't. And put your blade away. You never use it for anything other than skinning and gutting animals and you know it. Now, stand aside and let these kids go back to the city."

The Lawless man stared at her, his Herculean chest rising and falling with each fast breath. "We can't let her go. We need her to—"

"Pastor Alwyn just died," Aunt Reeva cut him off. "Which means we've got more important matters to attend to."

Upon hearing the news of Pastor Alwyn's death, the Lawless man's shoulders drooped, and he grabbed hold of the closest pew for support. He cast a weary glance at the church's entrance, as if searching for help that wasn't coming. "What do you want me to do, Reeva?"

"First, you're going to clean up this mess," she said, jabbing a finger at the muddy footprints leading into the vestibule. "Then you're going to apologize to Kira for frightening her."

He shuffled backward a few steps. "But—"

"And then you're going to bury Pastor Alwyn's body."

THEY WALKED BACK TO THE VAN IN SILENCE.

Kira wanted to talk to Will. To yell at him. To bombard him with questions. But her thoughts were too scrambled; her anger dulled by the realization that nothing in the Unregulated Zone was as she'd expected it to be.

Some people who lived outside of the barricade were regular people, not criminals. Even Brack, despite his rugged mountain-man exterior, wasn't as awful as he'd first seemed. He *was* a beast of a man, but he'd apparently been tamed by Aunt Reeva and now jumped at her every command. When Kira left the church, Brack had been on his hands and knees with a dirty rag, scrubbing his footprints off the floor.

As Kira stepped over him, he'd uttered a gruff apology. "Sorry about everything."

It wasn't much, but it was more than she had expected.

Emmitsburg seemed different now. Less frightening, but now she imagined eyes peering down at her from the broken windows. People crouching in overgrown alleyways and broken-down cars. It made her think of the scene in her mother's favorite movie, *The Wizard of Oz,* where the munchkins come out of hiding and Dorothy realizes that they'd been there all along, watching her.

When they finally reached the disposal van, Kira blurted out, "Who were those people at the church? How do you know them?"

Will leaned against the van, his arms hanging limp at his sides. "They're my friends. Even Brack. Believe it or not, he's a really decent guy."

"Your friends?" she repeated, as if she didn't know the meaning of the word. "How can those people be your friends? You told me you left the Unregulated Zone when you were twelve."

"That was true," he said. "But after I'd been driving the disposal van for a few months, I made my way back to my parent's house. I'm not sure what I was looking for. Pictures, I guess. Memories. Something to take back to the city with me.

When I went inside the house, Brack was there, looking for supplies. He almost shot me. It took me a half-hour to convince him I wasn't an undercover Patrol soldier. He's the one who introduced me to Aunt Reeva and the others. That was six years ago. Ever since that day, I've been helping their group out as much as I can."

"How big is this group?"

"Not big," Will said. "Less than twenty people divided into small groups and scattered around Emmitsburg, all hiding in different locations. The groups don't interact much anymore, for safety reasons, but they still look out for each other. They've assigned the stronger men and women to protect the town. We call them Watchers. If the Patrols get too close, the Watchers—like Brack—notify the others via radio and then draw the Patrols away. But their numbers are dwindling. Soon, there won't be enough Watchers left to protect the town."

"What happened to everyone else?"

"Some died." The muscles in Will's jaw tightened. "Others left and never came back."

Of all the questions cycling through Kira's muddled mind, one kept fighting its way to the front. "So, what was the *actual* plan today?" she demanded, her anger fueled by the sting of betrayal. The truth was, she'd felt something for Will back in the church when they'd nearly kissed, and although her feelings were inappropriate and self-destructive, they were still her feelings. "I know you didn't bring me all the way out here to show me flowers in an old church. What were you and your friend going to do with me?"

He stared at her for a few moments, not answering. Then he sighed and dropped his chin to his chest. "I wanted to tell you everything from the beginning—from right after we first met—but I didn't know if I could trust you."

"You didn't know if *you* could trust *me*? That's hilarious."

"Kira—"

"What do you want with me?" she demanded. "Just tell me."

Will rubbed a hand over his face, his eyebrows pinching together as if he was in pain.

"This isn't about you," he said. "It's about your father."

Chapter Eighteen

Kira's chest grew tight, as if a poisonous snake had coiled its body around her ribs.

"My father? I don't understand. What do you know about my father?"

Collapsing onto the van's metal bumper, Will rested his arms on his thighs. "I know who he is. He's the reason I volunteered. And he's the reason I picked you to be my advocate."

The invisible snake around her chest coiled tighter. "You *picked* me?"

"Yes. The day I came to see you at your office, I didn't have an appointment. That's why you couldn't find me in the system. I couldn't risk being randomly assigned to someone else. It had to be you."

"Why?"

Will's hands cut identical paths through his hair. "The defectors from last week? The ones found dead on the bridge? They weren't planning to leave the city. They weren't even defectors. Kira, they were just people. Friends of mine who worked in the Agricultural Sector. They knew about Aunt

Reeva and the others, and they regularly snuck me extra produce to deliver to the Unregulated Zone. Someone must've found out what they were doing, and now they're all dead."

"I don't understand. You think someone had them killed?"

"*Tortured and killed*, according to Sunday night's broadcast." Will wrapped his arms around his stomach, as if the thought made him sick. "I think the Patrols might've held them for a few days, trying to get information out of them. But if they ever got caught, they were going to say they were stealing extra food for themselves and their families. They probably figured they'd get off with a slap on the wrists."

"The Patrols?" Kira shook her head. "Will, I understand what happened to your parents, but why do you think the Patrols had anything to do with the deaths of those defectors?"

"Because I know what kind of people they are. When the Patrols come to the Unregulated Zone, they aren't just looking for resources. They're hunting, Kira. They hunt down survivors and kill them. A few weeks ago, two women and a man from Reeva's group were looking for supplies in a town just north of here when they encountered a Patrol unit. The Patrols shot the man on site, but they didn't shoot the women. I can only imagine why." He stared at Kira, his lips tugging into a grim line. "One woman, Deena, attacked the Patrols with her hunting knife, cutting up one guy's arm pretty good. She screamed for the other woman, Grace, to run, because Grace—that's Brack's wife, by the way—is pregnant. Grace got away, but we didn't know what happened to Deena until Brack found her body two days later. Someone had slit Deena's throat with her own knife."

Kira imagined the woman on the ground, her throat splayed open, a puddle of red expanding beneath her head. She closed her eyes until the image went away. "I can't believe the Patrols are killing people just for resources."

"That's what they did to my parents," Will replied without hesitation. "They also don't want a group to form out here that's strong enough to threaten the city. The citizens of Vita Nova certainly won't ever rise up against their corrupt government. They're perfectly happy dying, as long as they get their week of luxuries first. Meanwhile, the people living in the Unregulated Zone are slowly being exterminated...and that needs to end. And your father is the man in charge."

Everything snapped together in Kira's mind. Her father hadn't been lying about finding a note with her name on it in the defector's apartment, and Will had been a part of it. He'd intended to use Kira against her father.

"But how did you know?" she pressed. "How did you know I was Devlin's daughter? No one knows about me."

For several moments, Will only stared at his callused and oil-stained hands. When he finally spoke, he kept his voice low, as if someone in this dead town might hear him. "When I was fifteen, one guy at the sanitation lot got a vehicle. A battered Chevy that broke down a lot. I think his mother was a Volunteer, and she'd requested a car as a gift for him. Anyway, he said he would let me drive it as long as I didn't get caught and I kept it running. So, I went to the library and read every book I could find about fixing cars. And I kept that old clunker running. It's *still* running today. After I got it fixed up, I started using the car to follow Devlin."

Kira looked up at Will. "You followed my father?"

He nodded. "It wasn't that difficult. Everyone in the city knows where he lives. Plus, Jonesy was too busy to keep an eye on me, and I wasn't old enough to work yet, so I had most days to myself. I followed Devlin for the better part of a year, waiting for him to be outside of that fortified mansion of his without a security team. I figured if I was patient enough, I'd get an opportunity."

"An opportunity to do what?"

"To talk to him," Will said quickly. "To tell him what happened to my parents. One day, he left his mansion in that fancy Lincoln of his, and he was alone. I knew something big was going on because he never went anywhere alone. I followed him to the Residential Sector, where he stopped in front of a townhouse. He just sat there for a few minutes. I was about to open the door when I saw this young girl stroll across the street and climb into the Lincoln."

A gentle breeze stirred the thick vines covering each building, making the whole town appear to be moving. Kira shivered and drew her arms closer to her body. "That was how you knew about me? You saw us together?"

Will nodded. "It was obvious he was keeping you a secret. That's why he didn't bring his security team along. Or his wife and kids." He hesitated before finally saying the next sentence. "Plus, you have his eyes."

Her eyes. The one beautiful thing her father had given her.

"So, is that how the defect..." She stopped herself. "Is that how your friends from Agriculture knew about me? You told them?"

Another nod.

"And that's the only reason you volunteered? To use me to get close to my father?"

"Yes," Will admitted, his voice heavy with regret. "I'm so sorry, Kira. I was desperate. I felt like you were my only option to help Aunt Reeva and the others."

Everything he told me was a lie. Her heart ached with the realization. *He's been playing me from the beginning.*

"Once I got you to the Unregulated Zone," he continued, "we were going to notify Devlin that we'd kidnapped his daughter, and that if he wanted to see you alive again, he needed to publicly admit that the Patrols were murdering unarmed civilians in the Unregulated Zone. He also had to sign an Executive Order suspending all future Patrol operations, effective immediately. Once he did that, we would return you to the Market Street Bridge."

Kira's legs refused to support her anymore, so she slumped onto the van's bumper. "And if my father refused to comply? What would you have done?"

"Nothing. We were bluffing. We would never hurt you."

She gaped at him. "Really? What about your friend, Brack? Was he bluffing, too?"

"He wouldn't have hurt you, either." Will knelt in front of Kira and placed his hands on her knees. "After we spent time together yesterday, I knew I couldn't go through with the plan."

"But here I am, Will. You still brought me out here today."

"Because I wanted your help. I know you're a good person, and I thought if you met the people who live over here—if you saw they weren't bad—you might talk to your father. Maybe you could reason with him. Believe me, Kira. I would never hurt you."

Kira shoved his hands from her legs and hopped to her feet. "How can you ask me to believe you? You've been lying to me from the moment we first met." He opened his mouth to respond, but she wasn't finished. "You know what's really sad? You volunteered for this. You offered up your life for a mission that was doomed from the start, because it hinged on my father caring enough about me to do something that would hurt him politically. But he doesn't, Will. My father doesn't care about me. He would've let you kill me. And now you're going to die for nothing."

"Kira..."

He reached for her, but she swatted his hands away. "No. This is over. I'm done."

"What do you mean?"

"I'm not your advocate anymore. I'm not helping you at all. You're finishing the week out on your own."

The miserable expression on Will's face might've crushed Kira's heart, but her heart was already destroyed, trampled beneath the weight of his lies.

"Kira, I'm so sorry I hurt you."

But she didn't want his apology. She only wanted one thing.

"I want to go home," she said. "Just take me home."

Chapter 19

Wednesday

K ira lingered in The Riverfront's entryway, searching the faces scattered around the dining room, but she couldn't see Emma anywhere.

An ornate chandelier with tear-shaped baubles dangled overhead, the electric candles inside its shade glowing like fireflies trapped inside a glass. A carpeted stairway led to an overflow dining room on the restaurant's second level. To the right of the stairway, a narrow hallway lined with mirrors and decorative wall sconces led into a dimly-lit room, where she could see a dozen people gathered around a mahogany bar.

It was stuffy inside the restaurant, so Kira removed her leather jacket. One of her dress's straps slid down her shoulder, and she groaned and moved it back into place. The straps had been sliding down all evening, as if the dress knew that it didn't belong on Kira's body. At Emma's gentle nudging, Kira had worn a short black dress with spaghetti straps for their double date with the two Patrol soldiers. Emma had assured her that the dress would make her look amazing—and it did—but it also left her feeling exposed. So, she'd thrown on a pair of black tights, knee-high boots, and a black leather jacket that had belonged to her mother.

When she'd examined the entire outfit in the mirror, she'd realized that she looked tough. Like a woman you didn't want to mess with.

Or attempt to kidnap.

Since leaving Will Foster at the sanitation lot, Kira had done her best to slam the door on any lingering thoughts of him. Whenever he popped into her mind—which was more often than she liked, since she wasn't working this week and had nothing better to do—she would remind herself that he was a liar and a criminal who'd intended to kidnap her. So what if he only had forty-eight hours to live? If he wanted to escape his death sentence, he could leave the city and live with the others in the Unregulated Zone. If he'd stayed in Vita Nova, that was his problem, not hers. Kira didn't owe Will Foster friendship or companionship during his Final Week.

She didn't owe him anything.

"Good evening, Miss. Do you have a reservation?"

The hostess approached from the bar, her face flushed as if she'd been laughing. Or maybe she was a little tipsy. She looked to be about Kira's age, with pale skin, light-brown eyes, and curly blonde hair streaked with blue highlights. She wore her hair piled atop her head in an up-do that looked both messy *and* elegant.

"I think so." Kira hung the jacket over her arm and reached up to adjust the strap of her dress for the thousandth time. "I'm meeting a friend for dinner, but I don't think she's arrived yet."

The hostess flipped open her reservation book. "Name?"

"The reservation is under Emma Castile."

The hostess glanced up from her book, her smile fading. "Another member of your party has arrived. He's seated at the bar."

"Oh, really?"

Kira followed the woman down the narrow hallway into the bar area. Several couples huddled around the bar, leaning into one another and speaking in conspiratorial voices, but only one man sat alone. Glancing up from the glass tumbler in his hand, his eyes lit up at the sight of the hostess. Then he noticed Kira standing behind her and his smile faded. He gave her an awkward wave and slid off his barstool.

"That's him," the hostess said. "Good luck."

"Great. Thanks."

The hostess gave her an annoyed grunt and strutted away, the heavy clicking of her heels against the wood floor announcing her retreat.

The young man approached Kira with his drink in hand, the clear liquid sloshing around the glass. "Hey, gorgeous."

Kira extended her hand, expecting him to shake it, but he wrapped an arm around her shoulders and pulled her into a one-armed embrace. It was hotter inside the bar than it had been in the entryway, and the guy's button-down shirt was damp with sweat. His free hand—the one not clutching a tumbler of alcohol—grazed the bare skin of her shoulder blades. "You must be Kayla. Emma's friend?"

"Actually, it's Kira," she replied, pulling away from him. "And you must be Dayton."

He grinned at her. "Oh, you've heard about me, huh?"

"Not really." Kira shrugged. "Only your name."

Although her date was already drunk and a little touchy-feely, with his closely shorn blond hair, chestnut eyes, and muscular build, he wasn't *unattractive*. She had no trouble picturing him in his Patrol uniform with a rifle slung over one shoulder, trudging through the Unregulated Zone.

But he was also short—only an inch taller than Kira. With her boots on, they were the same height.

And the dark glint in his eyes made her uncomfortable.

Dayton took a sip of his drink and looked her up and down. "How old are you? You look really young."

Thirty seconds in, Kira thought, *and I'm ready to go home.* "Nineteen. You?"

"Twenty-five. That's not too old for you, is it?" Before Kira could reply, he continued, "You know what's the best part of living during the apocalypse?"

Kira sighed and stole a glance at her watch. It was five after seven. How long had this guy been drinking alone at the bar? "I give up."

He winked at her. "No minimum drinking age."

She fought the urge to roll her eyes. "Oh...right."

Dayton waved the bartender over. "Can I buy you a drink, gorgeous?"

Was he calling her gorgeous because she looked cute or because he couldn't remember her name? With this guy, she assumed it was the latter.

"I'll have a water, please," Kira said to the bartender, who gave her a knowing smile and walked away.

"*Water?*" Dayton looked disgusted, as if she'd requested a cup of blood. "You're drinking water?"

"I don't drink." One strap slid down her shoulder again. "I mean, I've drunk alcohol before, but I don't like how it makes me feel."

Before she could fix the strap, Dayton's hand found its way to her shoulder, and she tried not to cringe as he shifted the strap into place, his sweaty fingers brushing against her collarbone. "You know, this dress is great," he said, treating Kira to a whiff of the alcohol on his breath. "You're great, too."

"Kira!"

Oh, thank goodness.

Dayton stumbled back a few steps as Emma rushed out of

the hallway. An impossibly tall guy followed on her heels, all full lips and jet-black hair.

Exactly Emma's type.

"Render!" Dayton bellowed. "Good to see you, buddy."

"You're already drunk, aren't you, Cowell?"

Dayton laughed, holding his thumb and forefinger an inch apart. "Maybe a smidge."

While the guys shook hands and pounded each other on the back, Emma pulled Kira into a hug. "Girl, you look amazing. Does Dayton like your dress?"

"Oh, I'm sure he does."

Emma frowned. "What's wrong? Did he do something? Is he a jerk?"

"No, he's fine. Can we please sit down?"

"Sure." Emma's frown flipped into a grin, and she tugged at the dark-haired Patrol soldier's arm. "Alaric, this is Kira. She's my best friend in the universe and I'd do anything for her."

Dayton gave Kira a wink. "So would I."

Emma snorted laughter, as if Dayton was the funniest guy she'd ever met. "Okay, lovebirds. Let's eat. I got us the best table in the house."

The hostess directed them to a four-seater table with an incredible view of the river, and as their group sat down, Lizzy Currant's face flashed through Kira's mind. Was this the same table Lizzy and her husband had occupied the night before Lizzy's Sacrifice at Rolling Meadows?

Kira picked up a menu, but the words on the page blended into nonsense. She wasn't hungry, she realized, and she didn't want to be here. She didn't want to be eating dinner with these two men. Raising her eyes, she stared over the top of her menu at the decrepit buildings of the Unregulated Zone. She couldn't see Emmitsburg—the little town was too far north—but she knew it was out there, and an odd sense of longing filled her soul. She thought of Pastor Alwyn on his deathbed, one thin arm reaching toward the basement ceiling.

Let him reach, honey.

Dayton interrupted Kira's thoughts, leaning close to her and treating her to another whiff of his whiskey-soaked breath. "Have you eaten here before, Kayla?"

She tore her eyes from the Unregulated Zone and placed her menu on the table. "It's Kira. I've only eaten here once. Emma brought me here for my birthday last year, and I fell in love with it."

"Really?" Dayton barked laughter. "There are much better places to eat in this city. This restaurant is just..." He shook his head. "Well, to be honest, it's the kind of place my grandmother would choose...and she's been dead for twelve years."

Alaric shook his head, but he was grinning. "You're a moron, Cowell."

Biting the inside of her lip, Kira forced a smile and directed her attention to the napkin on her lap. She ran her hands over it. The fabric felt crisp and clean beneath her fingers, like the linens that had covered Pastor Alwyn's hospital bed.

"So, Dayton, how long have you been with the Patrols?" Emma asked.

He downed the last of his drink before responding. "I joined up when I turned eighteen. Render and I were in the same training platoon, which was a good thing for him. Without my help, he would've gotten himself kicked out and sent to Agriculture or Sanitation."

Alaric puffed out his chest. "You're full of it, man. The instructors hated you. So did most of the other recruits. They kept you in the program because you're a great shot."

Dayton winked at Kira. "I qualified as a marksman during our range training. That means I'm excellent at shooting bad guys from far away."

"Really?" The question spilled out of Kira's lips before she could stop it. "How many people have you killed?"

Emma's jaw dropped open, and she gave Kira a look that said, *What are you doing?*

"The Patrols don't kill people," Dayton muttered, banging his empty glass on the table for emphasis. Then he picked up his menu and perused the evening's specials, his jaw shifting in a way that reminded Kira of her father.

An uncomfortable silence followed, only broken when the bluish-blonde haired hostess materialized beside the table, pen and paper in hand, looking flustered. "I'm sorry about the wait, guys. One of our servers never showed up for work, so I'm pulling double-duty tonight."

Dayton's tipsy smile returned. "I guess it's our lucky night, huh?"

The hostess laughed and placed a hand on his arm. "Mine, too."

It was all Kira could do not to drop her menu on the table and walk out of the restaurant, but she couldn't leave Emma alone—not with these two guys.

After Alaric and Emma ordered their meals, the hostess turned to Kira and Dayton. "And what will you two be having tonight?"

"Separate checks for us, please," Dayton interjected.

Certain she'd misheard him, Kira shot a questioning look at Emma, and the shocked expression on her best friend's face told Kira that she hadn't been mistaken. Somehow, Emma had found a worse match for Kira than the infamous butter-slurper.

"I'll have the grilled Caesar salad with blackened chicken," Kira muttered, handing her menu to the hostess. She'd eaten the salad before and it was delicious. It was also one of the cheapest items on the menu.

"And to drink?"

Though she didn't want to encourage Dayton's drinking, she wouldn't survive the next few hours without an alcoholic beverage in her hand. "Red wine, please. And another glass of water."

"Wine," Dayton grumbled. "What happened to not liking how alcohol made you feel?"

"You've inspired me to make an exception."

The hostess rested a hand on Dayton's shoulder. Her blue nail polish matched the streaks in her hair. "And what can I get for you, sir?"

"The filet mignon. Rare. With a baked potato." He held up his empty glass. "And another one of these."

Kira's eyes widened. The guy couldn't shell out twelve dollars for her salad, but he could order the most expensive item on the menu.

"Very good choice," the hostess said, her hand lingering on Dayton's shoulder. "Would anyone like an appetizer? We're featuring a lovely bruschetta tonight. Or perhaps you'd like to place an order from our dessert menu?"

Dayton raised his eyebrows at Kira. "You want to share the bread pudding? The bartender told me it's the best thing on the menu."

Kira *did* like bread pudding. "That sounds great."

"Outstanding." Dayton cocked his head toward the hostess. "We'll take the bread pudding for dessert. Add it to Kayla's bill. I'm only going to eat a bite or two. I'm trying to eliminate sugar from my diet."

Kira didn't know whether to laugh or cry, but Emma looked mortified. And then Alaric tugged on her arm and she turned to him, all smiles and batting eyelashes.

As the hostess disappeared into the kitchen, Dayton rested his elbows on the table. "So, Render told me you're a volunteer advocate. Is there an extensive training process for that?"

"Not really." Kira used her fingers to carve trails through the condensation on her water glass. "I spent the first few weeks observing my co-workers, sitting in on their appointments and listening as they went over everything. After that, they set me loose."

"Why did you want to be an advocate?"

The last thing in the world she wanted to discuss with Dayton was her mother's death, so she left that part out of her explanation. "I wanted to make things easier for the Volunteers. What they're doing—sacrificing themselves for the good of all—it's such a brave decision, and I wanted to help them in whatever way I could."

Dayton looked at her. "A brave decision, huh? Most Volunteers are old or think they're sick. If they didn't Volunteer, they'd be Compulsories." His eyebrows pinched together. "What bugs me is that the Volunteers get the glory while people like Render and I go into the Unregulated Zone and put our lives on the line to find supplies for this city."

"My hero!" Emma gushed, chucking her napkin at Dayton. He tried to catch it, but the alcohol slowed his reflexes and the napkin landed on the floor. "You guys don't have to tell us how brave you are. I wouldn't be caught dead in the Unregulated Zone. No pun intended."

Kira picked up the napkin and handed it back to Emma. "So, Alaric..." she began, having decided to pretend that Dayton didn't exist. "Did you qualify as a marksman or whatever it's called?"

"Nah. Just a sharpshooter, but I'm getting better."

"He sure is, but he'll never be as good as me." Dayton raised both hands as if holding a rifle and aimed them at the river. "I'm hoping to find a long-range rifle during one of our Patrols. Maybe a Barrett M82 or something like that."

Kira glared at the invisible gun in Dayton's hand. "Why do you need a gun if you're looking for supplies?"

He exchanged a pointed look with Alaric before responding. "Because the Lawless are still over there. People don't like to talk about that, but it's true. They're over there, hiding in little holes like rats. They've attacked us plenty of times. Believe me, honey, you never want to go into the Unregulated Zone. It's a horrible place."

"If they're the rats, what does that make you guys?" Kira asked. "The exterminators, I suppose?"

Dayton smirked and ran his finger along the lip of his glass. "We risk our lives to find supplies. Things we need to keep this city running. We're not over there looking for trouble, but occasionally it finds us."

He was lying. Kira could see it in his eyes.

You're hunting them. Just like Will said.

Emma propped her chin on her palm. "Are there many Lawless left? Haven't most of them died off or moved somewhere else?"

"There aren't many left," Alaric replied. "We believe there's a small contingent of Lawless who refuse to leave the area, but it's only a matter of time before they're gone, too."

Every part of Kira's body tensed, as if preparing for a fight, and her collarbone still burned where Dayton's fingers had brushed against it.

Then she noticed the flesh-colored bandage on Alaric's forearm.

"Your arm," she asked. "How did you hurt it?"

Alaric's gaze briefly dropped to his bandage before rising again to meet hers. "This? Oh, it's nothing. I cut it on a broken window during a patrol."

"Not on a metal pipe?"

"No..." he said, drawing the word out. "Why?"

Will's words rushed back to her. *One woman, Deena, attacked the Patrols with her hunting knife, cutting up one guy's arm pretty good...Brack found her body two days later. Someone had slit Deena's throat with her own knife.*

"No reason. Just wondering."

Dayton picked up his glass and slammed it on the table. "Where's that pretty little hostess of ours? It doesn't take this long to pour a few drinks."

Kira picked at the fresh gray polish on her fingernails, her stomach rolling. She couldn't imagine eating anything—especially while sharing a table with the two Patrol soldiers—but she couldn't leave Emma alone with them, either.

Still, she had to get away, if only for a few minutes. "Would you excuse me?" she said, plucking her purse off the back of her chair. "I need to use the restroom."

"What?" Dayton glanced at her as she rose from her seat. "Oh. Sure."

She slipped away to the bathroom and locked the door. Bracing her hands on the porcelain sink, she stared at her reflection in the mirror. Her skin was unnaturally pale. The kind of pale that no amount of makeup could cover up. A strand of blonde hair clung to the side of her face, plastered there by sweat, and her hand trembled as she pushed it behind her ears.

Had Alaric murdered Will's friend, Deena?

She tried to tell herself that she was being paranoid. She had no proof that Alaric was the Patrol soldier that Will was talking about or that Will was even telling her the truth. He'd lied to her about other things, but no matter how hard she tried to convince herself otherwise, the truth was staring her in the face.

Kira had asked Alaric how he'd cut his arm for a reason.

He'd told Emma that he'd cut it on a metal pipe. And now he'd given Kira a different story.

Why would he lie?

Kira could only think of one explanation.

She took a deep breath, forcing herself to remain calm. When she returned to the table, she had to act normal. Whatever she did, she couldn't let on that she knew the truth.

Not just for her sake, but for Emma's.

Because she and her best friend were going to have dinner with a man who—a little over a week ago—had slit a woman's throat.

Chapter Twenty

"Who wants to go dancing?"

Outside the entrance of The Riverfront, Emma bounced on her heels, unable to contain her excitement. Downing several glasses of wine with her meal had loosened Emma's inhibitions, and she'd spent the last part of the dinner clinging to Alaric.

Kira locked eyes with her best friend and raised her eyebrows, trying to convey how much she *didn't* want the evening to continue. Hadn't Emma just sat through the same awful date as her? Why would she want to keep it going?

"Actually, I'm tired," Kira said, forcing a yawn. "Plus, it's a Wednesday night, Em. There won't be many people at The Grotto. Let's just go home."

"Kayla's right," Dayton agreed, slurring the two words into one. He'd finished four more tumblers of whiskey during dinner, and by the third glass, Kira had stopped telling him her name wasn't Kayla. "It's getting late. Might as well call it a night."

"Call it a night?" Alaric punched him in the arm. "You serious?"

Ignoring him, Dayton turned to Kira. "This was fun," he said, without a hint of sincerity in his voice. "Let's hang out again, m'kay?"

"Not too soon, though." Kira slid her arms inside the leather jacket. She couldn't wait to get home now that the horrible date had reached its conclusion.

Dayton watched as she shrugged the jacket over her shoulders, but made no effort to help her put it on. He patted his pockets. "Must've left my wallet inside. Better track it down. I'll catch up with you guys later."

Emma waved at him. "Bye, Dayton!"

As the Patrol soldier disappeared inside the restaurant, Alaric smirked at Kira. "Just so you know, he's going inside to pick up that hostess."

Kira couldn't bring herself to meet Alaric's eyes. "I'm sure he is, and I wish them all the happiness in the world." She turned to Emma. "You ready to go home?"

"No!" Emma stomped her foot like an impetuous child, her cheeks flushed from the alcohol. "I don't want to go home yet. It's too early."

"Relax. We don't need her, babe." Alaric slung a possessive arm around Emma's shoulders, and she snuggled into his embrace, placing one hand on his flat stomach as if they'd been a couple for years. "Nothing's stopping us from having a good time."

No way.

Kira wasn't about to let Emma go off by herself with the Patrol soldier. Plastering a good-natured smile onto her face, she grabbed Emma by the hands. "Come on. Tomorrow's a workday. If you go dancing, you'll drink too much, and you'll be hungover for work."

"Oooh, maybe they'll fire me!" Emma laughed. "Wouldn't that be just terrible? Gosh, I'm really going to miss hanging out with the soon-to-be corpses at the Compulsory Clinic."

The words hit Kira like a slap.

Emma knew about her mother.

She *knew*.

"Em. I'm not kidding. We're going home."

Emma's smile vanished, and she wrenched her hands out of Kira's. "What's wrong with you? You've been acting weird all night, like you're too good for us. You never even gave Dayton a chance. I'm sorry, Kira, but you can be a real snob sometimes."

Kira raised a rigid finger and pointed it at the restaurant. "That guy is a jerk. He called me Kayla all night. He made me pay for my dinner. And he charged his dessert to my bill."

"So what? He's a guy, Kira. They're all jerks." Her eyes flicked to her date. "No offense."

Alaric tipped an invisible hat at Emma. "None taken."

"Even if Dayton had been Prince Charming," Emma continued, "you still wouldn't have enjoyed yourself. You would've found something to hate about him because you don't know how to be happy."

This isn't Emma talking, Kira reminded herself. *She's drunk. This is how she gets when she drinks.*

But Emma kept going, her outburst fueled by alcohol. "You've been miserable ever since your mom died. You picked a depressing job so you could stay miserable. And no matter what I do—no matter how hard I try to help you—you insist on being unhappy. You came into this evening expecting the worst, and that's what you got. If you want to have fun, you're welcome to go dancing with us. But if you want to be unhappy, just go home. I'm nineteen. I don't need a babysitter."

Emma's words stung her deeply. Unable to look her best friend in the eyes, Kira stared over her shoulder at the lonely black strip of the Susquehanna River. For a moment, she considered abandoning Emma to Alaric Render and whatever evil intentions he had for her, but she couldn't do that. Emma was all she had left—the only person in the city who she trusted —and as painful as her words had been, there *was* some truth to them.

Alaric stared at Kira, waiting for her response, a slick grin on his full lips. He reminded her of a predator waiting to devour its prey. He was practically salivating. Her eyes flitted to the bandage on his forearm before returning to his face.

"Alright." Kira took a deep breath. "Let's go dancing."

ALTHOUGH THEY DIDN'T ARGUE ABOUT HER TAGGING along, Alaric and Emma made a point of ignoring Kira as they walked out to City Island. They remained a few paces ahead of her on the walkway—hands linked, whispering and laughing to each other—while Kira followed them like an obedient dog.

Either too loyal or too stupid to go home.

The booming of music reached Kira's ears before the club came into view.

On the northern tip of City Island, set against the backdrop of Vita Nova's skyline, the old bathhouse was a rectangular building with a blue and white facade and a red-shingled roof. It appeared out-of-place in its wooded Pennsylvania surroundings, as if someone had plucked it from the banks of the Mediterranean and dropped it on the edge of the Susquehanna River. All twelve of the arched windows on the first floor were boarded up, and the wood planks had been painted blue to match the rest of the building. A second-story balcony—big enough to accommodate a half-dozen people—extended over the arched entryway.

At the door, a burly bouncer with a blond goatee informed them it would cost five dollars a piece to get inside.

"But that's two dollars more than last time," Emma protested.

The bouncer gave her a disinterested shrug. "Inflation. Blame the economy."

As Kira dug into her purse, Alaric surprised her by pulling out his wallet and paying the entrance fees for all three of them, as if they were on a strange triple date. Once inside the club, however, he grabbed Emma's hand, gave her a quick twirl, and they disappeared into the crowd on the dance floor, putting to rest Kira's misconception that the three of them would be hanging out together.

Kira moved farther into the club, bypassing the crowded bar area and dance floor and heading for a quiet corner on the other end of the room. Three shallow wading pools occupied the center of the club, spaced several feet apart. The smaller pools on either end were empty, their metal ladders intact so patrons could climb down and dance *inside* the concrete basin. Only the center pool—the longest of them all—contained water. The club had no heat or air conditioning, so in the summer it was always sweltering, and in the winter it was always freezing. Tonight, it was a little chilly inside the room, but that hadn't stopped a few dozen young people from climbing into the unheated pool still dressed in their clothing, half of them shivering as they bounced in the water to the music.

Just looking at them made Kira cold.

Dozens of old-fashioned lanterns hung from the walls, casting yellowish light on the patrons gathered around the bar, in the empty pools, and on the dance floor. The surface of the water in the main pool shimmered, reflecting the light onto the turquoise walls and ceiling and making the entire room sparkle. The effect made Kira dizzy, and between the lights and the too-loud music, she needed to sit for a few minutes.

Long wooden benches ran the length of both walls. At the opposite end of the room, two neighboring doors led into the men's and women's restrooms. There was no line for the men's room, but eight women waited in a line outside the other restroom. When she found a spot that provided her with a decent view of the dance floor and the bar, Kira plopped onto the wooden bench and crossed her legs.

Soon, the night would be over.

Soon, she could go home.

As she watched other couples together, their arms wrapped around each other on the dance floor, Kira's thoughts inevitably turned to Will. To their time together in the Unregulated Zone and their almost-kiss in the church. Yes, he'd lied to her, and he'd hurt her...but she missed him.

She missed him *a lot*.

Out of nowhere, Emma passed in front of Kira, sweaty and dodging bodies as she stumbled toward the bathroom. The line was twelve deep at that point, and Emma's purposeful expression morphed into agony.

"Em!" Kira called out.

Emma spotted her and changed directions, veering to the right and plopping next to her on the bench. "Do you hate me?"

That was Emma. Straight to the point.

"I could never hate you."

"I know, but you should." She placed her hand on Kira's arm, above her elbow. "I'm sorry I said those things. I didn't mean any of it. You know that, right?"

Although she wasn't much of a drinker, Kira knew one thing about alcohol: It often acted as a liquid truth serum, and when people drank too much of it, their true feelings came out.

Still, she loved Emma, and she didn't want to make her best friend feel worse than she already did.

"I know you didn't mean it." Kira put a hand on top of Emma's. "And I'm not mad at you. I just wasn't comfortable leaving you alone with Alaric."

"Why not? He's nice. And he paid for us to get into the club."

"I know, but I don't trust him. He lied about his arm, remember? He told you he cut it on a pipe, and then he told me he cut it on a broken window."

Emma blinked at her, bleary-eyed and confused. "So? Why does that matter?"

"Why would he lie?"

"I don't know. Maybe he forgot how he got cut. I'm sure he gets hurt a lot out there."

"But what if he's hiding something?" Kira asked. "That's the only reason I could think of for him to lie. Maybe he doesn't want you to know how he got hurt. Maybe he did something bad out there."

"Like what?"

"I don't know. Maybe he hurt someone." Kira blew out a breath and glanced sideways at her best friend. "Or...maybe he killed someone."

Emma pulled away from Kira, her mouth falling open. "Killed someone? I love you, girl, but you sound super paranoid right now. Look, I get it. Dayton was a jerk. It's ridiculous that he couldn't get your name right, but that doesn't mean Alaric is the same way. He and I..." Her face dissolved into a goofy grin. "I think we're hitting it off."

Kira's heart plummeted into her stomach. It was no use. Emma would not change her mind about Alaric, and if Kira kept pushing the issue, she might even get upset and leave the bathhouse with him.

Kira couldn't let that happen.

"Don't worry, okay?" Emma patted her forearm, her eyes drifting to the bathroom line, which had grown by two people in the last five minutes. "Ugh, I *really* have to pee, so I better get in line. Do you want to dance after I come out? Alaric found this guy he knows from the Patrols, and they've been chatting in the corner for awhile. I'm bored."

"Actually, do you mind if I take a quick walk around the island? All these lights are making me dizzy, and I feel like I can't breathe. There's too many people."

Emma winked at her. "And on a Wednesday night. Can you believe it?"

"Whatever." Kira returned her smile, relieved they were back on track. "I'll be back in a half-hour. Promise me you'll still be here, okay? Don't go anywhere with Alaric."

"Do I look like a girl who would abandon her best friend for a guy she just met?" Emma batted her eyelashes and snorted laughter. "Actually, don't answer that. I'm totally that girl."

"Em, I'm serious. Don't ditch me. You better be here when I get back."

"I won't ditch you. Sheesh." She elbowed Kira in the ribs. "Why would anyone want to ditch a fun-loving chick like yourself?"

Just then, a group of five teenage girls exited the bathroom, stumbling on heels too high for their small feet. *No minimum drinking age,* Kira thought. Another group of girls slipped inside the bathroom before the door closed, and the line decreased dramatically.

Seizing the opportunity, Emma sprang off the bench and claimed a spot at the back of the line. "Have a pleasant walk," she called out, waving at Kira. "See you in thirty!"

Kira abandoned the bench and headed for the exit, eager to leave the club, if only for a few minutes. At the doorway, the bouncer with the blond goatee stamped the back of her hand so she could get into the club when she returned. Then he held up his pen and flicked on the light, revealing the hidden symbol on her skin. It was a blue rose, of course. Resisting the urge to smudge it with her thumb, she moved past the bouncer and stepped into the brisk night.

The old bathhouse was on the northern tip of City Island, and the Stadium was on the southern tip. A paved walkway circled the rest of the island, running alongside a small set of train tracks. In the days before the virus, a small steam train had transported visitors around the island—from the mini-golf course near the bathhouse, to the soccer fields in the center of the island, to the old carousel just outside of the Stadium. Kira had often wondered why her father hadn't made City Island a family-friendly place again. Aside from turning the old bath-house into a club, he and his administration had done nothing to the island. How much work would it take to get the train and the carousel running again? Why not hire people to clean up the soccer fields and the mini-golf course? Why was her father opposed to giving the people of Vita Nova anything good?

As she headed for the paved walkway, intending to follow the old train tracks around the island, a voice spoke up behind her.

"Kira."

Her first thought was that Dayton had changed his mind and decided to join them at the club, which would've made an already disastrous night so much worse.

But it couldn't be Dayton. He'd tossed Kira aside for the hostess.

Plus, Dayton thought her name was Kayla.

Slowly, she turned around, not allowing herself to hope until her eyes landed on the blue rose—a splash of brilliance against a backdrop of black. She raised her eyes to his face and all of her anger evaporated like the early morning fog on the river, her relief at seeing him so immense that she wanted to cry.

"You wore your rose," Kira whispered.

And then she fell into Will's arms.

Chapter Twenty-One

K ira pulled Will close, losing herself in his smell, which, after only a few days together, had already become familiar. Unlike Dayton, who had smelled as if he'd sprayed himself with alcohol instead of cologne, Will smelled like trees and flowers and freshly cut grass.

In a city filled with death, he always smelled *alive*.

Will's strong arms wrapped around her, his embrace conveying comfort and safety. He wore a lightweight puffer vest over a buttery-soft flannel shirt, and she buried her face in his chest, the Volunteer rose only inches from her nose.

"So?" he asked. "How's the date going?"

"Not good," she muttered. "Not good at all."

"Sorry to hear that. Where's Mr. Right?"

"I'm still looking for him, but my date is hanging out with the hostess from The Riverfront."

Will chuckled, sending a puff of warm air against Kira's neck. "The guy ditched you for the hostess?" He pulled away from her enough to look her up and down. "I can't believe your outfit didn't hold his attention. Do you think he thought you were trying too hard?"

"You're not funny. Emma made me wear this dress."

"Remind me to thank Emma. You look beautiful, Kira."

The blood rushed to her cheeks. When Dayton had complimented her dress at the restaurant, it had made her feel gross. But when Will did it, fireworks erupted inside her heart, the kind of spectacular display that Vita Nova could never replicate.

They remained near the entrance to the bathhouse for a few minutes, not speaking, just holding each other. Kira couldn't bring herself to let Will go, knowing her time with him was growing short. Thumping music reverberated from inside the club, the syncopated rhythm like the steady beating of her heart. Or the ticking of a clock. People came and went from the club, passing by the two of them as if they didn't exist.

Soon, Will wouldn't exist.

Less than two days. He's got less than two days left.

"What are you still doing here?" she demanded, pushing him away. "Why didn't you leave the city?"

He gave her a little shrug. "I thought about it, but I couldn't do it."

"Why not?"

"Can we take a walk?" he asked. "I want to show you something."

"The last time you said that, I ended up in the Unregulated Zone."

"Not this time. I promise, this is just a walk."

Leaving the bathhouse behind, they took the long way back to the Stadium, staying on the path that circled around to the desolate western end of the island. The steady thumping of dance music faded away, replaced by the songs of the insects who inhabited the far end of the island—the area closest to the Unregulated Zone. In that moment, it struck Kira that even the birds and the insects had more freedom than she did. They could travel across the river whenever they wanted. They could make their nests in whatever tree they wanted or burrow into the soil of the Unregulated Zone.

Barricades and blue roses did not define their lives…and she envied them.

When they reached the Stadium, Will surprised her by leading her onto the crippled western expanse of the Volunteer Memorial Bridge. Without a word, he strolled up to the chain-link fence, grabbed ahold of it, and began to climb.

"Hey!" Kira cried. "What are you doing?"

He looked down at her, a mischievous smile lighting up his face. "Haven't you ever climbed over to the other side? Everybody does this."

"Of course I haven't! What if we get caught?"

He nodded at the darkened walkway stretching out behind them. "No one's around. Don't worry. When Jonesy first brought me to the city, I used to do this all the time."

"It sounds like Jonesy should've supervised you better."

"No arguments there." Will continued his ascent of the fence, and when he reached the top, he swung both legs over and started down the other side. Halfway to the bottom, he let go, landing on his feet and staring at her through the fence. "Come on, Liebert. You snuck into the Unregulated Zone yesterday. You're a rebel now. I think you can make it over an eight-foot chain-link fence. Just be careful going over the top in that snug dress of yours."

"Very funny."

It took Kira twice as long to get to the top as it had taken Will. Halfway up, the fence swayed a little beneath her weight, and for one terrible moment, she thought it might tumble down and crush her.

"Will?"

"It's okay. It will not fall, I promise. Just keep climbing."

"You make a lot of promises," she grumbled.

But she kept climbing.

When she reached the top, she let out a little cry of victory. But the cry died in her throat when she realized she could not climb over to the other side of the fence. Not because of the constricting nature of her dress—although that didn't help—but because she couldn't swing even one leg over the top. Her body refused to cooperate.

"Will? I'm stuck."

"Just swing your leg over."

"I can't!"

Kira risked a glance at the ground. From her vantage point, it appeared to be one hundred feet away. Maybe more. Her brain knew it was only eight feet, but her brain and her body were no longer on the same page. She couldn't even bring herself to climb back down. Was this how she was going to die? Clinging to the top of a fence like a spider until she succumbed to dehydration or exposure?

The fence swayed as Will climbed up the other side.

"Don't do that!" she cried. "You'll make it fall!"

He ignored her and continued to climb, reaching her in seconds and bringing his eyes level with hers. "You're being ridiculous, you know."

"*You're* being ridiculous," Kira spat back. "I'm going to die because of you."

"Die? You're a few feet off the ground. You probably wouldn't even sprain your ankle. Are you always such a drama queen?"

"Are you always so rude?"

Will laughed and moved horizontally to make room for her. "I'm going to stay right here, okay? Just climb up a little higher and swing your leg over. I'll hold on to your arm the whole time. You're not going to fall."

"Will, I can't do it. My body won't move."

"Your body will do whatever you tell it to do. You're in charge. Now, listen...I've only got a few days left, and I'd prefer not to spend them hanging on this fence with you."

She didn't think she could do it, but when she tried to climb, her body obeyed. A few steps brought her to the top, and as soon as she got there, Will grabbed her arm and held her tight. "There. I've got you. Now, lean into me and swing your other leg over."

Because of her dress, she practically had to lie on the top of the fence to get both legs over, but Will held onto her the entire time, and she no longer felt as if she was going to fall. Once she had both legs firmly planted on the other side of the fence, climbing down was a breeze.

Will jumped off the fence and helped Kira down. When her feet hit the ground, he took her hand. "See? I knew you could do it."

"I almost died."

He led her onto the western end of the bridge, where only two of the old iron truss spans remained standing. It surprised Kira to see nothing at the end of the bridge—not even another fence. City leadership hadn't bothered to erect any additional barriers to keep citizens from plunging to their deaths in the swift-moving river, which a few people had done over the years.

Kira shuddered at the sight of all that deep water.

Even if she wanted to die, she couldn't imagine choosing a cold, watery grave over a Volunteer's peaceful death.

Will removed his vest and placed it on the cracked concrete walkway. He motioned for Kira to sit. After a moment's consideration, she picked up the jacket and moved it back a little from the edge. Then she sank to the ground, stretching her legs out in front of her.

Will plopped down beside her, his arms draped over his knees. "I come out here a lot at night. Honestly, I'm not sure why. I guess it makes me feel closer to home."

"You still think of the Unregulated Zone as your home?"

"It *is* my home," he replied in a soft voice. "Emmitsburg will always be my home."

"Then why live here?" she asked. "Why didn't you ever go back? You go to the Unregulated Zone several times a week. You could've easily left the disposal van for the Patrols to find. They would've assumed the Lawless had killed you. Or that you'd ran off."

He plucked a weed from the bridge and ripped it into pieces. "I've thought about leaving the city, but I know how much that would hurt Jonesy. Plus, I'm in a better position to help Aunt Reeva and the others if I live over here. My job enables me to transport food, supplies, and medicine to the Unregulated Zone. Things would be a lot worse for them if I didn't live in Vita Nova, but that doesn't mean I don't hate this city. I hate that I'm not over there to help protect them from the Patrols."

"But if you..." She swallowed, barely able to say the word. "If you die on Friday, not only will your friends lose you, but they'll also lose your help and support."

He tossed the stem of the weed into the river. "Yeah, I know. Nothing about this week has gone the way I'd planned. Yesterday, after I dropped you off at the sanitation lot, I considered going back to the Unregulated Zone and never coming back. But then I asked for guidance about what I should do, and I've been told that I need to see this week through."

That made zero sense to Kira. Why would anyone suggest Will stay in the city so he could die on Friday? "Who gave you this guidance?" she demanded, surprised by the anger she felt. "Was it Jonesy?"

Will looked at her. "God."

Kira waited for him to laugh, but his expression remained serious. "You talk to God?"

"All the time."

"And He answers you?"

He shrugged. "Sort of. Not in words, really. It's more like a feeling. For example, I'd much rather go back to Emmitsburg than stay here and die in two days, but when I prayed and asked God what to do, I got this powerful sense of peace about staying. I don't know how else to explain it."

Kira had never spoken to anyone about God before. She didn't know anyone who still believed in Him. Her mother must've believed *something*, if she'd gone to the trouble of hiding those devotional books in the back of her closet, but she'd never spoken to Kira about God or Christianity or faith. The devotionals had interested Kira because they'd meant something to her mother, but she'd only ever viewed them as stories. Practical little vignettes about how to live a good life.

Not something real. Not something worth giving up your life for.

"I don't understand," she said. "You believe God wants you to die as a Volunteer? Why would He want that?"

Will considered the question before responding. "I don't know. But I think He wants me to continue trusting in Him, even if His plans don't make sense to me."

Shivering, Kira pulled her knees into her chest. Even with her mother's jacket on, she couldn't get warm. "I don't know anything about God, Will. I don't know if He's real—I've seen no evidence of Him in this city—but if He exists, I can't imagine He would want you to die." She turned to face him. "You shouldn't be here. I don't care what God told you. I don't want you to die."

Will's eyes met hers, the lights from the city illuminating the left side of his face. "I told you I prayed for guidance and that God led me to stay. That's the truth, but it's not the only reason I stayed."

Her heart pounded against the inside of her ribcage. "What's the other reason?"

Tearing his eyes from hers, Will's gaze fell to his hands. "I couldn't make myself leave you. A big part of me wanted to ignore God's plan and run away, but I stayed for you, Kira."

Looking at him now, Kira could see the young boy he'd been. The one who'd watched his parents die and who'd survived a month alone in the Unregulated Zone. She wished she could've been there when he lost his parents. She would've hugged him and assured him that everything was going to be okay and that he wasn't alone.

Before she could change her mind, she scooted closer to Will and brought a hand to his cheek. The stubble on his chin felt prickly beneath her fingertips, but she knew the roughness concealed a gentleness underneath. A vulnerability that she understood on a deep level. A *soul* level. They'd both been orphans in different ways, and they were both searching for someone to love. Maybe she could be that person for Will, and maybe he could be that person for her. Maybe they could love each other for a little while.

For two more days.

Gently, she turned his face toward hers, forcing him to look at her. "Look at me, Will," she whispered. "Please."

Placing a hand on top of hers, Will shook his head. "Kira,

we shouldn't..." But then his eyes rose to meet hers, and he never finished his sentence.

It wouldn't have mattered if he had.

She would've ignored him.

Even as Kira's rational mind screamed at her to stop, she brought her lips to his, uncertain of what to do. She'd never kissed a guy before, and she didn't want to do it wrong. But when her lips touched Will's, he took over, wrapping an arm around her waist and pulling her close to him. Kissing Will felt like the most natural thing in the world, and all of her worries and insecurities disappeared as she melted into his arms.

I'd rather have this for two days than not at all, she realized. *I'd rather have Will for a moment than spend a lifetime wondering how it would've felt to be held by him.*

When they reluctantly pulled apart, Kira whispered, "What are we going to do? I can't lose you in two days."

Will pushed the hair from her face and shrugged. "What if we jumped?"

"Off the bridge?" she gasped, searching his eyes for any sign he was kidding and finding none. "Are you crazy? Anyone who's ever jumped off this bridge has died. There are huge rocks underneath the surface. Plus, the water is pitch-black right now. We can't see the rocks. What if we land on them?"

Another maddening shrug. "We've had a lot of rain lately. The river is higher than normal, so the rocks will be farther underneath the surface. Plus, it's not that far of a swim. We're already halfway to the other side. We could make it."

"But what about the undercurrent?" she demanded. "Even if we miss the rocks, won't the undercurrent drag us down?"

Will raked a hand through his hair, a frustrated look in his eyes. "You drive me crazy, Liebert."

"Why?"

"Because you're looking for a reason not to jump, and I'm looking for a reason not to kiss you again."

The world lurched to a stop. The night songs of the insects in the Unregulated Zone disappeared. Even the ever-present sound of the rushing river faded to a dull hum. Nothing existed inside Kira's world except for Will and the ghost of his kiss that still haunted her lips.

"I'm not jumping," she said, tapping a finger against her lower lip. "But I want you to kiss me again."

"Okay."

So he did.

Afterward, he brought her hand to his lips and kissed it. "Kira, I don't know what's going to happen this week, but if God brings me through this alive, I'm leaving Vita Nova forever. Would you want to come with me?"

"What? You want me to defect?"

The image of the six dead defectors appeared in her mind. Will assumed the Patrols had killed those people, but he didn't know that for sure. He *couldn't* know that for sure. Just because Will's friends in the Unregulated Zone were good people, that didn't mean the Lawless didn't exist.

"I don't want you to defect," Will whispered. "I want you to be free. Why would you want to stay? There's nothing holding you here anymore, except for that friend you told me about."

Emma.

In her surprise at running into Will, she'd forgotten all about Emma. Kira was supposed to be watching out for her best friend, and instead she'd been making out with Will.

She glanced at her watch. How long had she been gone?

Definitely over thirty minutes.

She launched herself to her feet. "We have to go back to The Grotto."

"Why? What's wrong?"

There was no good way to say it, so she blurted it out. "The two guys on my double date tonight were both Patrol soldiers."

"What?" Will rubbed at his forehead. "Are you serious?"

"Yes. One of them had a bandage on his arm. That was how he and Emma met. He'd gone to the Medical Sector a little over a week ago with a severe cut on his forearm. He told Emma that he cut his arm on a metal pipe, but when I asked him about it tonight, he said he'd cut it on a broken window. When I realized he was lying, I remembered the story you told me about your friend Deena. And I got this strong feeling that this guy might've killed her."

Will pushed himself off the ground, his nostrils flaring. "Where is he? Is he at the bathhouse?"

"I don't know. They might've left by now. We have to go!"

Emma. What if he hurts Emma?

No. She wouldn't let that happen.

Kira charged toward the island with Will following behind her. The chain-link fence had gotten no shorter in the last few minutes, but she made it to the top in no time, her concern for Emma overpowering her fear of falling. She hooked one boot over the top, slid the rest of her body over, and started down the other side.

An explosion lit up the night sky, and a guttural rumble reverberated through the ground, shaking Kira off the fence.

She landed hard on her back, her head smacking off the concrete.

The blanket of stars overhead blurred into a murky soup.

Will appeared in her field of vision, his face slowly coming into focus. "Kira?" He helped her into a sitting position and held her in his arms. "Are you okay?"

"I'm fine," she assured him. "I bumped my head."

As her vision cleared, she realized that the night sky had

taken on a strange reddish-orange hue. Even the stars hanging over the city had turned the color of dried blood.

She pointed at the sky. "What's wrong with the sky?"

"I don't know," he muttered. "There was some kind of an explosion. I think something's on fire."

"What? What's on fire?"

"The city."

Chapter 22

Thursday

Kira carried two glasses of ice water into the living room, the tiny rectangles of ice rattling in her shaking hands.

"Did you get ahold of your friend?" Will asked without looking away from the broadcast screen. The blue rose lay before him on the coffee table, its petals dark and wilting.

She nodded. "We just got off the phone. Emma left The Grotto with everyone else right after the explosion, and she's back at her apartment." After a moment, she added, "Alone."

"Good."

Kira handed him one of the glasses and then sank onto the couch next to him. Although it was after midnight, sleep was the farthest thing from her mind. She took a small sip of water and stared at the chaos and destruction flickering on the screen. It seemed impossible to comprehend that such a tragedy was unfolding only a few miles away.

After the explosion, Kira and Will had returned to The Grotto to search for Emma. Kira hadn't wanted to risk a confrontation between Will and Alaric, but she couldn't leave the island without her friend. But by the time they'd reached the northern end of the island, the bathhouse had already been evacuated and the paved roadway that circled the island was all but deserted. Will had grabbed Kira by the hand and they'd headed toward the city, running past the dark Stadium and onto the Volunteer Memorial Walkway. Drunken partiers had filled the walkway, staggering back to the city, all of them unsure of what was happening.

The crowds had increased once they'd reached Front Street, and word spread that there'd been an accident in the Eastern Sector. An explosion of some kind. People were speculating about a breach in the old natural gas lines that ran underneath the city.

Will's first concern had been for Jonesy, so he and Kira had headed for the Eastern Sector on foot, but they quickly discovered that Guards had blocked off every road leading into that area. After several failed attempts at slipping past the roadblocks, they'd given up on trying to find a way in and made the long trek back to Kira's townhouse, hoping to glean more information from the broadcasts.

What they'd discovered was that there *had* been an explosion at the Tenements, and one tower had been destroyed. The images on the screen looked like something out of a war zone: twisted metal, charred wood, and bodies draped in white sheets. Thankfully, the building where Jonesy lived—Tower 1 —had only sustained minor damage, and all residents of the building had been accounted for.

But Tower 2—Will's tower—was gone.

The broadcast screen flashed to a shot of the pile of smoking rubble that had once been a residential high-rise for the city's lowest classes of workers. *So many people,* Kira thought, remembering walking past the Tenements two days earlier and realizing for the first time just how many apartments were in each building. *And the explosion had happened at night when most people were home and asleep.*

Will placed his half-empty water glass on the coffee table. "I know so many people in that building, Kira. Randy—the soup guy from Market—he lived in my tower. So did most of the guys I work with. They've got families. Some have little kids..." He dropped his head into his hands. "I think I'm going to be sick."

Setting her own glass on the table, Kira reached for Will and pulled him into her arms. "I'm so sorry," she whispered, resting her head against his. "I'm so sorry this happened."

"I should've been there," he muttered into his hands.

"No." The idea was too awful to comprehend. "Then, you'd be gone, too."

Raising his head, Will looked at her with bloodshot eyes. "Earlier tonight, I was sitting on the couch in my apartment—doing nothing—and I couldn't stop thinking about you being on a date with some other guy. No matter what I did, I couldn't get you out of my mind. It felt like I had to go find you. When I couldn't take it anymore, I went straight to The Grotto, since you said you might go dancing after dinner." His voice cracked with emotion. "What if I hadn't left the apartment?"

"But you did," she cut him off, not wanting to consider what might've happened. She understood the reality of their situation. Soon, Will would be gone forever, but not until Friday.

Not tonight.

"I would be dead right now." He pointed at the broadcast screen. "I would be buried beneath all that rubble."

She smoothed the hair away from his forehead. "But you're not," she whispered. "You're not dead. You're still here. And I don't know what I'd do if you weren't."

Will stared at her for a long moment. Then he put a hand

on her cheek and kissed her long enough to leave her breathless.

When they reluctantly pulled apart, he brought a hand up and gently touched the back of her head. "Do you still have a headache? There's a decent-sized bump back here."

She winced a little, remembering the jarring sensation of her skull smacking against the pavement. "No, it's better. Just a little sore."

On the screen, Vita Nova reporter Barb Underwood stood in front of the rubble, holding a microphone to her burgundy lips. *"Authorities say that all fires are extinguished, and investigators are actively trying to determine the cause of the explosion. Based on preliminary reports that are coming in from several eyewitnesses, we believe the explosion originated in the basement of Tower 2. Immediately afterward, the building collapsed, with the lowest floors collapsing first and creating a devastating chain reaction that took the building to the ground in a matter of seconds. There was no time to evacuate. Rescue workers are searching the rubble for survivors, but so far, the situation appears grim."*

"No way this was a gas line," Will muttered.

"What do you think happened?"

"I don't know, but it wasn't a gas line."

The realization hit her out of nowhere, and a flower of hope bloomed in her heart. "They're going to think you're dead."

Will looked at her. "Who?"

"Everyone. The entire city. They have no reason to believe you survived the explosion. It could be weeks until they figure out that you weren't home when the explosion occurred, if they ever figure it out at all." She stopped short of stating the impossibility of identifying the remains of every resident, but she knew Vita Nova didn't have the resources for that kind of operation.

And what would be the point?

"I have a room at Rolling Meadows," he replied. "They won't believe I wasn't staying there."

"But you said that you haven't stayed there all week, right? The housekeeping staff will confirm that you haven't slept in your room, and the people at the front desk will know that you haven't been coming and going. They might not understand *why* you haven't been staying at Rolling Meadows, but they won't care. Besides, I'm still your advocate." Kira sat up straighter, allowing the plan to take shape in her mind. "I'll go to the Executive Mansion in the morning and I'll tell my father that you and I have been spending time with each other. I'll tell him we were together last night, and that I dropped you off at your apartment before the explosion."

"Kira—"

"No, just listen to me, Will. This is your only chance. If I convince my father that you're already dead—which shouldn't be difficult—then we'll just need Jonesy to sneak you back into the Unregulated Zone. And you'll be safe."

"Jonesy never goes out there anymore. He only does the schedules."

Frustrated, she pulled out of Will's arms and slid to the edge of the couch. "But he *could*, right? I don't want to sound heartless, but the sanitation department just lost a ton of workers. I'm sure the Guards on the bridge all know Jonesy. They aren't going to question what he's doing behind the wheel of a transport vehicle again. Not after tonight."

"I'm sorry, Kira...but I can't do that."

"Why not?" she demanded, her eyes filling with tears. "Didn't you just talk to me about God? Well, maybe this is His way of protecting you. Maybe He's giving you a chance to live."

Will turned away from her, his features hardening as he

stared at the broadcast screen. "God had nothing to do with this."

"You know what I mean."

He shook his head. "I'm not going anywhere. God wants me to see this week through to the end. I told you that."

Launching herself off the couch, Kira grabbed the blue rose off the coffee table and hurled it into the kitchen. It landed on the tile floor and skidded underneath the dinner table. "It's already Thursday! Don't you realize that? The city is going to kill you tomorrow and you don't even care!"

Rising, Will wrapped his arms around her, enveloping her in soft flannel. "Don't do that," he whispered into her hair. "Please. Don't cry."

She buried her face in his chest, dampening his shirt with her tears. "I already lost my mother, Will. I can't lose you, too. It's too much."

He held her as she cried, stroking her hair, his hand passing lightly over the bump buried beneath her hair. When her tears diminished, she pressed her ear against his chest and listened to the steady thumping of his heart. The sound comforted her, and she closed her eyes and silently thanked his heart for beating for twenty-two years.

A long time. But not long enough.

"I wish things were different," she sniffed, gazing at him through blurry eyes.

"Someday, they will be." Will used his thumbs to rub the tears from her cheeks. "I've been praying for you every day since we first met. The other day, after our fight in the Unregulated Zone, I asked God to give me a sign that you were going to be okay, no matter what happened to me. And that night, I ended up having this vivid dream about you."

Kira wiped her eyes. "You dreamt about me?"

He nodded. "You were standing in this beautiful garden

filled with dahlias. Not just the yellow ones Aunt Reeva grows, but all different colors. There aren't any dahlias in this city, so I knew you were somewhere else. Somewhere better. You were wearing this beautiful yellow dress and twirling around and dancing. You just looked so happy. When I woke up, I knew God had answered my prayer. That dream was my sign that you're going to be okay."

Kira went up on her tiptoes to kiss him, and their lips fit together perfectly.

Barb Underwood's shrill voice ruined the moment. *"Now, we're going live at the Executive Mansion for a statement from Mayor Devlin."*

They returned to their spots on the couch, and even though she was expecting it, Kira's stomach still sank as Victor Devlin's mottled face appeared on the screen. Her father sat behind his desk in his office, his hands clasped in front of him, his gray hair slicked back from his face.

Despite the early hour, and the unfolding tragedy, not a strand was out of place.

"Ladies and gentlemen of Vita Nova, it is with a heavy heart that I address you this morning. Two hours ago—just after ten p.m.—an explosion demolished Tower 2 of the Eastern Sector's Tenement high-rise apartment building. So far, rescue workers have retrieved fifty-six bodies from the rubble, but that number is certain to rise over the coming hours. We still have dozens of people unaccounted for, and we have yet to locate any survivors. We hope some residents weren't home at the time of the explosion, but given the late hour, that appears unlikely."

Kira reached for Will's hand, and his fingers closed around hers.

"As you're likely all aware, rumors have been circulating that a faulty gas line might be to blame for this tragedy. However, our on-scene investigators do not believe gas lines

caused this explosion." He paused and looked at his desk. After a few seconds, he lifted his head, took a deep breath, and continued, *"Ladies and gentlemen, I'm not sure how to tell you this, but preliminary evidence appears to point to sabotage."*

"Sabotage?" Kira glanced at Will. "What's he talking about?"

But Will said nothing, his eyes focused on the screen.

"Ten minutes after the explosion, we discovered a letter nailed to the front door of the Executive Mansion. The letter was from a group of Lawless, likely the same individuals responsible for murdering the six defectors last week. We can only assume they've discovered a way to access our city, probably as a result of their interrogation of the defectors. In the letter, this group takes full responsibility for tonight's attack, and they're now demanding that we deliver food and medical supplies to the Unregulated Zone via the Patrols on a weekly basis. Otherwise, more of our citizens will die. According to the last line of the letter, the bombing of the Tenement apartment building is only the beginning."

"He's lying," Will muttered, his face twisted in disgust. "No one in the Unregulated Zone did this."

"Then who did it? The Patrols?"

The camera zoomed in on Victor Devlin, highlighting the deep canyons in his cheeks. Those pockets had always reminded Kira of a treacherous and unforgiving terrain she could never hope to cross. *"Tonight's cowardly display of violence—perpetrated against the hardest working and most vulnerable members of our society—was designed to terrify us into compliance. However, I'm here to assure the citizens of Vita Nova that we will never give in to the demands of the Lawless. This attack is a test of our resolve. And we shall pass the test."*

Despite the early hour, the sound of cheers and clapping echoed through the streets outside Kira's townhouse. On the screen, her father dipped his head toward his desk, as if he could hear the applause.

He continued, *"Tonight's events have shown us we can no longer turn a blind eye to the imminent danger posed by allowing these murderers and criminals to exist just outside of our city. With that in mind, effective immediately, I'm authorizing the commanders of the Patrols to enlist and fast-track the training of regular citizens for an all-encompassing search-and-destroy mission of the Unregulated Zone. They will search every existing building and structure. Any buildings showing evidence of recent human inhabitation will be destroyed. Any Lawless found during this mission will be afforded the opportunity to surrender, and those who refuse will be executed on sight."*

"What?" Will leaped off the couch, both hands pressed against the sides of his head as if to block out the words. "What did he say?"

But Kira kept listening, her horror increasing with each sentence. Regular citizens being trained as Patrol soldiers? An all-encompassing search-and-destroy mission? She flashed back to Pastor Alwyn lying in the makeshift hospital ward. What would the Patrols have done if they'd found him? What would they do to Aunt Reeva?

Victor Devlin tilted his head toward the camera, his brows knitting together. *"Tonight's attack against the Tenements was an attack against us all. It was a brazen act of war, and we will respond to it as such. Make no mistake...this war will cost many lives. Like our brave Volunteers, many citizens will be asked to sacrifice their lives for the greater good. The price will be steep, but the reward will be great. Anyone who loses their lives fighting the Lawless will posthumously receive the title of Volunteer. Once we've reclaimed the Unregulated Zone, we will finally be able to expand beyond the barricade, and eventually, we will reclaim the rest of our lost world. For the good of Vita Nova, and for the good of all."*

Victor Devlin vanished from the screen.

A stunned looking Barb Underwood replaced him, staring slack-jawed into the camera, the microphone hovering inches from her burgundy lips.

Before the reporter could speak, Kira grabbed the remote and muted the broadcast screen. She plucked a throw pillow from the end of the couch and clutched it against her chest. So many innocent people had died tonight, and more innocent people in the Unregulated Zone would soon die for a crime they hadn't committed.

Would it ever end? Would the dying ever end?

Eventually, Will lowered himself down beside her. "This is going to be a massacre. You know that, right? They're going to kill everyone out there."

Kira pressed her elbows into her sides and wrapped her arms around her body, trying to make herself as small as possible. "It will take a few days for the Patrols to get this operation underway, right? So, we need to warn Aunt Reeva now. Tell her to get everyone out of Emmitsburg while there's still time."

"Warning them won't make any difference," Will replied. "They know it's not safe out there. People *have* left. I told you before that Aunt Reeva's group used to be bigger. The Patrols killed some people, but some left Emmitsburg over the years looking for a safer place. They all promised to come back if they found somewhere to go, but none of them ever came back."

"That doesn't mean anything. Maybe they traveled a long way and didn't want to make the trip again?"

"They wouldn't do that." Something flared in Will's eyes, and he hurriedly lowered his gaze to the ground. "Not all of them. If they could've come back, they would've. Something must've happened to them along the way. Maybe it was the Patrols. Or maybe it was something else."

"Then what?" Kira squeezed her arms tighter. "What are we going to do?"

For a long time, Will said nothing. He gripped his knees and stared at the floor, his knuckles slowly turning white. "We have to talk to Devlin," he finally said. "That's the only way to stop this. You're his daughter, Kira. Maybe you can make him change his mind."

Kira's mind raced through the possible things she might say to her father—the arguments she might use to convince him to call off the attack on the Unregulated Zone—but her brain kept reminding her of one certainty. "He won't listen to me. He never has. But even if he would listen, Devlin only sees me on his terms. I can't just march up to the Executive Mansion and demand to go inside."

Will studied her with ice-blue eyes. "You can tonight," he said. "At the Volunteer Ball."

"What?"

"Don't you see?" Will pried her icy hands from her arms and warmed them in his own. "Maybe this is why God keeps guiding me to see this week through. Volunteers get access to the Executive Mansion on their last night, which just happens to be tonight. And Devlin *always* makes an appearance at the Volunteer Ball." He rubbed at the scruff on his chin. "Unless you think he'll cancel tonight's ball because of the bombing?"

She shook her head. "He won't cancel it. My father is a horrible man, but he never cancels a party."

"Then will you go with me tonight?"

Kira gazed at the muted broadcast screen, just as the camera zoomed in on a white sheet covering a formless lump on the ground. Then she pushed herself off the couch and walked into the kitchen. Dropping to her knees, she reached underneath the table and grabbed the rose. One petal was hanging loose, so she plucked it off and placed it on the kitchen table.

She returned to the living room, knelt in front of Will, and pinned the blue rose to his shirt, careful not to pierce his skin. "You'll need to spend today at Rolling Meadows, whether you like it or not."

"Why?"

"The staff there will help you get ready for the Volunteer Ball. They'll have tuxes and dresses for the Volunteers, and hair and makeup people on site. When you guys are ready, one of the city buses will transport you to the ball."

"What about you?"

"I can't go to Rolling Meadows, but I'll meet you at the ball."

"Okay." Will put a hand on her arm. "Are we really doing this? You're sure?"

She answered with a resigned nod.

"We're going to the Executive Mansion tonight, and we're not leaving until my father changes his mind."

Chapter Twenty-Three

Halfway up the Executive Mansion's circular driveway, Kira paused and stared at her father's home, astonished that someone so terrible could live somewhere so beautiful. She caught glimpses of people through the multi-paned windows. The elite of the city, dressed in tuxedos and ballgowns, crystal flutes of champagne in their hands, the previous night's tragedy a distant memory.

Located on Front Street, across from the Susquehanna River, the Executive Mansion was impossible to access without an invitation, thanks to the private gate and armed Guards. Since Kira was coming as Will's guest, she'd reached out to her contacts at the mansion earlier in the day and had them add her name to the guest list. She doubted that her father ever bothered to look at the guest list before the ball kicked off, and that was a good thing.

She wanted to have the upper hand tonight.

The long driveway and thick border of trees in the front yard hid the mansion from view of anyone passing by on the street. White fairy lights hung from every tree and bush lining the driveway, giving the property a magical feel. The three-story brick mansion at the end of the driveway was perfectly symmetrical, with a single-story wing jutting off from each side of the main house. Two pine trees flanked the pedimented front door like twin soldiers standing guard over the house.

The Executive Mansion is a Georgian-style architecture design, her father had once described over a picnic lunch of sandwiches and chips, as if a twelve-year-old girl would know what that meant. *It's a classic, understated beauty. Just like you, my dear.*

She'd taken another bite of her sandwich, not believing him.

Although her father had lived in the mansion for most of her life, she had only seen the place in pictures and on broadcasts. Never in real life, not even during the artificial father-daughter days of her pre-teen years. None of those dates had included meeting his new family, but they would be inside tonight—all three of them. His gorgeous blonde wife and his two adorable blond children.

Not illegitimate children, like Kira, but *real* children.

She glanced at her watch.

Ten after seven.

The bus from Rolling Meadows hadn't dropped off the Volunteers yet, but that wasn't unusual. The bus arrived late so Deputy Mayor Graves could announce the Volunteers as they stepped inside the foyer.

Kira took a few hesitant steps closer to the front door, the sheer blue material of her chiffon gown swishing around her legs.

Finding a dress hadn't been too difficult. She'd contacted Desiree Parks, an eccentric dressmaker who had once fulfilled a wish for one of Kira's female Volunteers by creating five unique gowns that the woman could parade around the city in for each day of her Final Week.

The best of the five gowns had been gaudy, and the worst had been downright hideous, but Kira was desperate and she didn't know any other dressmakers in Vita Nova. So, she'd phoned Desiree after Will left her townhouse this morning and explained that she needed a gown for the Volunteer Ball.

"One of your clients invited you?" Desiree had gasped. "Kira! Do you love him?"

"I...uh..." Kira had stammered, caught off-guard by the question. "I'm...not sure."

Desiree responded with a delighted squeal. "Oh, how wonderfully and dreadfully romantic! Just give me your measurements and a few hours. I've got something that might work. I've been working on this dress for months. Always thought I'd gift it to a Volunteer, but your little Romeo and Juliet situation is too good to pass up. It's the perfect dress to highlight your doomed love affair. Just make sure to credit me at the ball, okay?"

Kira hadn't expected much from Desiree, so it had shocked her when she'd stepped inside the woman's shop and saw an eye-catching blue chiffon gown hanging on a rack near the door. Even more surprising was how perfectly the gown fit her, as if Desiree had designed it with Kira in mind. The halter neck style of the gown left her back exposed, and the color was a perfect match for the vibrant blue hue of the Volunteer roses. As if the Volunteer connection wasn't obvious, Desiree had attached a real flower in the center of Kira's lower back.

A blue rose.

When Kira asked her how she'd *gotten* a blue rose, Desiree had winked at her and said, "You aren't the only one with connections, honey."

A couple strolled past Kira, arm-in-arm, their heels clicking against the macadam driveway as they approached the mansion. Kira didn't recognize them, so they weren't Volunteers. Dignitaries, probably. People her father wanted to impress. When they reached the front door, it swung open, and the sound of classical music drifted up the driveway to Kira. The couple disappeared inside the mansion.

The screech of air brakes drew her attention to Front Street. Through the trees, she glimpsed a city bus idling outside the gate. Feeling exposed in her eye-catching dress, she abandoned the center of the driveway and moved closer to the hedges, where the dangling branches from the trees offered a little concealment.

A few moments later, a large group of people appeared in the driveway, heading for the mansion. All wore gowns or tuxedos, but only about half had blue roses pinned to their chests or attached to their wrists. The ones without roses would be immediate family members and loved ones—up to three per Volunteer—who would act as living buffers between their Volunteer and the events of the next twenty-four hours.

Although the group was going to a party, the overall mood was subdued. Few spoke. Several were crying.

And then—finally—Kira spotted Will near the rear of the group.

The sight of him took her breath away.

He wore a single-breasted black tuxedo with a white bowtie, and although Kira could tell how uncomfortable he was in the formal attire, he looked incredible. Not a trace of dark stubble remained on his chin, and although she'd loved the feeling of that scruff against her cheek when they'd kissed the previous night, she knew his soft skin would feel just as nice. A brave stylist had tamed Will's unruly hair for the evening, slicking it away from his face with a gel that made his golden-brown hair appear black.

Kira was so enamored by Will that it took her a moment to realize that he wasn't alone.

The little boy—Theodore Easton, the city's youngest Volunteer—strolled alongside him, wearing a tuxedo that was a perfect miniature version of Will's. Just like at the ceremony on Sunday evening, the boy had a lollipop in his mouth, the white stick bobbing from his red-stained lips as he babbled to Will.

Kira had almost forgotten about young Theodore and how Vita Nova was going to kill a six-year-old boy *for the good of all.* She searched the group for Trinity Easton and spotted her a few paces behind Will and the little boy. The young woman wore a skintight white gown that clung to her thin frame in all the wrong places, making her appear skeletal. She had dyed her choppy pink hair jet-black, and Kira suspected Trinity was already playing the role of grieving mother. She walked beside an older man, the two of them appearing to be deep in conversation. The man wasn't wearing a blue rose, which meant he was probably a family member. A heavyset woman followed close behind them, a gloomy expression on her face.

Theodore's grandparents, perhaps?

Kira blew out a nervous breath and emerged from the concealment of the trees.

Will spotted her immediately, his eyes widening as they traveled the length of her dress—from her face to her feet and back again. He blinked several times, the corners of his mouth curling into a smile.

"Wow," he mouthed.

Kira bit the inside of her lip, fighting to control the dopey smile that wanted to emerge at Will's obvious approval. As Will and Theodore approached her, she asked, "So, do you miss your sanitation uniform yet?"

"I did until a second ago," he said. "I didn't realize I liked that shade of blue until I saw it on you."

That was all it took. The dopey smile won the battle.

Even as Will and Kira flirted, Theodore hadn't stopped talking. He continued to prattle on about his favorite comic book characters until Will clapped a hand over his mouth, his fingers parting to accommodate the lollipop stick. "Quiet, kid. Didn't you notice the gorgeous woman standing in front of us?"

The little boy shrugged. Either he wasn't sure who Will was referring to, or he wasn't sure that Kira was gorgeous. "I'm Teddy," he said, his voice stifled by Will's hand. "Who are you?"

She knelt in front of him. "Hi, Teddy. I'm Kira. You look cute tonight. In fact, I think you might just be the cutest boy in the entire city. Maybe even the entire planet."

The boy raised both eyebrows as if to say, *That's quite a statement.*

Will removed his hand from Teddy's mouth. "Go ahead. Tell Miss Kira thank you."

"Thank you." The boy grinned at Will. "Is she your girlfriend?"

"Is she...what?" Will stammered.

"Do you guys kiss? Because you shouldn't kiss. That's how you get cooties. Momma says all girls have cooties, except for her."

A genuine laugh burst through Kira's lips. She didn't like many people in Vita Nova, but she liked Teddy Easton.

Will rolled his eyes. "I knew I shouldn't have taken my hand away from your mouth."

Trinity Easton strolled past them, her eyes narrowing with distrust as she saw Kira kneeling in front of her son. She patted her hip as if calling a dog. "Let's go, Teddy. You need to stay by Momma's side tonight."

The little boy's smile faded, and he glanced at Will, clearly not wanting to leave his new best friend.

"It's okay, buddy." Will squeezed his shoulder. "Go with your mom. I'll catch up with you inside, okay?"

"Okay."

Teddy darted to his mother's side and reached for her hand, but she shook him off and gave him a stern look, as if he'd been doing something wrong by talking to Kira and Will. The older man touched her elbow and whispered to her, and the anger on her face vanished as quickly as it had appeared.

"Does that woman care about her kid at all?"

"Not that I've seen," Will said. "During the bus ride over here, she was more interested in flirting than spending time with her son. Especially considering that her son has about twelve hours left to live."

"Flirting? That man isn't her father?"

"No. That's Tucker Morley. His wife is Edith Morley—one of the Volunteers." He nodded at the pudgy woman following a few paces behind Trinity and the older man.

Now that he mentioned it, Kira recognized Edith from the Reverence Ceremony on Sunday night. She remembered only a few details about the woman. Mid-fifties. Married. No children. But why wasn't she wearing her blue rose?

As if on cue, Edith reached up to touch her eye—wiping away a tear, perhaps?—and the bell-sleeve of her gown slid up to her elbow, revealing the blue corsage.

Will extended his right arm to Kira. "Shall we head inside?"

"Do we have a choice?"

"Not really."

She hooked her arm through his, and they headed for the mansion.

"I spoke to Edith for a long time this evening," he continued. "She volunteered after finding out that she was in heart failure. She didn't want to be a Compulsory, and she thought it might be nice to spend her Final Week at Rolling Meadows with her husband. I don't think she counted on this happening." He nodded toward Tucker Morley and Teddy's mom. "I get the impression that Tucker Morley is in the market for a new wife."

"And Trinity Easton is in the market for a better life."

Will nodded. "And her kid is nothing more than a pawn in her scheme. *That's* what really upsets me."

It broke Kira's heart to look at Teddy. The poor kid had no idea what was coming. He didn't have any concept of death or what it meant. He wasn't old enough to understand it, much less volunteer for it. And his own mother—the one person who was supposed to take care of him, no matter what—would not protect him.

She'd volunteered him to die.

As Will and Kira approached the group of Volunteers and family members gathered outside the front entrance of the Executive Mansion, the door opened and Sienna Graves emerged from inside. The deputy mayor pulled the door closed and shuffled down the steps in her ridiculous high heels.

At the Reverence Ceremonies, Graves wore sensible dark pantsuits, but for the Volunteer Ball, she liked to put on a show. Tonight's dress was bright yellow with a puffy petticoat skirt that ended above her knees. Coupled with her bright red hair, the whole ensemble made her look like a chicken.

When she reached the base of the stairs, Graves clasped her hands together. "Good evening to my brave Volunteers and their guests," she said. "Allow me to be the first to welcome you to the Volunteer Ball. As you know, it's tradition for each Volunteer to be announced as they step inside the foyer. As I call your name, please move through the door and walk to the other side of the room while the guests applaud your Sacrifice. Do not rush. *Glide*." Graves brushed a stray red curl from her forehead. "You will enter the mansion according to age, with the oldest Volunteer entering the Grand Hall first and the youngest entering last. This is to recognize that those of you with the most years of life remaining are sacrificing the most for this cause."

Several people cast uneasy glances at Teddy Easton, who was about to become the evening's most honored guest. He tugged at the hem of his mother's gown, trying and failing to get her attention.

"For those accompanied by loved ones, please remember that the mayor and other dignitaries of the city are here tonight to honor you, not your guests. Your guests should not attempt to speak to any dignitaries. That honor is reserved for the Volunteers."

Trinity Easton visibly balked at that comment, a strangled gasp escaping her lips. The older man, Tucker Mosley, put a hand on her shoulder and she quieted down.

Graves snapped her fingers. "Chop, chop, everyone. Let's get this party started. And remember...don't rush to the other side of the room. Glide." She disappeared inside the foyer, and after a brief speech which nobody outside the mansion could hear, she introduced the first Volunteer.

"Ladies and gentlemen. Please join me in welcoming tonight's brave Volunteers. Welcome, Edith Morley!"

The gentlemen removed his hand from Trinity Easton's shoulder and joined his wife on the bottom step. Without looking at her husband, Edith Morley took his elbow and allowed him to escort her through the door.

To Kira, she looked like a woman being led to the gallows.

One by one, Sienna Graves announced the Volunteers, and they retreated inside the mansion, greeted by the sound of cheers. Kira felt herself growing increasingly nervous as the group of Volunteers and their loved ones dwindled.

Everything was happening so quickly.

And then—suddenly—it was Will's turn.

"Ladies and gentlemen," Sienna Graves crowed into her microphone." Please join me in welcoming our next brave Volunteer: Will Foster!"

As they climbed the steps, the light from inside the mansion spilled over Will and Kira.

"We can do this," he whispered, squeezing her hand. "We have to do this."

"I know."

As they stepped into the light of the foyer, all eyes fell upon them. Dozens of faces lit up at the sight of the young couple. The elite of the city gasped, their greedy eyes raking over Kira's dress. They cheered and formed their fingers into V's and held them over their hearts. As she witnessed the delight in their eyes, Kira could almost hear the story they were cooking up in their minds.

Here come the star-crossed lovers, desperately in love but destined to be torn apart.

The fantasy would sustain them long after the ball ended.

Kira clung to Will's arm as he escorted her across the vast room, and gliding fell by the wayside as she increased her pace to match his. Most of the city was watching them on their broadcast screens. Emma was watching. Even the two Patrol soldiers from last night might be watching.

When Kira and Will reached the other Volunteers, two staff members directed them to their spot at the end of the line. Only when they settled into the line and the eyes of the crowd abandoned them did Kira release the breath she'd been holding.

As Sienna Graves made her final introduction, the gathered crowd greeted little Teddy Easton and his beaming mother with the biggest cheers of the night.

"Revere the Volunteer! Revere the Volunteer!"

As the little boy walked, wide-eyed, across the room, Kira glanced to her right, taking in the row of city dignitaries gathered on the other side of the room. She located her father immediately. He stood at the end of the line, in his own place of honor. Unlike everyone else in the room, he wasn't holding his fingers over his heart, nor was he cheering for the city's youngest Volunteer.

He wasn't even looking at Teddy Easton.

Victor Devlin's cold, gray eyes were locked on Kira.

Chapter Twenty-Four

Seated at a table inside the Grand Hall of the Executive Mansion, Kira took another bite of her dinner and gazed around the hall, awestruck by its unrestrained elegance. She'd seen it on her broadcast screen, but never in real life. The massive room featured twenty-two foot ceilings, enormous twin fireplaces, and floor-to-ceiling windows. At one end of the Grand Hall, twin wooden balustrades flanked a magnificent marble staircase. The staircase swept up to a wide landing before splitting off into two smaller staircases that ran in opposite directions, each leading to an upper level of the mansion, where Kira's father lived and worked and raised his family.

His *real* family.

In the center of the room, a crystal chandelier hung over the executive table. Seated at the table were Victor Devlin and his wife, Chandra, along with their children, Vance and Violet. Sienna Graves and her husband, Elton, also sat at the executive table. The remaining two chairs were empty.

When Kira had first noticed the empty chairs at her father's table, she'd naively expected that he'd arranged for Kira and Will to join him.

But, of course, he hadn't.

Victor Devlin would never acknowledge her in front of the city.

"Isn't this duck exquisite, dear? So tender and delicious. I imagine it's the most delightful thing you've ever eaten."

Kira looked up from her plate and noticed the wife of one of the city dignitaries watching her, waiting for an answer. Despite the layers of makeup plastered on her face, the woman was clearly older than sixty. She stared at Kira, as still as a photograph, a half-empty wineglass poised inches from her lips.

Each round table in the Grand Hall seated eight people, and every Volunteer and their guests had been seated at a different table. The staff had filled the remaining chairs at each table with various dignitaries from the city, including the older woman who was gawking at Kira. Aside from the woman, none of the other dignitaries at their table had bothered to engage Will or Kira in a conversation. For them, this evening wasn't about the Volunteers, no matter how much they tried to convince the public otherwise.

It was about celebrating themselves.

"Uh, yes," Kira managed. "It's wonderful."

Unnerved by the woman's penetrating stare, she returned her attention to the most elegant plate of food she'd ever seen. Pan-seared duck breast in a red wine sauce, served with a garlic mash and roasted baby carrots. As incredible as the food looked, it tasted even better.

She tried to think of something else to say to the woman. Something intelligent. Something more insightful than, "Yes, ma'am. This grub sure tastes good." But her mouth was full— she'd just taken a large bite of her carrots—and she couldn't get any words out, insightful or otherwise.

The woman seemed to enjoy Kira's discomfort, not unlike a cat playing with an injured mouse. She squinted at Kira as if observing a strange new species for the first time, a predatory glint in her eyes.

A thought popped into Kira's mind.

Duck isn't the only thing on the menu tonight.

Will stepped in to rescue her. "I agree. The food is wonderful. We don't get much duck in the Eastern Sector. We don't get much meat at all, actually, unless we catch it. Since there aren't ducks, chickens, or cows running around our part of the city, we make do with what we have. Have you ever eaten a rat, ma'am?"

The woman reared back, her face contorting in disgust. "I would imagine not."

Will popped another bite of duck into his mouth. "Oh, believe me," he spoke through a mouthful of food, "you'd remember if you had. It's a dark meat. Really gamey. Looks similar to rabbit, if you've ever had that, but rat meat is different. It's got this really distinct smell."

"Smell?" The woman wrinkled her nose and tipped her head down, giving herself an unfortunate double chin. "What sort of smell?"

"Excellent question." Will stabbed a piece of meat with his fork and waved it in the air. "Rats secrete this oil on their fur that makes their meat smell like urine. No matter how much you cook it, you can never get rid of that rodent-urine smell."

The other dignitaries seated at their table had ended their conversations and were all listening to Will, their mouths hanging open.

"Goodness gracious." The woman placed her wineglass on the table and brought a hand to her double chin. "I can't imagine eating such a dirty creature. That's revolting."

"It's not as bad as it sounds. When you're hungry enough,

you'll eat anything. You just have to add enough seasoning to cover up the urine taste. Or maybe a good sauce." He motioned to his plate. "Like this sauce, for instance. You wouldn't even notice the urine taste in a sauce like this one. Come to think of it, this duck even looks a little like rat."

The woman's eyes flicked from Will to the half-eaten plate of food in front of her, all the color draining from her face. She put her fork down and excused herself to the restroom.

Kira dabbed her lips with her cloth napkin, trying to hide her smile.

When the woman vacated her seat, the other dignitaries resumed speaking to one another as if the distasteful exchange had never occurred.

"So..." Kira leaned over to Will. "Rat, huh?"

"What?" He gave her a playful smile. "Aunt Reeva's cooked rat before. Every word I said was true."

"Yes, but you made the poor woman sick."

His smile dimmed. "Good. She deserves to be sick for making fun of you. She thinks all of her money and power make her better than you, but it doesn't. She's nothing compared to you."

Will's words—and the sincerity in his eyes—set her soul ablaze. More than anything, she wanted to kiss him. But she couldn't, could she? Not in front of the entire city. So, she reached underneath the table and held his hand.

As the Volunteers and dignitaries finished their meals, the string quartet gathered near the marble staircase played a song Kira had heard hundreds of times before while watching the Volunteer Ball on her broadcast screen. She'd always thought the song was pretty, but tonight, in the elegance of the Grand Hall with Will by her side, it was the most beautiful sound she'd ever heard.

Tonight, the music sounded like hope.

As if reading her mind, Will put his napkin on the table and turned to her. "Would you like to dance?"

She stared at his outstretched hand.

Was she really going to dance with Will in front of her father?

"Absolutely."

Will took her hand and led her to the rectangular dance floor at the base of the marble staircase, directly in front of the head table. All hope of blending in with the crowd had vanished the moment Kira put on the blue rose dress. She could feel the heat of her father's gaze against the bare skin of her back, probably wilting the blue rose Desiree had attached to the dress, but she didn't care.

With the music swirling around them, Will took her right hand in his left and hooked an arm around her waist, just above the rose. They weren't the only people dancing. Other couples were migrating onto the dance floor. A cameraman stood halfway up the marble staircase, broadcasting their dance to the entire city.

But when Kira closed her eyes and allowed Will to lead her, it felt as if everyone else had vacated the Grand Hall and only they remained.

"What are you thinking?" Will whispered into her ear.

She responded without opening her eyes, savoring the feeling of his hand in hers. "This music. I've heard it before."

"It's Pachelbel's Canon in D Major."

"How do you know?"

"Jonesy has an old record player in his apartment. I don't know where he got it, but he's had it for as long as I've known him. You wouldn't know it to look at the guy, but he loves classical music, and Canon in D is one of his favorite pieces of music. Mine too. They used to play it at weddings, back before..." Will's voice trailed off.

She opened her eyes. "Before what?"

Sadness flooded Will's features. "Before all of this," he said. "Kira, you have no idea how much I wish things were different. You have no idea how much I wish I could just dance with you tonight without feeling like I might never hold you like this again."

Pulling her face away from his chest, she met his eyes. "Are you really going to leave me tomorrow?"

"I don't know," he said. "But no matter what happens, I don't regret anything. I don't regret coming to your office that day, and I don't regret plotting to kidnap you and use you against your father." The tiniest hint of a smile found its way onto his lips, but the sadness in his eyes remained. "In my defense, I didn't go through with it."

She didn't want to ask the next question, but she couldn't stop herself. She needed to know. "Do you regret not leaving the city on Tuesday when you had the chance?"

He held her gaze, and she saw the answer in his eyes long before it reached his lips. "The only thing I regret is not spending more of this week with you."

It was the answer she'd longed to hear, but it broke her heart just the same.

As the music swelled around them and the song reached its crescendo, Will kissed her right there on the dance floor, in front of the whole city. She didn't try to stop him. She didn't care about the consequences. The kiss wasn't as passionate as their first kiss. This one was more understated. It conveyed something deeper. Something real.

Kira knew the cameraman would zoom in on their kiss, broadcasting it to every household in Vita Nova.

Even in a city that honored death above all else, people still understood love.

Pachelbel's Canon in D ended and a new song began, but

Kira and Will didn't stop dancing. She wasn't ready for this moment to end, and she couldn't bring herself to let him go. Not yet. Instead, she pressed her cheek against Will's chest and stared at the blue rose pinned over his heart, fighting back tears.

If only. If only. If only.

The words played over and over in her mind until they became the only words to the string quartet's new song. A song that sounded even more hopeful than the last.

If only. If only. If only.

And then a hand touched her shoulder, and she pivoted around to see a beefy man in a suit standing behind her, a somber expression on his face. She didn't know the man's name, but she recognized him as a member of her father's security detail.

The bodyguard stepped back and stood at parade rest. "Forgive the interruption, but the Mayor would like to speak with you in his office upstairs."

Kira's eyes darted from the bodyguard to Will. "Which one of us?"

"Both of you," the man replied. "Right now."

Chapter Twenty-Five

They followed the bodyguard to a private stairwell located off the foyer.

At first, Kira wondered why the man hadn't taken them up the marble staircase in the Grand Hall, but then she remembered her father cared only about appearances. He wouldn't want them using that staircase because it was within sight of everyone in the Grand Hall and those watching at home on their broadcast screens. People would certainly question why a young Volunteer and his date were being escorted upstairs to the private section of the mayor's house.

They emerged from the stairwell into a brightly lit hallway, its cheerful pale-yellow walls framed with white crown moulding. Red carpeting with a diamond pattern stretched to infinity, passing beneath several elegant arches that divided the hallway into sections. Halfway down, on the left side of the hallway, a set of double-doors hung open. The sound of crackling wood drifted out of the open doorway.

Will took her hand. "Remember why we're here," he said.

"No matter what happens tonight, I meant everything I said to you."

Her stomach did a queasy little flip—the duck wasn't sitting well with her—and the urge to run from that open door was overwhelming.

When they reached the office, she saw Victor Devlin standing in front of a stone fireplace, his back to the doorway. He stared into the flames, a glass tumbler filled with amber-colored liquid in his hand.

Will's hand squeezed hers hard enough to make her flinch.

She glanced at him, but his eyes were locked on Devlin.

The bodyguard cleared his throat. "Sir. I've brought Mr. Foster and Miss Liebert to see you."

Devlin turned away from the fire, his slate-gray eyes falling on Kira. Tonight, her father's pockmarked face had a crimson tinge to it, either from the alcohol flowing through his system or his proximity to the fire.

He waved them forward. "Come in. Please."

They obeyed, holding hands as they crossed the threshold into the balmy room. For no reason at all, one story from her mother's old devotionals flashed through her mind. It was the story of Daniel, who'd been thrown into the lion's den for disobeying the Babylonian king Darius's edict, which stated that he could not pray to anyone except for the king himself. Stepping into her father's office, Kira could imagine how frightened Daniel must've felt as the lions surrounded him, believing he was going to be devoured.

But God had closed the lion's mouths for Daniel.

Would He do the same for her?

Devlin nodded at the bodyguard. "Leave us, Brian. It's alright. Please close the door behind you."

The bodyguard looked uncertain but gave a quick nod and exited the room.

As the door clicked shut, Devlin abandoned his spot in front of the fireplace and approached Kira. He smiled at her, but something lurked beneath that smile. Something dark. "I have to admit that it caught me by surprise to see you tonight." His eyes dropped to Kira's hand, which was still entwined with Will's, and his smile faded. "I knew you took your job seriously, but I didn't realize that you took it *this* seriously."

Kira released Will's hand and stepped closer to her father. "I apologize if my coming tonight caught you off-guard, but I needed to speak with you."

"So you made out with a Volunteer on the dance floor? Was that embarrassing public display of affection designed to get my attention? Because it worked."

"We weren't trying to—"

But Devlin cut her off. "I tried to speak with you last week, remember? Outside your home. Unless I'm mistaken, you told me to get lost."

She swallowed hard, forcing her pride down her throat. "I know, and I'm sorry about that. I'm holding onto a lot of anger about my mother's death, but that's no excuse for taking it out on you. You didn't know about her situation until it was too late...and that's not your fault."

The words tasted bitter on her tongue, like chewed-up aspirin. She didn't believe what she was saying—not a word of it—but it was a means to an end.

Her father's face softened a little. "I'm glad you've finally realized that. Even if I could have helped her, it wouldn't have been the right thing to do. Your mother was sick, Kira...and in this city, sick people use up our resources and hinder our chances of long-term survival. The fact that she was your mother—or that she and I were briefly romantically involved—does not mean she gets to live forever. We cannot afford to make exceptions in Vita Nova."

What about the dozens of crusty old dignitaries in the Grand Hall? she wanted to say. *How many of them are over sixty? How many of them have secretly received medical care to prolong their lives?*

Instead, she said, "I understand."

"Do you?"

"I do. And I'm sorry."

Devlin took a long sip from his glass. "Good. I accept your apology." He turned his attention to Will. "Now, I'd like to hear from you, Mr. Foster. Would you care to explain the reasoning behind your sudden romantic involvement with my daughter? I don't suppose it has anything to do with the fact that you're scheduled to die tomorrow, and you've somehow discovered that your advocate's father is the mayor? You're not hoping to romance your way to a last-minute pardon, are you?"

Will's nostrils flared. "Absolutely not." After a brief pause, he forced the word from his lips, "Sir."

"Good. Because that would be in poor taste, and it wouldn't work. I was looking through your file a few minutes ago. You're a sanitation engineer, is that correct?"

"Yes, sir."

Devlin's lips curled into a smirk. "It's astounding, isn't it? You're standing here talking to me right now, and in a few brief hours, they will toss your body into the furnace for cremation. On Sunday, they will shoot your ashes into the sky over the river. Doesn't that frighten you? That you might still be *in there* somewhere when they set your body on fire?"

"What?" Kira gasped, horrified. "Why would you say that?"

"I'm only curious. If I were him, I'd be wetting my pants right about now."

Will's expression hardened like clay. "I'm sure you would be," he said. "But to answer your question, I'm not afraid of my body ending up in one of those furnaces. I don't fear death, sir. Not like you do."

Devlin peered into the fire, as if contemplating saving time and money by throwing Will into it. He glared at the young Volunteer. "I give you credit for bravery, son, but I wonder how brave you'll be tomorrow, when the doctor walks into your fancy room at Rolling Meadows with his needle full of death. Sometimes, we have to strap the Volunteers down to kill them. Did you know that? They're harder to kill than the Compulsories."

Lizzy Currant's face appeared in Kira's mind. The woman had been terrified of dying. Had she put up a fight during her last moments? Never had Kira imagined such a thing—she'd always imagined the Volunteers' last moments at Rolling Meadows as peaceful and serene—but now that her father had put the idea into her mind, she could see it no other way.

Anger pulsed through her veins. She wanted to scream at her father, to pound his face with her fists.

A soft voice whispered to her not to do it. *Don't forget why you came here. Don't fall into his trap.*

Of course, it was a trap. Her father was trying to bait Will into a fight by bringing up the crematorium, and now he was baiting Kira. The situation was disintegrating before her eyes, and if she still wanted to help Aunt Reeva and the others, she had to do something.

Something drastic.

She lunged forward and grabbed her father's hands. Despite the fire, his hands felt cold and clammy within her own. "Dad, I came here with Will tonight because we need your help. I'm begging you. Please help us."

Her father stared at her, too stunned to respond.

When he'd first come into her life when she was twelve, Victor Devlin had made it clear that he expected Kira to call him Dad. It didn't matter that he was a stranger to her or that he treated her with the same cold indifference that a person might show a stray dog that relieved itself on their porch. The pressure had increased with each father/daughter date until he'd come right out and demanded that she acknowledge him as her father. Even at twelve, Kira had been perceptive enough to know that Victor Devlin's continued love and attention were contingent on her doing this one thing for him. His ego required it. And he *was* her father, but no matter how hard she'd tried to force the word from her lips, she couldn't do it.

She couldn't bring herself to call this awful man Dad.

But for Will...

For Will, she would do anything.

"You've never called me that before," Devlin said. "Not even when you were a child. Why do I get the sense that you're throwing that word around now to manipulate me?"

As she stared into his eyes—which so closely matched her own—Kira realized they were the same dark-gray as the concrete barricade. "That's not what I'm doing. I should've said it long ago when you tried to have a relationship with me. You put everything into those dates, and I never gave you a chance. I'm sorry that I acted that way. I was angry about things that weren't your fault, but I need you to listen to me now. There's something going on in the city that you need to know about."

"Is that so?"

Releasing her father's hands, she moved closer to Will and linked her arm with his. "On Tuesday, Will snuck me into the Unregulated Zone. I hid in the back of one of the sanitation transport vehicles."

"He did what?" Devlin's eyebrows shot up, and he turned to Will. "You took my daughter out there?"

"Don't be upset with him, Dad," Kira rushed to explain. "I wanted to go. I've spent my whole life terrified of the people who live out there. I used to have recurring nightmares about them. The only way to be free of that fear was to see it for myself. And there weren't any roving bands of killers. No one threatened me. I met several people, and they were good people, struggling to survive. They don't mean us any harm."

Devlin slammed his glass on his desk, sending amber-colored liquid sloshing over the sides. "How can you say that? How can you stand here and tell me that those people don't mean to harm us after what happened in the Eastern Sector? Hundreds of people died last night, Kira. Crews are *still* pulling dead bodies from the rubble, all because of the Lawless. Of which I'm now assuming your new boyfriend is one."

"No! He's—"

"Don't be an idiot, Kira. With all due respect, you were out there for one day. I hardly think that qualifies you as an expert on the Unregulated Zone and its inhabitants. Just because the people you met put on a friendly face for you, do you honestly think that means you can trust them? Did it occur to you they might try to manipulate you to get close to me? Or that your boyfriend might be in on the scheme?"

Kira rested her fingertips on her chest. "The bombing last night...that wasn't them. I *know* it wasn't them." She took a deep breath. This was where things got complicated. "I don't know who blew up that building, but it wasn't anyone from the Unregulated Zone. Maybe the Patrols had something to do with it? There are bad people in the Patrols, Dad. *Terrible* people."

"The Patrols?" Something flashed in Devlin's eyes. Something she couldn't identify. "That's quite an accusation."

"I understand that, but you have to believe me. The people living in the Unregulated Zone didn't do this. They didn't. If you carry out this search-and-destroy operation, you'll be responsible for the deaths of dozens of innocent people. It will be a massacre," she said, repeating the word Will had used the previous night.

Her father stared at her for a long time, his upper and lower jaws sliding back and forth. Grinding his teeth, as he always did when he got angry. Finally, his jaw relaxed, and he smiled. "As much fun as this discussion has been, my guests are expecting me downstairs. Forgive me, Kira, but I don't have the time to entertain hysterical theories about the Patrol soldiers. Especially hysterical theories that aren't backed up by a shred of evidence."

"I have evidence, sir."

Her father's eyes shifted to Will, as if he'd forgotten the young man was still in the room. "Is that so? What evidence do you have?"

Will unlinked his arm from Kira's. "I used to live in the Unregulated Zone with my parents until the Patrols showed up at our house. I was twelve years old when a Patrol soldier murdered my father right in front of me. And then you murdered my mother."

"What?" Kira brought a hand to her lips. "What did you just say?"

With lightning speed, Will bent and snatched a small pistol from underneath the cuff of his pants. Before Kira could react, he raised the gun and aimed it at Devlin's chest.

"I'm sorry, Kira," he said. "But I've been waiting ten years for this."

Chapter Twenty-Six

"Will?" Kira froze in place. "What are you doing?"
"He did it, Kira," Will said. "He killed my mother."

Victor Devlin raised both hands, his jaw twitching. "Calm down, son. You're obviously confused. I've never killed anyone."

Will's eyes darkened to the color of the Susquehanna at night. "I'm not confused. After a Patrol soldier shot my father, my mother ran outside. The Patrols held their fire. I don't know why, but they didn't shoot her. Then, a man stepped out of one of the Humvees. He wore a suit...and I'll never forget the ugly pockmarks all over his cheeks."

Devlin's face blanched, but he said nothing.

Tears brimmed in Will's eyes. He rubbed them away. "You walked over to my mother. She was on the ground with my father. I thought you were going to comfort her—I really did—but you never said a word. You just pulled out a pistol and shot her between the shoulder blades."

Kira clapped a hand over her mouth. "No."

Devlin glared at him. "Son, you need to—"

"'They're all sick out here,'" Will cut him off. "That was what you said, wasn't it, Devlin? You said, 'They're all sick out here. Kill everyone you find.'"

The canyons in Devlin's cheeks deepened, and his jaws resumed their tectonic sliding. "I've never set foot in the Unregulated Zone. You think I would risk exposing myself to the diseased filth that exists out there?"

"What about the bombing in the Eastern Sector last night? Did you orchestrate that? Did you murder those people?"

"You're crazy." Devlin uttered a hollow laugh. "Why would I murder my own people?"

"To get everyone behind your search-and-destroy operation in the Unregulated Zone. You found out from the so-called defectors from Agriculture that there are still a bunch of people alive out there. You can't have that, right? A group that's avoided the Patrols for this long might one day threaten your control over this city. They need to be eliminated, but for that kind of operation, you'd need more Patrols and the city's support. If an entire apartment building of people had to die for your cause, no big deal. They're expendable, right? Everyone is expendable to you."

Tears flooded Kira's eyes. She didn't want to believe Will. She didn't want to believe that her father could murder those people or shoot an unarmed woman in the back. But there was a coldness about Victor Devlin. An emptiness. A dark void where his soul should've been.

Did the blood of a monster course through her veins?

Finally, she found her voice. "Will, put the gun down. You don't want to do this."

"You should listen to my daughter," Devlin said. "She's a smart young lady. Put the gun down before you get hurt."

"Whose going to hurt me?" Without taking the gun off its

target, Will backed up to the office door and turned the dead-bolt. Then he dragged a chair from the desk and jammed it underneath the doorknob. "You? What are you going to do, Devlin? You don't have a gun this time, and you don't have a security team to protect you. There's nothing stopping me from shooting you dead where you stand."

"You'll never make it out of this building," Devlin muttered.

A vein pulsed in Will's neck. "I'm scheduled to die tomorrow. I have nothing to lose. Literally nothing."

"I wouldn't say you have *nothing* to lose." Devlin tapped a finger against one canyon in his cheek. "Right now, you're scheduled to die a Volunteer's death. Quick, Painless. Pleasant as death can be. However, if you're arrested tonight and thrown into the Confines, your last hours won't be nearly as pleasant. Do you think your dead mother would want you to suffer such a terrible fate?"

Will lunged forward and grabbed the mayor by his suit, shoving him into the wall next to the fireplace. Devlin's leg bumped into the metal stand holding the fireplace tools, sending a poker and pan sliding across the floor. The room filled with the sound of metal clanging against marble.

That sound, Kira thought. *It will bring others.*

Her father's lead security goon, Brian, wouldn't be far away.

"Will, don't!" Kira's words came out as a whisper. Weak and powerless, like her. Lightheaded, Kira put a hand against the wall to steady herself. She wanted to pull Will away from her father before he did something awful, but her legs wouldn't cooperate.

On the other side of the room, Will dug the gun into Devlin's temple. "Do you want to die tonight, Devlin? If you do, keep talking about my mother."

Devlin continued to sneer, as if Will didn't have a gun pressed to his head. The only sign of his fear was the glaze of sweat coating his forehead. "I know nothing about your mother. Now, if you're going to kill me, get on with it. Or do yourself a favor and put a bullet in your own head before security breaks down that door and makes you wish you had."

Will shook his head. "Not yet. Before you die, I want you to transfer the Volunteer Ball broadcast up here. I know you can broadcast from this room. Tell the city that you've just discovered the Patrols are behind everything, including the bombing in the Eastern Sector. I don't care if you take personal responsibility or not, but I want you to call off this search-and-destroy operation before it starts."

"Or what? You're going to shoot me in front of my daughter? With my wife and young children downstairs?"

"I will if I have to."

A heavy pounding on the door made Kira jump. She spun around to see the office door rattling on its hinges as someone tried to get inside the room.

"Mayor Devlin?" It was Brian's voice. "Sir? What's going on?"

Instead of responding to the security guard, Devlin regarded Will with cold eyes. "This is over, son. My men are right outside that door. This has all been for nothing."

"Your men might be outside," Will said, "but you're in here with me. Do what I'm asking or I'll kill you before they get inside."

The banging grew louder.

It sounded as if multiple people were kicking the door at once.

Will drove the pistol harder into Devlin's temple, and Kira's father winced in pain.

"Transfer the broadcast, Devlin! Tell them the truth! Do it now or you die!"

Her father shook his head. "I won't do it. You're going to have to kill me."

Frozen halfway between the door and the fireplace, Kira watched as Will's finger tightened around the trigger. Would he actually do it? Would he actually shoot Devlin in the head? And then what? What would happen when security broke the door down? What would they do when they saw Will standing with a pistol in his hand, and their mayor lying dead on the floor?

They'll kill him, she realized. *They'll shoot him, and he'll die right in front of you.*

No.

She couldn't let Will die.

Not like that.

As Will continued to shout at her father, demanding that he transfer the broadcast to the office, Kira ran to the door and unlocked the deadbolt. She grabbed the chair with both hands and pulled it from the door.

The door burst inward and Brian—along with three other members of her father's private security detail—rushed into the office, their weapons drawn. They zeroed in on the two men struggling near the fireplace and aimed their weapons at Will's back.

"Drop the gun!"

Will's body went rigid. He turned his head slowly, his brows knitting together in confusion as he noticed the four men standing inside the room, their pistols aimed right at his back. Then, he noticed the chair, which had been pulled off to the side.

Finally, his gaze landed on Kira.

She was still gripping the chair with both hands.

"You let them in?"

The sadness in Will's voice broke her heart.

"You've got five seconds to drop the gun, pal," Brian said. "One...Two..."

Tears carved pathways down Kira's cheeks. "Please, Will. Put the gun down."

Will's eyes darted from one security goon to another, and Kira didn't have to read his mind to know how badly he wanted to pull the trigger. This was his only chance to kill the man who'd killed his mother and so many of his friends.

But if he pulled the trigger, he'd be dead a second later.

They'd kill him right in front of her.

With a heavy sigh, he pulled the pistol away from Devlin's head, leaving behind a dark-red bruise on the mayor's temple. Then he dropped his arm to his side. The gun dangled from his fingers for a moment before clattering to the marble floor.

Immediately, the four security goons surrounded Will and took him to the floor. He landed hard on his stomach, his arms twisted behind his back. Brian drove a knee between his shoulder blades while one of the other guards put him into handcuffs.

"Take him to the Confines," Devlin ordered, grabbing a handkerchief from his breast pocket and dabbing the beads of sweat from his temple. "I want this young man kept under full sedation prior to his execution tomorrow, which will now be as a Compulsory. Better make it nice and early. Eight o'clock."

"Yes, sir."

Devlin strode across the room to his security detail, and Kira flinched, expecting him to punch Will. Instead, her father tore the blue rose from Will's chest and crushed it in his hands. Then he tossed the petals into the fireplace. "In the morning, they're going to transfer you to the Compulsory Clinic. When you arrive, the nurses will put you to sleep, and you won't ever wake up. You should thank me. That's a far better fate than you deserve."

"No!" Kira launched herself at the security guards, but her father grabbed her and held her back. "Let go of me!"

As the security guards led him into the hallway, Will screamed over his shoulder, "Don't let him do this, Kira! You have to stop him!"

Then her father kicked the door shut, and Will's screams faded to nothing.

Chapter Twenty-Seven

"I'm not angry with you, Kira," Victor Devlin said. "That young man manipulated you, and he should be ashamed of himself. But don't worry. He won't bother you ever again."

Seated on the couch in her father's office, Kira brought a glass of water to her lips. Bile climbed her throat, but she swallowed it down with a sip of the water. Then she placed the glass on a wooden coaster on the end table and wrapped her arms around herself, trying to get warm.

It had been thirty minutes since her father's security detail had dragged Will off to the Confines, but her body wouldn't stop shaking.

Had she made a mistake by opening the door? What else could she have done?

"Are you cold, sweetheart? Here."

Devlin grabbed a blanket from the arm of the couch and draped it around her shoulders. It wasn't much, but it was the most fatherly thing he'd ever done.

"Thank you."

"Of course. When you're ready to go, I'll have my driver take you home." Her father collapsed onto the couch beside her and stared into the fire. "I'll do my best to keep this quiet. That young man's name will no longer be listed among the Volunteers. People will want to know why. I'll wait a few days before publicly addressing what happened tonight, and when I do, I'll try to leave you out of it."

"He never would've done it," Kira whispered. "Will never would've shot you."

Frustration crinkled Devlin's eyes. He rested his hands on his thighs, palms up, blue residue from the crushed rose staining his right hand. "You and I agree he lacked the spine to pull the trigger, but the fact remains that he threatened an elected official with violence, and he will be put to death tomorrow morning." He softened his face and put a hand on her shoulder. "It's important that you know I don't blame you for anything. You couldn't have known what that young man was planning. Besides, I've always wanted a relationship with my oldest daughter. Chandra is dying to meet you, and so are the kids. What do you think? Is there a path for us to build a relationship?"

Kira wanted to believe her father. She really did. It would be the easiest choice to believe him. It would mean a return to normalcy, to the life she'd been living prior to last Thursday, when Will had walked into her office and turned her world upside down. Believing her father would mean having a relationship with her half-brother and sister, something she'd always wanted. She would finally have a family.

But she couldn't get Will's accusations out of her mind.

She blurted out the question without thinking. "Is it true what Will said? Did you order your Patrols to kill people in the Unregulated Zone?"

"Kira—"

"Please. We can't have any kind of relationship if you don't tell me the truth. Right now. No matter how ugly it is."

Devlin stared at her, his lower jaw gliding back and forth like the pendulum of a clock. Without saying a word, he rose from the couch and crossed the room to his desk. He picked up the tumbler and emptied the glass, his Adam's apple bobbing as he swallowed the brownish-yellow liquid. Then he placed the tumbler on his desk and regarded Kira with wary eyes. "What we talk about tonight stays between us. Do you understand?"

In that moment, Kira would've agreed to anything her father asked. The urge to know the truth—the whole truth—was overwhelming.

She nodded. "I understand."

Devlin's limbs gave out, and he sank into the chair behind his desk. The same chair from which he did most of his newscasts. "Almost two years after this city went into lockdown, they elected me mayor. Above all else, my job was to keep people safe. The citizens of Vita Nova continue to re-elect me every four years because I've done a phenomenal job of protecting them. Just as you take your job as a volunteer advocate seriously, I take my position as mayor seriously. Like it or not, you get that intensity—that single-minded focus—from me."

Kira looked away. She didn't enjoy thinking that she shared anything more than her DNA and her strange eye-color with her father.

Devlin continued, "I always knew that our biggest threat would come from the Unregulated Zone. That's why I formed the Patrols and sent them out with the mission of scouting the area and reporting the number of people still alive. The people out there weren't in hiding back then, so it wasn't hard to find their camps and observe them from a safe distance. I couldn't believe it when I got the actual numbers. Hundreds of survivors, Kira. *Hundreds of them*, scattered in dozens of camps around the Unregulated Zone, all within miles of the barricade. We'd been in lockdown for more than two years at that point, so I'd expected any survivors outside of the city to have died of starvation or disease, but that hadn't happened. And I knew those people would eventually become a problem for Vita Nova."

"A problem?" Kira interjected. "Why would hundreds of healthy survivors be a problem for the city?"

"Simple." He ran his fingers along the rim of the empty glass as if trying to make it hum. "Resources. We have them. They don't."

"But they hadn't done anything. They hadn't attacked the city."

"No, but they would not be content to stay on their side of the barricade forever. Anyone who says differently is a fool. I couldn't sit back and wait for them to get desperate enough—or strong enough—to attack us."

Kira didn't like where this was going. "So, what did you do?"

Devlin folded his hands over his chest. "Nothing, at first. I needed time to formulate a plan that would keep everyone safe, but would also be accepted by the majority of the city. And then a plan fell into my lap."

"What plan?"

"Word got out, as it does, that the Patrols had located camps of survivors in the Unregulated Zone. You were too young to remember this, but a small faction of do-gooders in the city started riling everyone up, saying we needed to send food and supplies with the Patrols to help the people in the Unregulated Zone." Devlin rolled his eyes and shook his head in disgust. "It was total lunacy. They acted as if we had an unlimited supply of resources to go around. But those do-gooders presented me with an opportunity. If something happened to them during their humanitarian mission, maybe that would convince the rest of the city that the people out there were dangerous. So, I sent a group out with a limited amount of supplies...and they never came back."

An uncontrollable shudder swept through Kira's body. She remembered the awful story of the citizens slaughtered by the Lawless. Every kid in Vita Nova knew that story. It had been the basis for her nightmares. Some bodies had been decapitated. Others had limbs missing. "So, they weren't killed by the Law—" She stopped herself from using the term because it meant nothing to her anymore. "Who killed those people? The Patrols?"

Devlin's lips curled into a sad smile. "Don't look at me like that. I never wanted you to know any of this. You asked for the truth, so that's what I'm giving you. Everything I've done as mayor, I've done to keep the people of this city safe. That includes you, Kira."

"No." Kira leaned forward and wrapped her arms around her waist. "Oh, no."

There had been *women* in that group.

"After the failed humanitarian mission," Devlin continued, ignoring Kira's distress, "I began to refer to the people out there as the Lawless in my broadcasts. The name was Sienna Graves's idea. People became terrified of the Unregulated Zone, but fear dims over time. We discovered those kids from Agriculture were sneaking food to the Lawless. I still don't know how they got the food over there. My interrogators weren't able to get much information out of them. But people in this city are volunteering to die so the rest of us don't run out of food, and then you've got a bunch of traitors from the Tenements stealing our precious resources and giving them to the enemy. As penance for that crime, the traitors gave up their lives for their city."

Kira lifted her head and met her father's gaze. "They didn't give them willingly. You took them. You *murdered* them."

Devlin's body stiffened at the remark. "Nobody in Vita Nova gives their lives willingly. Certainly not the Compulsories. Not even the Volunteers. We knew the Compulsory Program wouldn't keep our population at bay long-term, but throwing healthy people over the barricade wall wasn't going to work either. If you send too many people out there, you risk creating an army that might threaten your city. So, we created the Volunteer program. We incentivized people to sacrifice their own lives by appealing to their hedonistic desires." Abandoning his desk, he walked to the fireplace and picked up the metal rack. Then he retrieved the pan and poker and returned them to the rack. "And you're a part of that, if you'll admit it. You're not really advocating for the Volunteers. You're advocating for Vita Nova. You're advocating for our survival. If I'm a murderer, Kira, then so are you."

She closed her eyes, trying to block out his words. It wasn't true. She wasn't like him. The next question lodged in her throat like a bone, and she knew that if she didn't force it out, she would choke on it. "And the Tenements?" she asked, opening her eyes. "Did you kill those people so you could get the city behind your search-and-destroy mission?"

Devlin stared at her, his lips pressed tightly together, as if trying to keep the words from spilling from his mouth. Finally, he said, "There are other forces at work here, Kira. Forces much stronger than you and I."

"What are you talking about?"

He returned to his desk chair and sank into it, the leather groaning beneath his weight. "There are people in Vita Nova. People with more power and influence than I could ever hope to have. They are no longer content to stay within the barricade. They want what's over there." He nodded toward his office window, which faced the river. "There's an enormous world out there—resources, land, weapons—and it's all ripe for the taking. However, convincing people to expand beyond the barricade will not be easy. Not unless we assure them we have eliminated the Lawless, and we can't do that without a large-scale military operation."

It all came together in her mind, the last few puzzle pieces falling into place and revealing a terrible picture. "So, you and these mystery people—these *forces*, as you call them—created this myth of the Lawless to keep people from wanting to go outside the barricade, but now the city isn't big enough for you anymore, so you're going to slaughter anyone who's survived outside of the barricade." Suddenly, the office felt unbearably hot, making it difficult for her to breathe. "You spent years convincing people that the Unregulated Zone was filled with monsters when the real monsters were right here all along."

"You think I'm a monster?" Devlin fixed his eyes on her. "I'm not a monster. I'm your father."

Something came to her then. Something her mother had said at the Compulsory Clinic as the Somnumbutal systematically shut down each of her major organs. "Can I ask you one more question?"

"Of course."

"When my mother was dying, one of the last things she said to me was, 'They made him leave. He wasn't sick.' Do you know what she was talking about?"

One pockmarked cheek twitched almost imperceptibly.

But Kira had seen it.

Then Devlin's eyebrows bunched together in manufactured confusion, and he shook his head. "I have no idea what she meant by that."

He's lying.

Kira couldn't remain inside the room any longer. It wasn't

only the heat from the fire, or the hellish revelations from her father. But the office felt as if it had shrunk in the past half-hour. Or perhaps she'd grown larger. The mansion itself felt too small to contain her.

"I should go."

Devlin didn't rise from his desk. "I'll let my driver know. Be safe getting home, Kira."

Rising from the couch, she headed for the office door, the wrinkled skirt of her gown clinging to her damp legs. She couldn't wait to peel the dress from her body. It no longer made her feel beautiful. Now, the vibrant blue gown and the rose at the base of her back reminded her of all the dead Volunteers she'd let down.

All the Volunteers she'd let die.

When her fingers grazed the doorknob, Devlin's voice stopped her.

"Kira? Who is this young man? Why does he matter to you?"

Her hand fell away from the door, and she turned to meet her father's eyes.

"Everyone matters."

ONE LEVEL BELOW, THE SOUNDS OF THE VOLUNTEER BALL drifted up to greet her.

Violins. Dancing. Laughter. Blue Roses.

The occasional cries of, *"Revere the Volunteer!"* and *"For the good of all!"*

To avoid being seen, she took the hidden stairwell to the foyer, where she and Will had strolled arm-in-arm a few hours earlier as doomed lovers. A lone security guard stationed at the front door looked up from the book he was reading and gave her a quick nod as she approached. She ignored him and stepped outside.

A black sedan idled in front of the mansion, waiting to take her home.

As Kira passed the car, she glanced inside and saw the young driver asleep behind the wheel, his mouth gaping open. She kept walking until she reached the end of the driveway and the dark blue ribbon of the Susquehanna River came into view. Inhaling the fishy stench of the river, she stared into the darkness of the Unregulated Zone.

It might've been her imagination, but she thought she could see a single, flickering light on the other bank, signaling her like a beacon.

Then she took off her heels, picked up the bottom hem of her blue rose dress, and ran all the way home.

Chapter 28

Friday

Friday morning broke dark and dreary. A steady rain pattered Kira's bedroom window like drumming fingers, as if the clouds themselves had conspired to remind her of the shortness of time. She watched, bleary-eyed and exhausted, as fat raindrops slid down the glass, converging into tiny, winding rivers before plummeting to the ground.

The sky groaned. A low rumble of thunder. Distant, but powerful enough to rattle the window in its frame.

A storm.

Still far away, but growing closer.

Gliding over the uninhabited parts of the Unregulated Zone.

Heading for Vita Nova.

She hadn't gotten much sleep, nor had she expected to. A tearful late-night conversation with Emma hadn't made things any better. Nothing could. But she had forced herself to remain in bed all night instead of pacing around her townhouse like a captive animal.

The few times she'd drifted off, she'd slipped into the nightmare from her childhood. She was back in the river, strapped to the back of a drowning man. As he sank, he pulled her down with him, their bodies linked as they descended toward a watery grave at the bottom of the river. As the surface receded from view, the struggling man glanced over his shoulder, and Kira glimpsed his face. Only it wasn't the brutish cannibal from the Unregulated Zone dragging her to her death.

It was her father.

Kira threw back the covers and climbed out of bed. Her blue gown lay crumpled on the floor, and she stepped over it on her way to her dresser. Moving quickly, she stripped out of her pajamas and pulled on the comfy sweater, worn jeans, and black boots she'd laid out the night before. Then she brushed her teeth, put on a little makeup so she could pass for a human, and twisted her hair into a messy bun before heading downstairs.

In the kitchen, the digital clock above the stove read six-fifteen.

Another rumble of thunder. The lights dimmed.

She grabbed a green apple from the fridge and ate it leaning against the sink, her eyes lingering on the wilted blue rose petal lying on her kitchen table. Sour juice dribbled down her chin, and she wiped it away with a kitchen towel. After she finished the apple, she filled a cup with water from the sink and swallowed the whole glass in five big gulps.

The lights flickered again. The power would almost certainly go out. Vita Nova often lost power during thunderstorms. Occasionally, it stayed out for days. As a child, Kira had dreaded stormy nights because she didn't like the dark.

But the dark no longer frightened her.

Worse things lived in the light.

She pulled on her raincoat, flipped the hood over her head, and stepped into the storm.

A short walk through the mostly empty Residential Sector brought her to her regular bus stop. The six-thirty bus pulled up on time, sending a mini-tsunami of rainwater onto the sidewalk. Bulky windshield wipers flung rain into the streets and onto the small group of waiting passengers.

The interior of the bus was warm and dry, a welcome change from the damp city streets. Kira found a seat near the front, next to an older woman clutching an oversized purse on her lap. As the bus pulled away from the curb, Kira could sense the woman studying her, but she kept her eyes locked on the driver's back.

"That was you last night," the woman finally said. "It was, wasn't it?"

Kira scrunched her shoulders, trying to disappear inside the hood of the raincoat. "Excuse me?"

"At the Volunteer Ball. I saw you on the broadcast. You were dancing with one of the Volunteers. Quite a good-looking young man."

"Sorry." Kira shook her head. "I don't know what you're talking about."

"Sure you do. I never forget a face." The woman held her purse tighter against her chest. "I don't know that young man's reasons for Volunteering, but if it makes you feel any better, you two looked beautiful on the dance floor. That kiss of yours had me in tears. Been a long time since I've seen anything that romantic at a Volunteer Ball. Is he already gone?"

Kira clenched her teeth, struggling to hold back tears. She was exhausted—both emotionally and physically—and the nosy woman wasn't helping.

"I don't know," she said, as the bus lurched to a stop.

The woman rose from her seat and squeezed past Kira. "Your dress was gorgeous, by the way. The most beautiful gown

I've ever seen. I'm sure you made that young man very happy during his Final Week."

Then the woman trudged into the rain, leaving Kira alone on the bus, too exhausted to cry.

———

WHEN THE DOOR TO HIS OFFICE SWUNG INWARD, THE wiry-haired man seated behind the cluttered desk glanced up from a mountain of paperwork, a toothpick jutting from one corner of his mouth. He had thick eyebrows—multicolored—like twin caterpillars. He peered over the rim of his glasses at the young woman in his doorway, his eyes sliding down her sodden raincoat to the puddle of water collecting around her boots.

"Help you, miss?" he asked, the toothpick dancing as he spoke.

Shock stole the words from her mouth. Everything she'd intended to do—and all the things she'd planned to say—went out the window when the nerdy man with the red-tinted mustache brought his beady eyes to rest on her.

It's him, she realized. *It's the same man.*

When she could speak, she asked, "You're Jonesy?"

The expression on the man's face hovered between mild interest and confusion. "That's what the nameplate on my desk says." He pointed at the small sign in front of him which read, *Hank Jones.* Then he squinted at her until understanding dawned in his eyes. "You're her, aren't you? The girl. Kira. The one Will's been talking about?"

A stab of pain in her chest. Brief but unbearable. "He told you about me?"

Jonesy leaned back in his chair and folded his hands over

his stomach. "More than I cared to know. So, you're Devlin's daughter? His *secret* daughter?"

Kira put her hood down and moved closer to the desk. She couldn't get into everything that had happened the night before. Not now. She didn't have enough time to explain it all. "They're going to put Will to death today as a Compulsory."

Contempt replaced the smile on Jonesy's face. "Yes, I'm aware," he said. "Rumors spread quickly in this city, especially in the Eastern Sector." He leaned over and spat his toothpick into the trashcan. "Why did you come here, young lady? It's no secret that I care about that boy, but I can't do anything to help him."

"Maybe you can." She kept her voice low, even though none of the other sanitation engineers had arrived for work yet. "I want you to pick up his body from the Compulsory Clinic this morning. They're going to put him to death at eight o'clock, so that's when you need to be there."

Jonesy's fuzzy eyebrows shot up. "I don't go into the Unregulated Zone anymore, young lady. I haven't for a long time."

"I understand that," she said. "But no one is going to question you. Not after what happened at the Tenements."

"Young lady...*I can't* do it." The man pounded a fist on his desk. "You don't understand. I can't see my boy like that."

Kira wanted to tell Jonesy her plan, but there were so many things that could go wrong. She didn't want to give this man hope because she feared losing that hope might shatter him.

"Please," she begged. "You're the only person who can help me. You're the one who brought Will into the city. It's only right that you are the one to take him home."

An internal struggle played out on Jonesy's face, and Kira could practically hear him weighing his loyalty to Will against his fear of being caught. Perhaps it was wrong to ask this man— who'd already done so much for Will—to do one more thing.

But he was the only person Will trusted, so he was the only person Kira trusted.

Jonesy removed his glasses and rubbed his eyes. He appeared to have aged five years in the five minutes Kira had been in his office. With his eyes on his desk, he shook his head, and Kira's heart plummeted to the floor.

But then he looked up at her. "Alright. I'll do it for Will."

Relief flooded her body, and the urge to climb over the desk and throw her arms around the sanitation engineer was overwhelming. No matter what happened today, someone who loved Will would take care of him. That was all that mattered.

"Thank you," she said. "Eight o'clock. Please don't be late."

Kira headed for the door, eager to get to the bus stop. The next bus would arrive soon, and she had to be on it.

"Wait a minute," Jonesy called after her. "What are you planning to do?"

Kira answered without looking back.

"Whatever I can."

Chapter Twenty-Nine

The Compulsory Clinic was tucked away on a side street behind the main hospital complex in the Medical Sector. Its location seemed deliberate, as if city leadership had intentionally hidden the building, hoping people would forget about it.

Kira gripped the wet handrail and climbed the narrow concrete steps to the clinic's front door. She hadn't been back to the Compulsory Clinic since her mother's death, but the boxy brick building looked as ominous as she remembered. A dome-shaped awning hung over the small porch—dark green with white lettering that identified the clinic for anyone lucky enough to have never set foot inside it. Two small windows flanked the front entrance, each topped with smaller versions of the same green awning, giving the clinic the appearance of an upscale inner-city apartment building. The clinic had multiple floors, each with a dozen patient rooms.

Kira lifted her eyes to the darkened windows. How many people had died in this building? How many would die today?

She didn't believe in ghosts, but if any building in Vita Nova was haunted, it would be this one.

Pulling the glass door open, Kira stepped into a reception area that belonged in another building. While the exterior of the clinic hadn't changed in fifty years, the modern reception area featured crisp lines, freshly painted walls, and laminate wood flooring. Cheerful touches that would've been more at home in a chic hotel than a clinic where people went to die.

Glass vases filled with white roses occupied both ends of the reception desk. Emma poked her head between them and did a double-take when she noticed Kira standing inside the front door. She wore a pair of black scrubs, her dark curls piled atop her head.

"Kira? What are you doing here?"

The intricate metal clock hanging on the wall behind Emma's head was fancy, but impossible to read, so Kira glanced at her own watch.

Seven-thirty-six.

The ride across the city from the sanitation lot had taken longer than she'd expected. Lots of people were riding the buses this morning, thanks to the rotten weather. At each stop, it had taken forever to load and unload the sopping-wet passengers.

But she'd made it in time. Barely.

"Have they transferred him here yet?" she asked.

Emma gave her a blank stare. "Who?"

Flipping down her hood, Kira approached the reception desk. She'd always deferred to Emma, letting her hold the reins of their friendship, but not today. Not anymore. "You know exactly who I mean. Did they bring him over from the Confines yet?"

Something flashed in Emma's eyes. Not fear, exactly.

Emma wasn't easily intimidated by anyone or anything, but she looked nervous. Kira was asking her for information that she wasn't allowed to give, and if she got caught, the consequences could be severe.

Gripping the edge of the reception desk for support, Kira leaned closer to Emma. "Please," she said, her voice husky with emotion. "I need to see him one more time."

Emma's cheeks and neck flushed red. She reached out and grasped Kira's hand. "You know I would do anything for you, but seeing him again is just going to make it harder. It won't change anything."

It might, Kira wanted to say. *It just might.*

But she swallowed the words before they could slip past her lips.

Emma couldn't know what she was planning.

If she did, she would never let Kira go through with it.

The front door pitched open, accompanied by a sharp crack of lightning that lit up the entire street. A young woman rushed into the building as if trying to outrun the lightning, shaking the water droplets from her umbrella onto the lobby's non-skid rug. An older woman followed close behind her, and as the door clicked shut, the woman turned and cast a sorrowful gaze at the glass, as if she'd rather be standing outside—in the middle of the storm—than in the lobby.

Once they were both inside, the two women linked arms and stared expectantly at Kira, as if waiting for her to greet them. They looked so much alike. The same jet-black hair, pale complexion, and rosebud-shaped lips. They could've been sisters, if not for the age difference.

But they weren't sisters.

They were mother and daughter. They *had* to be.

Of course.

"Good morning." Emma pulled her hand from Kira's and smiled, but the fake perkiness of her smile didn't make its way into her voice. "Welcome to the Compulsory Clinic. How may I assist you today?"

The young woman spoke in a shaky voice. "I'm Kat Miller. I'm checking my mom in." Her lips drew into a paper-thin line as she struggled not to cry. But the young woman lost the battle, disintegrating into a puddle right in front of the reception desk.

The mother took over, her voice all business. "We're checking in for my appointment. My name is Celeste Miller."

Kira wanted to wrap her arms around them, to console them with the promise that everything was going to be alright, but that wasn't true. Everything would not be alright. Kira knew that better than anyone. In a few hours, Celeste Miller would be dead. Just like Kira's mother. Another beautiful, healthy woman put to death by the same city that claimed to be protecting its citizens.

And her daughter would be left alone to navigate a world that no longer included her mother.

Emma punched the woman's name into her computer. "Okay. I've got you right here, Ms. Miller. Your appointment is scheduled for eight-thirty, so you can go into the waiting room." She motioned to a set of double doors beyond the reception desk. "Have a seat inside and one of our intake officers will finish getting you checked in. While you wait, there's coffee and an assortment of cookies in the waiting room. Help yourselves."

"Thank you." The mother wrapped an arm around her sobbing daughter and led her toward the double doors. "Be strong for me, honey," she whispered. "It'll all be over soon."

As mother and daughter withdrew into the waiting area, Kira turned to Emma, her anger boiling the blood in her chest. "Coffee and cookies?"

Emma nodded. "Do you see why I hate this place?"

"Then stop playing their game. These people killed my mother, Emma. And now they're going to kill Will. I didn't even have time to say goodbye to him. If you hate this job so much, then do something about it. Help me find Will before it's too late."

Another peal of thunder punctuated Kira's plea, and the lights in the building flickered and went out, bathing the reception area in darkness. They came back on a moment later, and Kira saw that Emma's expression had changed. She no longer looked worried or nervous.

Now she looked resigned.

"They brought him in a little while ago," she admitted, her shoulders sagging. "But it's too late, Kira. He's sedated. I wish I could help, but there's nothing I can do to—"

"Which floor?" Kira demanded. "Which room is he in? Could you add me to the list as a family member so I can be with him?"

Shaking her head, Emma said, "Inmates from the Confines aren't allowed to have anyone with them. Not even family members. Plus, they keep them under guard until the doctor shows up for the procedure."

That wasn't good. Kira hadn't realized that Will would be kept under guard, considering they'd already drugged him into unconsciousness. "But you work here. Can't you escort me to see him?"

Emma brought a pink fingernail to her mouth and chewed on it. "No. The only people allowed on the patient floors are nurses and doctors. And the sanitation engineers who transport the bodies. Unfortunately, you're none of those things...and neither am I."

"But you're wearing scrubs? Won't they just—?"

"No." Emma's voice was firm. "People know me around

here, Kira. They know I'm the front desk receptionist. I can't pass for a nurse."

Kira felt time ebbing away like sand running through an hourglass. She couldn't bring herself to look at her watch again, but it had to be a quarter of eight by now. If she didn't get to Will's room in the next five minutes, it would be too late.

Time. She needed time.

"Emma, I need you to do something for me, okay? I need you to change Will's appointment time to nine o'clock."

"What?" Emma's eyes widened. "No way. I can't do that."

Kira stabbed the reception desk with one forefinger. "Yes, you can. I *know* you can. You've told me before that you sometimes have to change people's appointment times. Well, I need you to do it now, before it's too late."

Emma sank deeper into her chair. "Absolutely not. You can't ask me to—"

"I've never asked you for anything in my life," Kira pleaded. "And I wouldn't be asking you to do this if there was another way, but there isn't. You're the only one who can help me."

Emma unleashed a dramatic sigh and dropped her head into her hands. After a few moments, she lifted her head and blew out a breath. "Do you have any idea how much trouble I could get into? I could get fired. Maybe even arrested."

But her fingers were already moving, typing something into the computer.

Kira closed her eyes, allowing herself to hope.

"Thank you," she whispered. "Thank you so much."

She opened her eyes as Emma finished typing.

"There," Emma said. "It's done. Can I do anything else for you today?"

"Just one more thing."

Emma groaned. "I was being sarcastic."

Kira's eyes drifted from her best friend's face to her black scrubs.

People know me around here, Kira. They know I'm the front desk receptionist. I can't pass for a nurse.

"Do you have an extra pair of scrubs I can borrow?"

Chapter Thirty

Keep your eyes forward. Move with a purpose. Act like you belong.

Kira tried to follow Emma's advice, moving swiftly through the sterile hallway, her boots heavy against the recently waxed tile floor. Thankfully, there weren't many doctors or nurses in the third-floor hallway this morning, but Kira avoided eye contact with everyone she passed.

After changing into Emma's scrubs in the restroom off the front lobby, she'd stashed her damp clothing behind the large plastic garbage can in the restroom's corner, where she hoped no one would discover them until she returned. *If* she returned. After a quick glimpse in the mirror, she'd exited the restroom, slipped silently past Emma, and taken the elevator to the third floor.

He's in Room 323. The last room, at the end of the hallway.

Of course, it had to be the third floor.

But—Kira—there will be a Guard.

The seed of a plan that had sprouted in her mind early this morning had grown into something more substantial, but there were still so many variables. So many things she couldn't predict. Would the Guard believe her? What about Jonesy? What if he was late or didn't show up at all? Kira had no choice but to step out in faith and place her trust in the God she'd read about in her mother's devotionals. The One Will and Aunt Reeva believed in.

Hopefully, He would light the way for her.

The last time she'd walked this hallway, each room had been occupied. Today, however, the rooms were all empty. The doors hung open, revealing the same bare walls. The same crisp, white bedsheets. The same powder-blue blankets.

As Kira approached Room 317—the place where her mother had drawn her final breaths—a nurse emerged from the room cradling an armful of blue blankets.

The nurse paused outside the doorway, her eyes narrowing in suspicion. "Can I help you?"

Act like you belong.

Kira lifted her eyes to the nurse's face and forced an exasperated smile. "I'm sorry. It's my first day working here, and I just noticed the numbers above the doors. I think I got off on the wrong floor. I'm assigned to the second floor today."

Emma had told her what to say if someone stopped her. Every nurse was assigned to a specific floor, and there wasn't much interaction between the floors. The only problem would be if whoever stopped her questioned why she wasn't wearing any identification. Or if they escorted her to the proper floor themselves.

Luckily, this nurse was too busy for any of that. "No worries," she said, her expression relaxing. "Welcome aboard, by the way. This old building is a maze, but you'll get used to it." She lifted a finger toward the end of the hallway. "The stairs are over there. Just take them down one level and you're all set."

"Thank you."

The nurse gave her a quick nod and rushed away, tossing the blue blankets into a laundry bin on the other side of the hallway before disappearing into another room.

Kira had to hurry. She'd gotten lucky with this nurse, but she couldn't expect the next one to be as distracted. And Will's room was *right there*, a few paces away, the only closed door in the hallway.

But before she could take another step, she forced herself to look into the room.

Her mother's room.

The room was identical to every other room on the floor. Nothing indicated that a seismic shift in Kira's life had taken place in this room. Her gaze settled on the bed, and for a moment, she could see her mother lying beneath the blue blanket, her hands crossed over her stomach, a serene expression on her face.

It was the first time her mother hadn't looked worried about something.

"This is for you, Mom," Kira whispered. "This is what I should've done for you."

Then her legs moved, propelling her away from the door, and away from the past, which could not be changed.

Toward the future.

Toward Will.

Chapter Thirty-One

When Kira entered the room, a Guard leapt out of the high-back chair next to the window and stuffed a paperback book into the cargo pocket of his uniform. He was young—likely still in his teens—with closely shorn reddish-blond hair and a smattering of freckles across the bridge of his nose.

He cleared his throat and puffed out his meager chest. "Something I can do for you, ma'am?"

In Kira's peripheral vision, she saw the hospital bed pressed up against the left wall of the room, and the outline of Will's body beneath the blue blanket. His chest rose and fell in the slow, steady rhythm of the heavily sedated.

She didn't allow herself to look at him.

Not yet.

Lifting her chin, Kira tried to slip into the role of a fearless, no-nonsense nurse. "Yes, I'm here to prep the patient for his procedure. The doctor should be in shortly, but in the interest of full disclosure, I should tell you we're already running behind this morning. As you know, this patient wasn't supposed to be a Compulsory, so we had to squeeze him in at the last minute."

"Okay..." The Guard scratched at his temple, clearly not sure what Kira expected him to do with this information. "I guess...just...do whatever you need to do, ma'am."

"Well, that's the thing. We're unable to continue with the procedure until all the necessary paperwork has been filled out."

Creases formed on the young man's forehead. He scratched his temple harder, as if someone had buried the solution to this problem underneath his skin. "Ma'am, there must be a mistake. I signed a bunch of papers when we arrived."

Kira held up her palms. "Yes, but I just spoke with my boss, and she says you still need to complete two more documents or we can't move forward with the procedure. All the paperwork is with the receptionist at the front desk. You can run down to the lobby, fill everything out, and we'll be good-to-go."

The Guard shook his head. "I'm not allowed to leave the prisoner's side until the procedure is complete, ma'am. That's against regulations."

This was taking longer than Kira had expected. If Jonesy held up his end of the bargain, he would be here at any moment. "I understand that you've got a job to do, but so do I. And it's nearly eight o'clock. The doctor will be in soon, and if those documents aren't signed, he won't give this guy his injection. Then, you're going to have to transport him back to the Confines and explain to your superiors why they've got to feed and house this prisoner until Monday." Before the Guard could argue, she motioned at the figure in the bed without glancing in that direction. She didn't trust herself to not get upset at the sight of Will lying there, unconscious. "This man is no threat to me or anyone else in this clinic. He's on another planet."

The Guard's eyes darted from Kira to the hospital bed, his

mouth twitching as if he wanted to argue. Then he grabbed his cover from the windowsill and popped it onto his head. "Alright. Where am I supposed to go?"

"Front desk, first floor lobby. Ask for Emma."

The Guard walked past her and vanished into the hallway, the door drifting shut behind him.

She was alone with Will.

Steeling herself for whatever she might see, Kira allowed her eyes to fall on the figure in the bed.

A soft gasp escaped her lips.

Nothing could've prepared her for how terrible Will looked. Instead of the crisp tuxedo he'd worn to the Volunteer Ball, he wore the shapeless, olive-drab uniform of the Confines inmates. Either Will had fought the Guards or her father had ordered him beaten, because the left side of his face was so bruised and swollen that he was almost unrecognizable. The purplish-blue discoloration and inflammation of the skin around his left eye was evidence of a direct punch, but despite the beating he'd obviously endured, he appeared to be sleeping peacefully, his lips hanging apart, as if he had only drifted off for a few moments.

He isn't asleep, Kira reminded herself. *He's unconscious.*

The drugs seeping into his body via the IV in his arm would keep him that way until the doctor arrived to end his life with a deadly injection of Somnumbutal.

Her father had claimed it was a peaceful death. Better than Will deserved.

But Kira couldn't imagine a worse fate than being drugged into a sleep that never ended.

The rooms didn't have locks on the doors, for obvious reasons. The staff at the Compulsory Clinic didn't want a Compulsory barricading themselves inside their room in a last-ditch effort to avoid being put to death. So Kira couldn't do anything to prevent the young Guard—or anyone else—from barging in. But Emma had promised to keep the Guard occupied for as long as she could, and she'd also moved Will's appointment back an hour, which would hopefully give Kira enough time.

She went to work, hurrying over to the small sink area and opening cabinet doors until she found the right one. A pile of black squares occupied the farthest cabinet to the right. She grabbed one and shook it open. The rectangular sheet of plastic crinkled loudly in her hands, and she held her breath, her eyes darting to the closed door.

Footsteps walked past the room, not slowing.

Kira released the air from her lungs and her hands tightened around the black bag.

She'd known where to find the body bags because—two years earlier—she'd watched as a sanitation engineer gently maneuvered her mother's body into one.

Only now, she knew the man's name.

Jonesy.

She hadn't said anything to him at the sanitation lot, but she'd recognized him instantly. The man had been so gentle with her mother's body. Watching him wheel her mother out of the room on the stretcher had been awful, especially knowing that her mother's final destination was a burial pit in the Unregulated Zone, but the kindness in the sanitation engineer's eyes had made a horrible experience a little easier.

She closed her eyes and held the body bag to her chest.

If her mother hadn't died as a Compulsory, Kira wouldn't have known how the process worked. She wouldn't have known the sanitation engineers placed the Compulsories inside body bags for transport. She wouldn't have known where the body bags were stored or the best way to get a dead person into one. And she wouldn't have known that the sanitation engineers transported the dead Compulsories to the lower-level parking garage via a rear service elevator, where no one coming into the front lobby would see them.

Had her mother died for this?

So that, one day, she could help Will?

Kira didn't know what to do with that thought, so she buried it in the back of her mind, where it wouldn't distract her from what she needed to do. She would exhume it later—if there *was* a later—and figure out what it all meant.

Hurrying over to the bed, she traced the line of the IV to the spot where a strip of medical tape covered the cannula protruding from the back of Will's hand. She grabbed the edge of the medical tape and peeled it off. Then her eyes settled on the cannula buried inside Will's skin. She had no clue what she was doing—no clue if she could hurt him by removing it herself —but she had no other options. With a shaking hand, she grasped the cannula and pulled, nausea twisting her insides as the needle-like protuberance slid out of his skin.

Disgusted, she tossed it away.

Blood pooled at the hole in the center of his hand, and since she had no bandage, she used her right thumb to put pressure on the spot. She tried to count to sixty but only made it to twenty-nine before she pulled her finger away. A little blood leaked from the hole in Will's hand, but a little blood was the least of her worries.

It was five minutes past eight.

Jonesy was late.

Or maybe he wasn't coming at all.

Shoving the insidious thought away, she pulled back the covers, revealing the entirety of Will's body. His feet were bare, and she couldn't see any shoes in the room, which meant that they had probably transported him to the clinic in a wheelchair. That wasn't surprising. According to Emma, Guards at the

Confines drugged the prisoners into a zombie-like state for transfer to the clinic.

She unzipped the body bag.

Sliding his feet and legs into the bottom of the bag wasn't a problem, but when she got to his torso, she discovered she couldn't lift him at all. She tried rolling him onto his side, as she'd seen Jonesy do with her mother's body, but Will felt impossibly heavy in her arms.

He's dead weight, she thought. *Literally.*

Frustrated, she collapsed against the side of the bed, beads of perspiration running down her face.

I can't do this.

But she *had* to do it. She couldn't afford to quit.

If she quit, Will died.

Summoning every ounce of strength she possessed, Kira again tried to lift him, fully expecting the guttural sounds coming out of her throat to draw the attention of a passing nurse or aide. She worked the body bag underneath his right hip, but when she sprinted around to the other side of the bed and tried to lift him, his body shifted and the bag slid out from underneath him.

"No!"

Exhausted, she draped her body over Will's legs and closed her eyes.

"I'm sorry," she whispered.

She'd failed to save her mother, and now she'd failed to save Will, too.

The sound of approaching footsteps drew Kira's attention to the door.

The footsteps slowed...and then came to a stop.

Turning away from the bed, her eyes fell on the narrow gap at the bottom of the door...and on the two black shadows that hadn't been there before.

Her breath caught in her throat.

Would it be a doctor? A nurse? Or the Guard?

So close.

She'd been *so close* to getting him out.

Kira positioned herself between bed and the door, a human barricade between Will and the people who sought to take his life. His last line of defense. But she had no gun. No knives. There weren't even any needles in the room. Only the discarded cannula, which dangled uselessly from the IV pole, a drop of Will's blood blooming from its tip.

Three soft knocks on the door. Two quick ones, followed by another knock a few seconds later, like an afterthought.

Or like a code.

She'd first heard that knock two years earlier when the sanitation engineer removed her mother's body from the clinic.

She ran to the door and flung it open.

Jonesy stood in the hallway, one leathery arm extended behind him, his hand gripping the stretcher. He glanced at Will's battered body—sprawled on the hospital bed, legs half-stuffed inside a body bag—and the blood left his face.

His eyes filled with tears. "My boy." He choked out the words, sinking against the stretcher and putting a hand on his stomach. "What did they—?"

"He's not dead," Kira whispered, grabbing Jonesy's hand and pulling him into the room. "They haven't done it yet. He's sedated."

Jonesy wiped at his eyes. "He's...what? He's alive?"

"Yes, but he won't be for long unless we get him out of here."

Without warning, Jonesy grabbed Kira and pulled her into a bone-crunching embrace. Tears leaked from his eyes and fell onto the shoulders of Emma's scrubs. "He's like a son to me," he whispered. "Did he tell you that?"

Kira hugged him back. "He said you're like a father to him." She almost thanked him right then for handling her mother's body with such care and respect, but their time was almost up. The young Guard might return at any minute.

Jonesy released her and rolled the stretcher into the room, closing the door. "Help me."

Together, they got Will into the body bag. The entire process went much smoother with two sets of hands, but Kira knew Jonesy would've done just fine on his own. When they were nearly done, Kira lifted Will's head and worked the bag underneath his neck. A quiet moan slipped through his lips, and she held his head in her hands, willing him to wake up, but he didn't open his eyes.

The drugs hadn't worn off yet.

Jonesy tipped his head toward the stretcher. "Help me lift him."

Using the handles on the body bag, they slid him from the bed to the stretcher. Then Jonesy zipped the bag around Will's head, leaving a tiny gap in the black plastic.

It's not enough.

Kira reached for the zipper, intending to open it a little more.

"Leave it," he commanded. "Or someone will notice."

She pulled her hands away. "Are you sure he'll be able to breathe?"

Jonesy went to the bed, tossed the blanket aside, and removed the top sheet. He shook the sheet out and let it drift over the body bag. "He's getting enough air. I'll unzip it once I get him into my van. But I've got a bad feeling about this. We need to get him out of this building right now."

As he turned toward the door, Kira gripped his gaunt arm. "You won't be able to stay in the city after this. You know that, right?"

He swatted the idea away. "Eh, I'm too old to run, and I've got no desire to survive in the Unregulated Zone. Plus, I'm fifty-nine, which means I've got less than a year of life left, anyway. If I end up checking out a little early, so be it. At least I'll have done something good for this hellion of mine." Jonesy tipped his head and gave her a pointed look. "What about you? There's room in the back of my van for one more."

Kira placed a hand on the bottom of the sheet that covered Will's body. "I can't go. Not yet. When he wakes up, tell him I had one more Volunteer to help. He'll understand."

Jonesy scratched at the bridge of his nose. "How do you plan on getting out of the city? Because Will's going to ask me when he wakes up, and I better have an answer ready for him."

She considered his question for a moment. "Tell him I'll go to the place where he and I first kissed." Her cheeks warmed as she remembered that tiny flame of happiness that the bombing of the Tenements had so quickly snuffed out. "If we make it, that's where we'll go."

Jonesy's caterpillar eyebrows joined in the middle. "We?"

Ignoring his question, Kira stepped past Jonesy, pulled the door open, and stuck her head out of the room. Two nurses in black scrubs stood at the opposite end of the hallway, chattering in animated voices. One of them tossed back her head and laughed—a high-pitched cackle—as if she wasn't standing in a place where countless people had drawn their last breaths. Then, the nurses slipped through a set of double doors, both of them still laughing as the door clicked shut behind them.

Kira nodded at Jonesy. "The hallway's clear."

Jonesy gripped Will's stretcher with both hands and pushed it into the hallway with the practiced ease of a man who'd done the same job for years. He turned to the right and guided the stretcher toward the service elevator at the end of the hallway.

Kira followed him.

Twenty feet to the elevator. Fifteen. Ten.

A soft whisper in her mind found its way to her lips. "Please, God."

Jonesy reached the elevator and hit the down button with one shaking, arthritic finger. When the doors opened right away, he glanced at Kira, a smile tugging at the corners of his lips. "Will would say that God is on our side today." He winked at her. "Either that or someone fiddled with the buttons to hold the elevator on this floor."

Together, they steered Will's stretcher onto the elevator, and Jonesy climbed in beside him. "Last chance, young lady. You sure about staying?"

She nodded. "I'm sure. Just take care of him, okay? Get him out of this city."

Jonesy reached for the bank of buttons next to the elevator's doors and undid whatever he'd done to keep the elevator stuck on the third floor. The elevator dinged, and the doors began to shut, but then Jonesy reached out a hand to keep them open. He squinted at her for a few moments and then gave her a slight nod. "I remember you. About two years ago, was it?"

"What?"

"You should know that I said a prayer for your mother. Never been much for praying, but I guess Will has rubbed off on me over the years."

Kira felt her chest expand, and two years of pent-up emotions threatened to burst from her lips. "You remember me?"

He nodded. "Of course I do. You broke my heart with those tears of yours. Don't go breaking Will's, okay?"

Before Kira could respond, Jonesy released the button and the elevator doors whooshed shut.

Chapter Thirty-Two

"Excuse me? Who are you?"

Kira froze at the top of the third-floor stairwell, one hand gripping the smooth metal railing.

The voice belonged to the nurse with the catlike face that Kira had just passed when she'd entered the stairwell. She'd held the door for the nurse. Smiled. Tried to be polite. Doing otherwise would've drawn attention to herself.

But she'd still caught the nurse's attention.

Kira had considered taking the main elevator back to the lobby, but the stairwell had felt safer. Less traveled. Plus, she hadn't wanted to run into the Guard from Will's room. He might still be in the lobby with Emma, and if he was, Kira didn't want the elevator to announce her arrival with a loud ding. Her plan had been to hide out in the stairwell until he left.

But she hadn't expected to run into a nurse. One who looked as if she'd been around for a while and knew who belonged in this building...and who didn't.

"Miss?" The nurse wasn't going anywhere. "Miss? Who are you?"

Fixing an exasperated expression on her face, Kira spun around to face the woman. "Ugh. It's my first day working here and I'm *so* lost. I have absolutely no idea where I'm going."

The nurse's face didn't soften at all. If anything, she looked more suspicious. "I didn't realize we were getting anyone new." She tucked a wisp of blonde-gray hair behind one ear, her blunt pixie-cut accentuating her sharp features. "What floor have they assigned you to?"

"Uh...I'm supposed to be on the second floor today," Kira said, repeating her lie from earlier. "I don't know if I pressed the wrong button on the elevator or something, but I ended up on three."

The woman wasn't buying it. "They assign every newbie to one of our charge nurses for their first few weeks on the floor. What's the name of your supervisor?"

Stupid, stupid, stupid. Why hadn't she asked Emma for the names of the charge nurses on each floor? She didn't know anyone in the building except for Emma.

Kira brought both hands to her cheeks. "Honestly, I don't remember. My best friend, Emma, just got me the job here. She works at the front desk. I don't want to mess things up for her."

"Emma Castile?" The woman's ice-cold demeanor thawed so fast that Kira expected to see a puddle of water at her feet. "Oh, Emma's a darling. Just go back downstairs to the lobby and check with her. She'll be able to pull up the information on her computer and tell you who they've assigned you to. I'd walk you down, but I don't have time. They're about to bring my first patient back."

"No problem." Kira unleashed a nervous laugh. "I *should* be able to find the lobby without too much trouble. I'll check in with Emma and find out where I need to be. Thank you for your help."

The woman waved a hand at her. "No problem. Good luck today. Working here can be tough at first, because of the nature of the job, but you'll get used to it."

Never, Kira thought. *I could never get used to watching people die.*

"Thanks. Have a good day."

"You too."

The nurse exited onto the third floor, and Kira hurried down the dimly lit stairwell, eager to get out of the Compliance Clinic before anyone else confronted her. She felt terrible for dropping Emma's name to the nurse, but she'd been desperate and it had just slipped out. Kira didn't want anything to come back on her best friend once the authorities realized that one of their condemned prisoners had escaped, but Emma had already done so much that she couldn't cover up.

When Kira reached the first floor, she pushed the door open just wide enough to see Emma seated behind the reception desk. The Guard was nowhere in sight.

"Kira?" Emma rose from her seat as Kira approached. "What happened?"

"I got him out. How long ago did the Guard leave?"

"Two minutes. Maybe three."

Which meant he would be reaching the empty clinic room right about now.

"Okay. I have to go...and you need to come with me."

"Come with you? Are you crazy?" Emma rolled her eyes. "I love you, babe, but I don't want to be involved in whatever you're doing."

"You're already involved. They're going to know you helped me. You let me into the building. You changed the time in the computer for me. For goodness' sakes, you even gave me your scrubs."

Emma shrugged. "I'll say you threatened me. That I did it under duress."

"They won't believe you!"

"I don't care," Emma insisted, her tiny nostrils flaring. "I'm not going anywhere. This city is my home. And since we're being upfront with each other...you're not leaving either. This whole mission of yours is crazy. They will never let you out of the city. You're going to end up in the Confines and then they'll send you here. You just sacrificed yourself to save Will."

She couldn't bring herself to argue because everything Emma had said was true. Kira had no actual plan of escape. No hope of success. Had she gone with Jonesy, maybe she could've gotten out of the city, but she'd chosen to stay. She had to do one more thing that mattered. Not just for her mother or Will, but for everyone.

For all the Volunteers she could've helped, but didn't.

Kira slipped into the restroom and retrieved her clothes from behind the garbage can. She didn't have time to change, so she pulled her rain jacket on over Emma's scrubs and tucked the rest of her clothes under her arm to keep them dry.

She emerged from the bathroom to find Emma standing outside the door.

"Here." Emma slid a set of car keys into Kira's palm. "Take my car. She's in the side parking lot. You've got no chance riding the buses, but in a car...maybe."

"Are you serious?"

"Yes." Emma winced as Kira closed her fingers around the keys. "But please treat her right. She's a good girl. Loves her momma."

Kira smiled. The only thing Emma loved more than her car

was Tom Petty. "Thank you, Em. You've done so much to help me. I don't know what else to say."

"Don't say anything." She grabbed Kira and hugged her tight. "You're insane, but I love you. Whatever happens, don't forget that."

"I won't." Kira clung to her best friend, not wanting to let go. "I love you, too."

Over Emma's shoulder, Kira saw a jar on the front desk filled with something resembling tiny, colorful flowers on white stems.

Only they weren't flowers.

When Emma released her, Kira walked over to the desk, selected a red one, and slipped it inside her pocket.

As she headed for the door, Emma called out after her, "I just hope this Will guy is worth all the trouble."

Inside her chest, Kira's heart fluttered. A tiny butterfly of hope.

"He is."

Chapter Thirty-Three

When Kira was halfway across the parking lot, the Compulsory Clinic's alarm began to blare.

The discordant shrieking spurred her into a run, and she reached Emma's Porsche in seconds, tossing her clothes onto the passenger seat and sliding behind the wheel. She jammed the key into the ignition. The engine sputtered and growled, as if voicing its frustration that Kira, and not Emma, was in the driver's seat. Slamming the driver's door, she shifted the car into gear and floored it out of the parking lot, desperate to put distance between herself and the clinic before more Guards arrived.

As she passed the rear of the building, she glanced at the loading bay. No disposal vans idled outside the rear entrance, which meant that Jonesy had gotten Will out of the area before the alarm went off. Getting out of the city would be a whole different problem for Jonesy, especially if the Guard from Will's room had been smart enough and fast enough to alert the Guards at the bridge checkpoint.

The worst of the rain and thunder had ended, but the slate-gray sky refused to lighten. The thick blanket of clouds over-head rumbled its discontent. A low, menacing sound, like a threat. Massive puddles of standing water from the earlier rain-storm littered the city streets, making it dangerous to drive fast. She couldn't risk hydroplaning and losing control of the vehicle.

She turned onto Division Street as a bus lumbered past, traveling in the opposite direction. Blank-faced passengers stared at her from the windows, the breath from their nostrils fogging the glass. Most would be on their way to work. Others might be on their way to the Medical Sector for their semian-nual health screening.

A week earlier, Kira had been among them.

But everything had changed.

With both hands gripping the steering wheel, she navigated the rain-drenched city streets, the Porsche's tires spraying water onto the sidewalks. As she turned from Division Street onto North 7th Street, she kept checking her mirrors for flashing lights. Part of her expected the Guards to track her down before she reached her destination.

If that happened, at least she'd saved Will.

But the road behind the Porsche remained empty, and soon after Kira reached Elmerton Avenue, a driveway came into view on the left-hand side of the road.

She eased her foot off the gas, and the Porsche slowed, but Kira's pulse sped up at the sight of the wooden sign with its time-faded white letters.

Welcome to Rolling Meadows.

Home to Our Brave Volunteers!

Despite its upbeat message, there was something unsettling about the sign when compared with the extravagance of the property located beyond, concealed by the trees. The sign dangled from two rusted metal chains, one longer than the other, giving it a slightly crooked appearance, like the smile of a card player who flashes you his hand before taking you out of the game.

Kira turned the Porsche onto the gravel driveway, and the vehicle limped through a dense grouping of pine, oak, and ash trees, their limbs extended over the road as if to greet the Volunteers. Beyond the trees, the driveway sloped into the peaceful valley where Rolling Meadows existed in its own world—a lone ship floating in a sea of green. The natural slope of the land, as well as the narrow strip of woods from which Kira had emerged, blocked the two-story lodge from all views of the city, as if to fool the Volunteers into thinking they had escaped the borders of Vita Nova.

In a way, Kira supposed they had.

Ignoring the main parking lot, she continued around the side of the lodge, heading for a single-story annex that jutted out from the main part of the building. Although the annex had no windows—only skylights—Kira parked near a set of double doors she knew opened into the lodge's indoor swimming pool. The doors couldn't be opened from the outside, but that wouldn't be a problem.

She planned on entering through the lobby.

Stripping down to her tank top and underwear, Kira tucked Emma's black scrubs underneath the driver's seat, where they hopefully wouldn't be seen by anyone passing by. Then, hurrying, she changed back into her own clothing, pulling on jeans that were still damp from the rain. Once dressed, she checked her reflection in the visor mirror. By some miracle, she looked significantly better than she felt. The bit of makeup she'd applied before leaving the townhouse to conceal the dark lines under her eyes was holding up despite the rain and humidity. Her hair looked a little rough, so she tugged it out of its messy bun. Blonde waves tumbled past her shoulders, and she raked her fingers through her tresses until they looked halfway decent. Leaving her raincoat on the passenger seat, she stepped out of the car, locked the door, and headed for the main entrance.

Like at the Compulsory Clinic, anyone entering Rolling Meadows had to check in with the staff at the front desk, so Kira breathed a sigh of relief when the double doors whooshed open, and she recognized the young woman watering plants in the lobby. She wore the uniform of the female Rolling Meadows staff members: a black long-sleeved bodysuit tucked into a pleated skirt. Blue stripes the same color as the Volunteer roses adorned the skirt. Male staff members wore black slacks and button-down shirts with blue ties.

The petite brunette glanced at Kira, her mouth falling open. The watering can in her hand spilled water onto an already-drenched plant. "Kira?"

"You're over-watering that plant, Kimber."

Kira had been in the same class in school as Kimber Worley, and although they hadn't run in the same social circles —Kimber had been popular and outgoing, while Kira had been shy and invisible—they'd always been friendly with one another. That friendliness had carried over into their professional lives, and they often saw each other when Kira visited her Volunteers on the morning of their Sacrifice.

Kimber lowered her eyes to the watering can, which was spilling water and soil onto the glass table beneath the planter. "Oh! Oh, no!"

The supply closet behind the front desk had extra towels and wash clothes for the lodge's guests, and Kira hurried inside and grabbed a towel. Returning to the lobby, she lifted the plant and mopped up the water beneath it.

She wrinkled her nose at Kimber. "You're staring at me."

"I can't believe you're here," the young woman whispered,

as if they weren't alone in the lobby. "I mean...I saw you at the ball, Kira. You were dancing. With *him*. With that cute Volunteer."

She couldn't deny her connection to Will. The night before, their doomed love story had played out on broadcast screens all across the city. "I'm his advocate," Kira said, soaking up the last droplets of water with the towel. She pulled the towel away and stared at her reflection in the glass. "And I fell for him."

Kimber bounced on her heels, chirping like an excited bird. "Really? This is going to sound weird, but I think that's *soooo* romantic." Then her smile dimmed as the realization settled into her blue eyes. "Oh. You fell for him...and now they're going to—"

"They already did," Kira finished her sentence. "Earlier this morning."

Kimber's hand flew to her mouth. "Oh, Kira. I'm so sorry."

"Thank you. But I came today because of another Volunteer. The little boy."

"Teddy? Yes, he's so sweet. Honestly, I don't think he should—" Kimber caught herself before she finished the sentence. "I mean, it's sad because he's young, but I totally respect his decision."

"Totally," Kira agreed, resisting the urge to roll her eyes. "I'm not Teddy's advocate, but I was wondering if I could see him before his appointment. I didn't get to say goodbye to him last night, and I'll feel terrible if I don't see him one more time."

Kimber chewed the inside of her cheek. "I don't know," she said. "I'd have to check with his mother, but to be honest, I'm not exactly sure where she is."

"Certainly not with Teddy, right?" Kira arched an eyebrow. "From what Will told me, that woman has been spending most of her son's Final Week soaking up the benefits of this place and enjoying the company of the husband of another Volunteer."

"Kira..."

"Please. I didn't get to say goodbye to Will. This has been a horrible day. I can't leave here without saying goodbye to that little boy."

Had it been anyone else at the front desk that morning, Kira wouldn't have been allowed any farther inside the building. Yes, she was friendly with the other staff members at Rolling Meadows, but only Kimber knew her on a personal level and trusted her. Kira felt a twinge of guilt at taking advantage of Kimber's trust, but the guilt wasn't enough to deter her from what she needed to do.

"He's in the game room," Kimber finally said. "That's where he hangs out when his mother is busy...doing other things."

"Thank you!" Kira threw her arms around the young woman's shoulders, surprising both of them. "Seriously. Thank you so much."

"You're welcome. But be quick, okay? His Sacrifice is at eleven."

"Don't worry. I'll be gone before then."

And—God willing—so will Teddy.

Chapter Thirty-Four

Unlike the lodge's quiet hallways, the first-floor game room at Rolling Meadows was alive with lights and sounds.

A foosball table stood along the wall closest to the game room's entrance, the miniature figures hanging motionless from their metal rods, as if someone had pressed pause in the middle of their game. Next to the foosball table was an ancient-looking pinball machine, its screen flashing and emitting little melodic dings as if to draw attention to itself. On the other side of the room, a shooting game stood next to a claw machine loaded with a variety of cheap-looking stuffed animals. The animals stared through the glass at Kira with painted eyes, like inmates in a glass prison, the metal claw hovering menacingly above them.

Beside the claw machine was a side-by-side racing game. Teddy Easton reclined in one of the driver's seats, surrounded by the stuffed animals he'd liberated from the claw machine.

One stuffed animal—a panda bear—had the place of honor on Teddy's lap.

The blue rose hung crooked on his chest.

On the screen in front of the little boy, a red Corvette barreled through the dark streets of an unnamed city, smoke belching from its exhaust pipe, narrowly avoiding collisions with buses and parked cars. As Kira watched, awed by the boy's driving skills, a black Humvee surged forward and bumped the Corvette, sending it spinning out of control. But Teddy recovered quickly, his tiny hands clutching the wheel in a white-knuckled grip.

Kira approached the little boy carefully, not wanting to startle him, her chest tightening with each step. Even though his Sacrifice wouldn't occur for another few hours, she felt a strong sense of urgency. Time was running out.

For both of them.

"Teddy?"

He glanced up at her before returning his attention to the screen. "Oh. Hi."

"Do you remember me from last night?"

His nod surprised her. "You're Will's girlfriend," he said. "Kira."

Will's girlfriend.

His words tore a hole in Kira's heart. The pain was palpable. Her legs felt incapable of supporting her weight, so she lowered herself into the other driver's seat, facing Teddy.

"Everything is free in here." Teddy swerved to the left to avoid hitting a parked motorcycle. "You don't even have to put money in the machines. I've been playing games all week."

"That's really nice."

"Wanna race?" he asked. "I'm getting good. I beat Will four times in a row yesterday, which is weird because he drives all the time and I've never even been in a car."

Kira smiled. She could imagine Will sitting where she was now, going head-to-head with Teddy in a racing game and letting the little boy win. "Actually, I was thinking maybe we could go somewhere."

"Who?"

"Just you and me."

The little boy shrugged. "Like where?"

"For a little ride in my friend's fancy car. Would you like that?"

He broke out in a grin, his eyes sparkling. "Sure! But can you ask my momma first?"

The fractured remains of Kira's heart shattered into a thousand tiny pieces. Despite everything, the little boy still trusted his mother. And why shouldn't he? Until now, she'd kept him safe and loved him, as much as a selfish woman like Trinity Easton could love anyone. His little mind couldn't comprehend that his own mother would ever do anything to hurt him.

"Teddy? Do you know what's going to happen to you today?"

The boy's smile dimmed. "Momma says I'm going to be a superhero for the city. She says I'm going to save the world with my Sacrifice."

"Yes, but do you know what that means?"

The red Corvette crossed the finish line, and the screen lit up with the words *Winner - 1st Place!* Teddy dropped his hands into his lap and looked at Kira, his little face growing serious. "Momma says they're going to put me to sleep."

Like a dog. Like an animal.

Like your precious life means nothing.

Tears rushed to Kira's eyes, but she blinked them away. "That's right, buddy."

"Momma says it'll only be for a little while."

"No." She couldn't let Teddy believe his mother's lies any longer. "Not for a little while. If they put you to sleep, you're going to sleep forever, but I don't want that to happen. That's why I'm going to leave Vita Nova today. I'm going outside the barricade for an adventure. I know you really liked Will, and I think he's going to be there, waiting for us. Would you like to come with me?"

He tipped his head to the side, looking thoughtful. "Can Momma come?"

"She can't, buddy. I'm so sorry, but she has to stay here in the city." Teddy stared at her, uncertain, until she added, "Only heroes get to leave."

The little boy's face crumbled, and his eyes shone with tears. "But I'll miss her."

Kira reached up and wiped away the tears on his cheeks. "I know you will, buddy. Mommas are special, aren't they? I miss my momma every day, and she's been gone for two years. But I don't want you to go to sleep forever, and that's what's going to happen if you stay here. You're a really special little boy, and I need you to stay awake, okay? Heroes have to stay awake if they want to save the world."

More tears escaped his eyes. Furiously, he wiped them away and pinched his lips together, trying to look tougher and older than his six years. Finally, he gave Kira a nod. "Okay, but can I take Pandy with me?" He held up the stuffed panda bear. "That's his name. Pandy."

"Of course. Pandy's welcome to come."

"And can we drive really fast when we leave?"

She couldn't help but smile. "We certainly can."

Kira held out her hand, and Teddy took it. Together, they headed for the exit to the game room. A few feet down the hallway, a windowless door led to the indoor pool area, and another set of double doors opened into the side parking lot.

On any other day, Kira would've avoided the indoor pool area, which would've been swarming with Volunteers and their families.

But not today.

She'd been to Rolling Meadows enough to know that people rarely spent the last few hours of their lives swimming.

As they stepped into the hallway, Kira reached into her pocket and pulled out a red lollipop. The same one she'd grabbed from the jar on Emma's desk at the Compulsory Clinic. She handed the lollipop to Teddy, and he accepted it with a smile.

Kira smiled back.

"Let's stay awake together."

Chapter Thirty-Five

T he Porsche tore down the driveway, spitting out gravel and generating a cloud of dust that blocked Rolling Meadows from view.

In the passenger seat, Teddy clutched his stuffed panda against his body and squealed with delight. "Go faster, Kira!"

Before leaving the parking lot, Kira had buckled Teddy into his seat. The little boy did not know what a seatbelt was. He had spent his entire life riding the buses, and the buses didn't have seatbelts. So Kira had done it for him, feeling like a protective mother as she snapped the buckle into place and tugged it tight against his chest. He'd squirmed and complained, not liking the feeling of the seatbelt against his body, but as Kira backed out of the parking place and started to drive, he'd forgotten about his discomfort.

When they reached the end of the driveway, she barely let her foot off the gas as she made the righthand turn onto Elmerton Avenue.

When the Porsche merged onto the highway, she saw them.

Guard vehicles racing up from the city, the blue and red lights in their windshields flashing like lightning.

They passed her heading in the opposite direction, and for one hopeful moment, she thought something had distracted them and they hadn't seen her. But as she approached the intersection of Elmerton and Cameron, she glanced in her rearview mirror and saw the lead car executing a u-turn. The Guard vehicle raced up behind her, and the others followed, their cars filling the Porsche's rear window.

"Teddy, hold on, okay? I have to drive faster."

He laughed and bounced in his seat. "Go! Go! Go!"

For the little boy, this wasn't any different from his racing game. He had no idea what might happen to him if they crashed. Or if the Guards caught them.

Kira whipped the Porsche onto State Street, the pack of Guard vehicles sticking to her like fleas on a dog. Overhead, the menacing clouds opened up once again, not yet finished unleashing their fury on the world below. She flicked the windshield wipers on and turned them as high as they would go, but she couldn't see more than a few feet of road through the downpour. The raindrops came at the windshield hard and fast, attacking the car with sinister intent, as if the clouds themselves had conspired with the Guards to stop her from getting Teddy Easton out of the city.

She was traveling too fast to navigate around the puddles of water, and she felt a momentary loss of control as the car hydroplaned.

This is too dangerous, she thought. *I'm driving too fast.*

She eased her foot off the gas, and the car slowed.

The Guard vehicles closed in.

We're not going to make it.

No. She pushed the thought away, unwilling to allow it to put roots down in her mind. She'd done all she could for Will and Teddy. Even knowing that she probably would not make it out of the city if she went to Rolling Meadows, she'd still tried to help the little boy.

Not rescuing Teddy hadn't been an option.

She'd spent the last two years of her life making her Volunteers as happy as possible before the city killed them, which made her an accomplice in their deaths. Her father had been right about one thing. She wasn't advocating for the Volunteers —she was advocating for the city. For the leadership's ability to continue slaughtering its citizens, while the elite and powerful of the city continued to hoard precious resources for themselves.

As the chase entered the heart of the city, Kira saw a red light glowing at the intersection of State and Walnut.

She jammed the accelerator to the floor.

The Porsche barreled onto Walnut Street, barely avoiding a collision with a city bus coming from the opposite direction.

The lead Guard car wasn't so lucky.

It slammed into the side of the bus, pushing the bus to the other side of the road. The sickening crunch of metal was so loud that Kira felt it in her bones.

"Whoa!" Teddy's eyes widened. He pulled the white lollipop stick from his mouth and dropped it into the center console. "What was that sound?"

"It's okay. We're okay."

She glanced in her rearview mirror and saw the damaged bus and Guard vehicle blocking the intersection, preventing the other Guard cars from following them.

"We're going to make it," she whispered, more to herself than Teddy. "We're almost there."

But then she saw it up ahead, on the left side of the road.

The concrete bulk of the Guard Headquarters.

There was a flurry of activity outside the building. A half-dozen Guards, rushing to their vehicles. Activating their blue and red lights. Joining in the chase.

The Volunteer Memorial Walkway came into view. Blue lights shimmered through the rain on the windshield, giving her something to aim for. She shot across Front Street without slowing and drove the vehicle onto the pedestrian walkway, hoping the metal section was wide enough to accommodate the Porsche.

It was.

Barely.

The car rattled as the Porsche's tires tore across the walkway's rough metal grate. The intense vibrations made Teddy laugh, but Kira felt them in her whole body, jolting her bones, shaking her teeth in their sockets. Her hands slipped off the wheel, and the Porsche veered to the right, toward the river.

"Kira!" Teddy screamed, no longer laughing.

She jerked the wheel hard to the left, and the tires briefly went up on the concrete before dropping back to the metal grate. The car swerved toward the guardrail again, but Kira regained control a fraction of a second before impact.

There's no room for error, she reminded herself. *Not in Vita Nova.*

When they reached City Island, Kira parked the Porsche sideways at the end of the walkway, hoping to block the Guard vehicles from following them onto the island. Then she stepped out into the driving rain and hurried around the car, opening the passenger door and unbuckling Teddy from his seat.

"Come on, buddy!" She grabbed his hand. "We have to run!"

Holding hands, they raced onto the destroyed section of the old bridge, their shoes smacking against the iron girders. Icy rain poured from the sky, drenching them both before draining into the river below.

Kira didn't let herself look at the river, which would be higher and faster than the last time she'd seen it because of the morning's torrential rain. She didn't let herself consider what she was about to do. If she thought about it for even a moment, she would lose her nerve. Instead, she shut off her brain and put her body on autopilot, tugging Teddy along with her as they ran for the fence.

"Where are we going?" Teddy asked, struggling to keep up with her.

"To see Will. But we have to climb the fence, okay?"

Behind them, sirens wailed, growing louder every second.

Kira risked a look back.

The Guard vehicles were on the walkway, barreling toward the Porsche. They didn't appear to be slowing down.

When they reached the fence, Kira released Teddy's hand and crouched so she was eye-level with the boy. "I need you to climb for me, buddy. Okay? I need you to climb over the fence."

Pushing wet hair from his eyes, Teddy gawked at the fence. He looked at her and shook his head. "It's too high. I can't do it."

"Yes, you can. I climbed this same fence with Will the other night, and I was afraid too, but it really wasn't that scary. I'll be right here if you have any trouble, I promise. But I need you to climb as fast as possible. Okay? Can you be a superhero for me?"

She expected him to continue to protest, and if he did, there would be no escape from the city. Not for either of them. If she couldn't get Teddy over the fence, she would also remain in Vita Nova. She would not leave him.

But Teddy surprised her by hooking his little hands into the fence and climbing.

"That's it, buddy! There you go!"

Just as he reached the top, a deafening crash rocked the island.

Kira whirled around, her mind transporting her back to the awful night of the Eastern Sector bombing. What had her father blown up now? How many more people had he killed?

Nothing had exploded.

But the Porsche wasn't where she'd left it. The lead Guard vehicle had crashed into it, pushing it out of the way, and now a half-dozen other Guard vehicles were pouring onto the island, slamming on their brakes just before the destroyed bridge.

She returned her attention to Teddy, who was clinging to the top of the fence like a frightened monkey. His arms were shaking, either from the driving rain soaking into his clothes or the effort of holding himself up.

Or from fear.

"Great! Now, just swing your leg over the top! You can do it!"

The little boy followed her instructions, putting her to shame with how quickly and effortlessly he scaled the fence and climbed down the other side. Within seconds, Teddy was on the ground and staring at her through the holes in the fence.

"Are you coming?" he asked.

Shouts from behind her: *"Stop! Stop right there!"*

She glanced back.

Guards. On the destroyed section of the bridge. Closing in on her.

She had nowhere to go. Nothing to do but climb.

Kira grabbed the fence and pulled herself up, moving swiftly despite the rain-drenched clothes weighing her down. She pictured Will waiting for her at the top with his dimpled smile and kind eyes. Holding a hand out to her. Telling her she could do it.

When she reached the top, she couldn't see anything. Her

rain-soaked hair hung in her face, so that she couldn't see the approaching Guards, the ground, or the fence itself. Swinging her leg over the top, she found her footing and started down the other side as the first Guard reached the fence.

He drew a pistol from his holster and leveled it at her. "Don't move!"

Kira let go of the fence and dropped the last few feet to the ground, landing hard. Her eyes focused on the barrel of the pistol, and that black hole stared back at her—an unblinking black eye of death. Her hands defied her, rising into the air against her will.

It was over. She would not make it out of the city.

"Kira?" Teddy cried. "What's happening?"

And then she remembered.

This is his only chance. Teddy only has one chance.

And you're it.

She lifted her gaze from the pistol to the eyes of the Guard holding it. "You'll just have to shoot me."

Pushing the mop of wet hair from her eyes, she grabbed Teddy's hand and shoved him in front of her, hoping to protect his body with her own in case the Guard fired his weapon.

"Run, Teddy!" she cried. "We have to run!"

So, they ran.

Kira braced herself, expecting to feel the impact of a bullet slamming into her back. Waiting for it. Wondering if she would feel the impact, or if she would be dead before she hit the ground.

Better than a needle in the arm.

But the Guard didn't fire, and the edge of the bridge raced up to meet them, a severed finger pointing toward the Unregulated Zone like a warning. Or the finish line of a race.

Coming to a sudden halt at the edge, Kira peered into the churning river fifty feet below. Rain pelted its dark surface,

making it appear alive. A hungry monster waiting to swallow
them both.

From the moment Kira had rescued Teddy, she'd known
this moment would come. There was no other way out of the
city. Not for them. The river was their only option, but now
that it was daring her to step into its endless, gaping mouth—
she couldn't do it.

She couldn't jump.

"Stop right there!"

Spinning around, she saw the first Guard on her side of the
fence, sprinting toward the end of the bridge. Still others were
coming, scrambling over the fence and dropping into the
puddles of water below. One splash after another. All coming
for her.

Teddy's voice, filled with fear. "Kira? What do we do?"

Not wanting him to be afraid, she picked the little boy up
and held him against her chest. He clung to her, wrapping his
legs around her waist and burying his face in her neck. She
closed her eyes and hugged him as tightly as she could.

"I'm sorry," she whispered. "I'm so sorry, buddy."

He lifted his head from her shoulder. "They're coming."

The little boy could see Guards, but Kira refused to turn
around. She couldn't bear to see the contempt in their eyes.
When they reached her, they would pry Teddy from her arms.
Take him back to Rolling Meadows and his mother. Back to the
doctors and their poison needles, and to the people who wanted
to end this precious little boy's life for no reason.

"Are they mad at you for taking me away?" Teddy asked.
"Are they going to put me to sleep forever?"

Lizzy Currant's whispered voice filled her mind.

Stay awake, Kira. Stay awake.

She opened her eyes.

And that's when she saw him.

Across the river, on the edge of the broken western span.
Will.

"Kira!" He cupped his hands to his mouth and shouted at her. *"Jump!"*

Was it really him? She wiped the water from her eyes and squinted at the other bridge, but the rain was relentless, cascading down her face, intent on blurring her vision.

"Will?"

She hadn't imagined it, had she? She'd heard his voice. Heard him calling her name.

Swift, heavy footsteps pounded up behind her. Gruff voices commanded Kira to put the boy down and move away from the edge.

Everything was ending, right here at the edge of the city.

"Hold on to me, buddy," she whispered into Teddy's ear. "Don't let go, no matter what."

He tucked his head against her neck and nodded. "Okay."

"Let's stay awake together."

Then she closed her eyes and stepped into nothing.

Chapter Thirty-Six

A jarring impact, like slamming head first into the concrete barricade, and then the ice-cold river swallowed them whole, gulping them down its bottomless throat.

Kira tumbled through the murky blackness, dragged deeper by the fierce undercurrent. She kicked for the surface, but her legs were dead stumps, powerless against the insistent pull of the river. She hung suspended in black space, feeling as if she were both motionless and falling. Her arms were unnaturally heavy, and though she couldn't see a thing, she knew they were wrapped around Teddy's body.

But he wasn't moving. He wasn't kicking or struggling like he should've been. Instead of being coiled around her neck, the boy's arms hung at his sides.

Her boots plowed into the silt and rocks at the bottom of the river, and a white-hot flash of pain in her ankle lit up the emergency circuit boards in her brain. Her lungs shrieked for air, and the tremendous pressure and weight of the river spawned sharp, stabbing pains behind her eyes, as if someone was driving a scalpel into her brain. The pain was unbearable, and when she opened her mouth to scream, gritty water gushed past her lips and into her mouth.

Ignoring the shrieking pain in her ankle, her head, her chest...she summoned her strength and pushed off the bottom of the river as hard as she could, kicking for the surface. She could see it above her, an indigo blanket cast over a pitch-black bed, raindrops pelting the surface of the water, creating a million tiny ripples, like bulls-eyes.

She aimed for one of them.

Just when she thought her lungs might explode, her head broke the surface and she inhaled a mouthful of blessedly cold air. A violent spasm wracked her chest, and she coughed up the water that had seeped into her throat.

A distant crack, like thunder, then another.

Splashes in the water.

Not raindrops. Something else.

Treading water, she saw the Guards poised on the bridge, their weapons aimed at the water. More cracks and splashes.

Bullets, she realized. *They're shooting at me.*

But the current had carried her far from the edge of the bridge. Too far. They could shoot all they wanted, but their bullets wouldn't reach her. Or Teddy.

Teddy.

The moment she thought of him, she noticed his weight in her arms, as if he hadn't been there the entire time. Her eyes fell on the pale shape cradled against her chest, his body limp and lifeless, his lollipop-stained lips turning the same ice-blue as Will's eyes.

And the blue rose on his chest.

"Teddy!" she cried, shaking him. "Wake up!"

His head lolled on his shoulders, hanging backward at an

impossible angle, revealing a bone-white neck that resembled the belly of a dead fish.

He's not breathing, she realized. *Teddy isn't breathing.*

Her legs stopped scissoring beneath her, and no matter how hard she tried, she couldn't make them move. Her body began to sink.

Sopping clothing. Heavy boots.

Teddy's body.

All of it...dragging her down.

Her first instinct—pure survival—was to let the boy go, to ease her arms of that terrible burden and use whatever strength remained in her body to swim for the shore. It was too late for Teddy. He was gone, but it might not be too late for her. Her legs would give out before she made it to land, but without Teddy in her arms, she had a fighting chance.

Kira's arms loosened around the boy's body, and she felt the determined tug of the river as it tried to pull him from her. To claim him—Vita Nova's youngest Volunteer—as its own. How far would he go? How far would the river carry him? Into the Chesapeake Bay? All the way to the Atlantic?

At least he would be free.

But as the river tried to snatch Teddy away from her, Kira's instinct to save him overcame her instinct to survive. She held him against her body, his light-blond hair floating around his head like a crown.

Even though she couldn't feel them, her legs must've been scissoring enough to keep her afloat this long. But she had nothing left to give, and she sank deeper into the water, the water claiming her one inch at a time. For no reason, she thought of the little man in the house. The one who'd gone from one part of her mother to another, switching off the lights.

Death was a horrible thing.

The world faded away as she submerged beneath the surface.

She'd heard that drowning was a peaceful death, but the fire raging inside her throat and lungs, and the vice-like pressure in her head, was anything but peaceful.

But even worse was the realization that, after all she'd done, she'd failed to save Teddy. That was the worst pain of all.

Beneath the river, light speckled the darkness. Stars winked all around her. Was she still underneath the river or had she slipped through a black hole into another realm? Into outer space? She was cold—unbearably cold—but she couldn't feel the water rushing around her. All she could see were stars.

Stars everywhere. Multiplying. Growing brighter.

It was the most beautiful sight she'd ever seen.

Her lungs took over, and she gasped for air. Air that wasn't there.

Of course. Air didn't exist in space.

Her whole body shuddered. Brief but violent. The stars dimmed and grew brighter. Impossibly bright. Brighter than the sun.

Still, she held onto Teddy.

And in that star-speckled darkness, she saw something.

Hands. Reaching for her.

Suddenly, she was no longer under the surface of the river but inside the old church, surrounded by dahlias, her nostrils filled with the scent of them.

The scent of life.

Aunt Reeva spoke up inside her head, her words composing Kira's last cognizant thought before the stars exploded and enveloped her with their blazing light.

Reach, honey. Reach.

So she did.

Chapter 37

Saturday

Kira opened her eyes and saw flowers.

Dahlias.

Ringed petals. Curled edges. Brilliant yellow blooms that reminded Kira of an explosion of fireworks.

She lifted her head high enough to see the row of empty beds on the other side of the windowless room. The cabinet filled with medications stolen from Vita Nova. The metal rolling tables and battery-powered lanterns.

The church.

Her head slumped onto the pillow.

She wasn't dead.

She was in the Unregulated Zone.

Every part of her body hurt, including her right ankle. Yet the pain in the center of her chest put all of her other aches and sore spots to shame. Each breath brought on a fresh wave of anguish. Tears spilled from her eyes and soaked into the pillow beneath her head.

A familiar voice spoke. "Are you alright, honey?"

Slowly, Kira turned away from the flowers.

Aunt Reeva sat on a wooden chair beside Kira's bed, a tattered Bible lying open in her lap. Her eyes filled with concern. "How do you feel? Are you in pain?"

"My...chest." Speaking hurt, so she chose her words carefully. "Pain. Really bad."

The old woman nodded grimly. "Yes, I'm sorry about that. I can't be certain, since we don't have any x-ray machines lying around, but I think you've got a hairline fracture in your sternum. Not to worry—it'll heal on its own—but you've got a few rough days ahead of you. You've also got a sprained ankle, much as I can tell. Think you can swallow a few Tylenol? It'll help with the pain."

"Yes."

Crossing the room to the medicine cabinet, Aunt Reeva opened the door and grabbed a bottle from the bottom shelf. Then she returned to her chair and shook several white pills into her palm. "Here," she said, placing them in Kira's outstretched hand. "Take four. You've earned it."

After Kira popped the pills in her mouth, the old woman handed her a cup of water. She swallowed them in one big gulp, the room temperature water soothing against her sandpaper-dry throat.

"Just relax, honey. Shouldn't take too long for those pills to kick in."

"What happened?" Kira managed. "I was...in the river."

She remembered very little. She remembered jumping off the bridge to get away from the Guards, and she remembered the terrible, helpless feeling of sinking into the murky depths of the Susquehanna.

And hands. She remembered hands.

"You drowned yesterday," Aunt Reeva explained, never one to mince words. "You've been in and out of consciousness for the last twenty-four hours. When they pulled you out of the river, you were as cold as ice and you weren't breathing. Thankfully, the CPR worked, and they brought you back. Believe me when I tell you, it's a miracle that you pulled through. God is so good."

"Who? Who pulled...me out...of the river?"

A tiny smile settled on the old woman's lips. "Will did, honey," she said. "Well, him and Brack. It took two of them, seeing as how you wouldn't let go of that boy. Once they got you out, Will did CPR on you. He only knows how to do it because I taught him, by the way."

Will's alive.

The pain in Kira's chest vanished as she realized she hadn't imagined Will on the other section of the bridge. Jonesy had gotten Will out of the city. He'd really been there, yelling for her to jump, and he'd known where to go because Jonesy had told him.

And then she remembered Teddy—poor, sweet Teddy—and a crushing wave of grief swept over her, pushing her beneath the surface.

Drowning her all over again.

Aunt Reeva jumped up and pulled Kira into an embrace. "Goodness! What's wrong, honey? Why are you crying?"

But the words wouldn't come. For the longest time, Kira could do nothing but sob in Aunt Reeva's arms, even though it made the pain in her chest that much worse. She should never have gone after Teddy. Yes, he would be dead either way, but he would've had a peaceful death. He wouldn't have suffered in his last moments. She couldn't imagine the terror he must've felt as a total stranger clutched him against her body and jumped into the river.

"Kira, talk to me." Aunt Reeva rested her forehead against Kira's and whispered into her ear. "Please. Tell me what's wrong."

"Teddy," she gasped, through choking breaths. "I...killed him."

"What?" The old woman jerked away from Kira, her eyes growing wide. "No, honey. They brought the boy back, too. They got him back easier than you. No fractured sternums for that little tiger. He spent most of yesterday resting right over there." She pointed at the bed next to Kira's. "Will read him a bunch of books to keep him quiet so you could rest, but when Teddy woke up this morning, he decided he wasn't having anymore of the bed. Strong-willed boy, that one. If you ask me, he should rest, but he's acting fine, so what do I know? Last I checked, he was upstairs with Will."

Kira stared at Aunt Reeva, tears stinging her eyes, too stunned to speak.

Will and Teddy were both alive.

Somehow, she'd gotten them both out of Vita Nova.

And now she was out, too.

She was free.

"I can't...believe...it worked," Kira rasped.

It didn't seem possible, yet she knew Aunt Reeva wouldn't lie to her. Because of her friendship with Emma and knowledge of the facility, she'd gained access to the Compulsory Clinic to save Will. Because of her job as an advocate and relationship with Kimber, she'd gained access to Rolling Meadows to save Teddy.

She'd become a volunteer advocate to help the Volunteers, and that's exactly what she'd done.

"If I...wasn't...an advocate..."

Aunt Reeva's face broke into a smile. "*And who knows but that you have come to your royal position for such a time as this?*"

Kira stared at her. "What does...that mean?"

"Another time, honey." The woman patted her on the arm. "You need to rest."

A creaking of hinges drew Kira's attention to the other side of the room.

Will hovered in the open doorway, his face still bruised from the beating he'd endured at the Confines. But the swelling had gone down and he looked like Will again.

When their eyes met, his lips parted, but he didn't speak.

Teddy stood beside him, holding his hand.

"Your girl finally woke up," Aunt Reeva called out to Will. "She's alright. A little emotional for my taste, but physically, she's fine."

"Kira!"

Teddy darted across the room and leapt onto the edge of Kira's bed.

"Careful!" Aunt Reeva grabbed for Teddy, but it was far too late to catch him. When she saw Kira was fine—that Teddy hadn't hurt her—the old woman leaned back in her chair and closed her eyes. "Son, my old ticker can't take much more of you."

He looked embarrassed. "Oh. Sorry."

"It's...fine...buddy," Kira croaked, pushing Teddy's fine blond hair away from his forehead. "How...are you feeling?"

"Great!" Unable to contain his excitement, Teddy bounced on his knees, shaking her bed. "Miss Kira? Do you remember your promise?"

Of course she did. How could she forget?

Each word was a struggle, but it was worth it for Teddy. "I promised...we'd stay awake...together."

The little boy stopped bouncing. Carefully, as if afraid to hurt her, he wrapped his arms around her shoulders and squeezed. "I'm glad you're awake now."

"Me...too."

When Teddy released Kira, Aunt Reeva took the boy's hand and helped him off the bed. "We'll leave you two alone for a little," she said, pulling Teddy toward the doorway. "Come on, Teddy Bear. We've got a lot of flowers to water."

After they left, Will approached Kira's bed and pulled the wooden chair closer. He pressed a hand against the side of his chest and winced as he lowered himself into the chair.

Concerned, Kira reached for his hand. "Are you...feeling okay?"

He interlaced his fingers with hers, but instead of meeting her gaze, he kept his eyes on their hands. "I'm good. Just a broken rib."

"From the...Confines?"

"From jumping into the river." He gave her a little shrug. "I guess I hit the water wrong."

She remembered the hands in the water. The ones that had broken up the stars. Reached for her. Pulled her to safety. Those had been Will's hands. She stared at his strong fingers, entangled with her own smaller ones.

Those hands had saved her life.

"Aunt Reeva said...you pulled us...both out."

"Brack jumped in, too." Will lowered his eyes to the floor. "I'm so sorry, Kira. I wish I could've gotten to you sooner."

Reaching out with her free hand, she lifted his bruised chin and forced him to look at her. "Are you...seriously...apologizing...for saving my life?"

He rubbed his eyes, anger darkening his features. "I told you to jump," he said. "I put you and Teddy into a dangerous situation, and then I almost didn't get you out of it. What if we hadn't been able to reach you? What if the current had swept you away?"

"But...it didn't."

"But what if it had? You jumped for me, and I almost got you killed."

Even though it hurt to move, Kira hooked his shoulder with her hand and pulled him closer. "I didn't jump...for you," she whispered into his ear. "I jumped...for me. And...for Teddy."

Will kissed her forehead and then closed his eyes. "Kira..." he said, his breath warming her cheek. "You can't go back to Vita Nova. You know that, right? You and I...we can't go home ever again."

She closed her eyes and pictured those hands.

Reaching.

Pulling her out of the depths.

Then she put a hand behind Will's neck and drew his lips to hers.

"We *are* home."

Chapter 38

Epilogue

Fireworks rode into the heavens, exploding in magnificent starbursts of color and light, bright enough to blot out the stars.

To Kira, they resembled handfuls of glitter flung onto a child's easel.

Or dahlias.

Each thunderous explosion drew a fresh round of applause from the crowd gathered inside the Stadium. The colors in the night sky ran like paint, sprinkling the cremated remains of the previous week's Volunteers into the river below. Vivid halos on the river's glassy surface twirled like dancers at a ball before breaking apart and disappearing altogether.

On the opposite side of the river, Kira leaned back on her palms, her boots dangling over the severed edge of the old Walnut Street Bridge. She stared into the night sky as the vivid display of colors lit up the Unregulated Zone. It was all so beautiful—so hypnotizing—that she almost found herself missing her life in the city.

Until the breeze carried the acrid scent of sulfur from the fireworks across the Susquehanna.

The humidity was high—the air as thick and dense as the inside of a wet sponge—and for a moment, the gentle breeze against Kira's cheeks felt like whispers from heaven. But the accompanying stench of fire and sulfur reminded her that the barricaded city was not heaven.

Vita Nova was closer to hell than heaven.

Noticing a patch of purple aster wildflowers growing nearby, she leaned over, plucked one from its stem, and tucked the flower into her hair above her right temple. She'd never seen an aster growing anywhere in the city, but they littered the Unregulated Zone. The most beautiful wildflowers grew everywhere she looked, punching through cracks in the sidewalks and coloring the broken streets in shades of purple and blue and yellow.

There was more color—more life—in the Unregulated Zone.

She hadn't noticed that when she'd first toured the Unregulated Zone—she'd been too blinded by fear—but it was true.

"Asters spread like dandelions," Aunt Reeva had explained after Kira pointed out a patch of the daisy-like flowers growing behind the church. "The seeds act like tiny parachutes. The wind carries them."

Wincing at the pain in her chest, Kira had knelt beside the woman to examine the flowers, searching for the tiny seed pods hidden among the petals.

"Asters are hardy little things," the old woman had continued, her eyes drifting from the patch of wildflowers to Kira. "To look at them, you might say they're pretty but dainty. Maybe even a little weak. But God—in His wisdom—designed them to survive. Often, those things we do to destroy life are precisely the things that cause it to spread."

On the other side of the river, the fireworks continued their assault against the sky. As she often did, Kira found herself thinking of Emma. Was she inside the Stadium right now, her eyes on the heavens, wondering what had become of Kira? Or was she locked away in the Confines, awaiting the imposition of her punishment for her role in last week's escape?

Kira hated thinking about Emma, so she tried not to do it. She could do nothing to help her best friend. Not now. Maybe not ever. But if the opportunity ever presented itself for her to sneak back into the city and rescue Emma, she would take it.

Leaning over the edge of the bridge, Kira gazed at the water. All of that murky blackness should've frightened her even more than it used to, after her near-drowning a week earlier, but it didn't. She wasn't eager to go for a swim in its gloomy depths, but now she saw the river for what it was—a natural barricade.

Not from those outside of the city walls, but from those *inside* it.

Since Kira's escape from Vita Nova, more Patrol vehicles had been coming into the Unregulated Zone every day, the tell-tale rumbling of their engines echoing through the empty streets long before the vehicles themselves came into sight. The Patrol soldiers—many of whom had probably been civilians only a few days earlier, judging by their tactical skills—walked alongside the vehicles, breaking off to go door-to-door with pistols and automatic rifles, searching the abandoned buildings and houses with a thoroughness Aunt Reeva and the others hadn't seen before.

But they weren't looking for the Lawless. Or for Will. Or for Teddy.

Kira's father had sent them. They were looking for *her*.

She didn't know how she knew that, but she did.

Thankfully, they weren't searching the right area yet, but

Raena Rood

their perimeter continued to expand, edging closer every day to their little refuge in Emmitsburg.

It wouldn't be long now.

A sound of crunching leaves came from behind her. Turning, she saw a familiar shape approaching. As he drew closer, an explosion of light in the sky illuminated his beautiful face, and she couldn't help but smile.

"The show's almost over."

Will lowered himself next to her, his eyes sparkling. They sat with their shoulders and arms touching, his long legs swinging next to her own. "Good thing I didn't walk all the way out here for the show."

As the final barrage of fireworks exploded in the night sky, Will put a hand on Kira's cheek and kissed her deeply, the tips of his fingers lightly caressing her neck.

Kira didn't mind missing the end of the fireworks display. Nothing Vita Nova could shoot into the sky—no matter how breathtakingly beautiful—could compete with Will's dimples when he smiled, or the soft angles of his face, or the look in his eyes the moment he finished kissing her.

When they pulled apart, those three words—*I love you*—prodded at the inside of her lips, trying to find a way through.

But she wouldn't allow herself to say them yet.

Maybe someday, but not today.

Instead, she asked, "Are we still on for tomorrow?"

Will's smile faded, and he cast a weary glance at the Stadium. The lights were back on. The residents of Vita Nova would soon return to their homes to prepare for another week of revering Volunteers before putting them to death. "Looks that way. Brack thinks we might see a few storms roll through the area later tonight, but the plan is still to head out before dawn. I've told the other groups in the area that we're leaving, but none of them want to come with us. They'd rather take their chances here, hiding from the Patrols."

The idea of leaving Emmitsburg behind both thrilled and frightened Kira. Tomorrow, she and Will—along with Aunt Reeva, Teddy, Brack, and his wife, Grace—would begin their expedition to find out what existed farther out in the Unregulated Zone. None of them wanted to embark on this journey, but soon, hiding in Emmitsburg would no longer be an option—not with the Patrols inching closer.

There was only one problem.

When people left the Unregulated Zone, they never returned.

"So, I was just thinking—"

"Will..." Kira interrupted, knowing what was coming.

He mimicked her admonitory tone. "Kira..."

"Let's not do this again."

But he couldn't help himself. "You don't want to talk about what a bad idea it is for you to come with us?"

"There it is." Kira rolled her eyes. They'd had this same argument fifty times over the last few days, and it always ended the same way. Still, she admired Will's persistence, even if it annoyed her. "Go on. Tell me about my fractured sternum."

"What?" His eyebrows bumped together in a scowl. "You *do* have a fractured sternum."

"So what? It barely hurts anymore," she lied. "Plus, you've got a cracked rib and you're going. Allow me to remind you that *you* are responsible for fracturing my sternum, so you're not allowed to use it against me."

"You mean when I saved your life?"

"Uh-huh." She lifted her chin in defiance. "Right after I saved yours."

Without missing a beat, he continued through his litany of reasons she needed to stay behind. "Plus, you shouldn't be walking on that ankle. Aunt Reeva says you should rest it or you're going to make it worse."

"Aunt Reeva *also* says that I should be fine as long as I keep it wrapped and rest it whenever we stop, which I fully intend to do."

Will's eyes darted from her face to the side of her head. Reaching out, he plucked the aster from her hair. He held the flower in his hand and studied it for a few moments. Then he flung it into the river.

Kira bit on the inside of her lower lip, struggling not to laugh. "Why'd you do that?"

He shrugged. "Because you're impossible to deal with. And I'm immature."

Under a night sky glazed with smoke, Kira kissed Will again, their lips communicating something deeper than want or desire. She pressed one hand against his strong chest, feeling the steady rhythm of his heart beneath her palm. Afterward, she rested her head on his shoulder and allowed her eyes to follow the faint line of the barricade wall as it wrapped around the city like a snake.

"Will?" she asked. "Do you think we're going to find people out there?"

He considered her question for a long time before responding. "I'm sure we're going to find people. I'm just worried about what kind of people they might be."

That was a valid fear, given that no one had ever returned from one of these expeditions. But she closed her eyes and imagined a happy ending. "I'm hoping we find a little settlement of people. A quaint town with no barricade wall, where children play games in the tree-lined streets. There will be lots of dogs, of course. Maybe even a few cats, as long as they don't have attitudes. In this town, they only shoot off fireworks on the

Fourth of July, like normal people. Oh, and they don't kill each other all the time."

"Of course. That would be nice."

"What about you?" Kira asked, her eyes still closed. "What are you hoping to find out there?"

Will picked up her hand, brought it to his lips, and kissed it.

"I've already found it."

Acknowledgements

To my dear readers: From the bottom of my heart, thank you for making all my childhood dreams come true. Thank you for spreading the word and telling others about my books. Thank you for taking the time to post reviews, which are so important to authors. And thank you for your wonderful emails and messages, which always seem to arrive when encouragement is needed most. Please know that God is using each of you to bless me, and I pray that He's using me to bless you as well. If you've enjoyed this book, please consider leaving a review on Amazon, Goodreads, or wherever you wish. I appreciate each and every review!

To my inner circle of usual suspects: I could list your names, but you know who you are. Thank you for continuing to love and support me. God's word says, "Plans fail for lack of counsel, but with many advisors they succeed" (Proverbs 15:22). Thank you for being my advisors along the way, and for helping me with the editing process when funds suddenly became unbearably tight. God is so good. He made a way for this book to be published by providing each of you with special gifts that could help me. I am forever grateful for your love and friendship.

Thank you to my husband and children, who have sacrificed time with me so that I can pursue the calling the Lord has placed upon my heart. Aside from my salvation, the greatest gift I've ever received has been my family. You are the reasons I continue to write. To my children: I pray that my pursuit of my writing dreams will inspire and encourage each of you to chase down your own dreams, no matter how crazy they seem.

To my son, Ben Rood: Thank you for using your artistic talents to create my first ever book map! I can't wait to see what God has in store for you.

Finally, to my Lord and Savior, Jesus Christ: Thank You for equipping me to write for You. And—above all—thank You for giving up Your perfect and blameless life in the greatest Sacrifice that has ever been made *for the good of all.*

— Raena Rood
   July 2022

About the Author

Raena lives with her husband and three children in rural Pennsylvania, where her hobbies include raising chickens, singing off-key while cleaning, and introducing her kids to cheesy 80's movies. When she's not writing, she spends way too much time thinking about buying more chickens. And possibly a goat.

Also by Raena Rood

The Subversive Trilogy

Subversive: Book 1 of The Subversive Trilogy

Sanctuary: Book 2 of The Subversive Trilogy

Salvation: Book 3 of The Subversive Trilogy

Made in the USA
Middletown, DE
12 September 2024